TERMS OF ENGAGEMENT:

STORIES OF THE FATHER AND SON

* * *

A SHORT STORY COLLECTION

PAUL ALAN RUBEN

"Who deserves sympathy and who is a jerk? Maybe Oedipus *should* kill his father on purpose? Maybe father Abraham should ignore the ram and plunge the son? Can we ever know anything, or are we each forever imprisoned in the cave of our own impenetrable skull and/or the ironic conventions of our culture? Engage with Paul Alan Ruben's book and you'll be left reeling. It sizzles."

—**Sena Jeter Naslund**, author of seven novels, and two collections of short fiction. Her novels *Ahab's Wife* and *Four Spirits* were each named a *New York Times* Notable Book of the Year.

"With wrecking-ball force and brilliant energy, Paul Alan Ruben reveals his characters' fraught terms of engagement. In galloping sentences that are yet intricate and nuanced, we see the sometimes breath-catching and sometimes haunting frictional force of these father-son relationships. These men converse, argue, and kibbitz and in doing so, wondrously negotiate shaky peace or declare no-holds-barred war."

—**Mary Clyde**, author of the short story collection, *Survival Rates*, which received The Flannery O'Conner Award for Short Fiction

"In Paul Alan Ruben's sharply drawn world, sons are sons forever, and no father ever rests in peace."

—**Jay Heinrichs**, *New York Times* best selling author of *Thank You For Arguing*.

Published by Larkin Books, a division of Alison Larkin Presents.

www.alisonlarkinpresents.com

ISBN-13: 978-1-64255-207-2

For Paula
For Brandon

* * *

Those into whose lives you are born do not pass away.

—J. M. Coetzee, *Slow Man*

CONTENTS

I

STORIES OF THE FATHER
AND SON

FATHER, SON, AND THE HOLY OBIT

MY FATHER SUCCUMBED to lung cancer on December 29, 2010.

An hour after my brother, Terry, and I left hospice that morning—having learned that he would not regain consciousness —I sat down in my home office to prepare his obituary. I had planned it as an addendum to "Family Connections," my Sunday column for *The New York Times*: a brief announcement of his passing to follow that week's feature story.

The words emerged from me as I had always intended them to: respectfully and faithfully reflecting my self-administered oath to never publicly criticize my father while he was alive, or posthumously. But after the first two sentences I was overwhelmed by regret.

I had never disclosed to my father the true feelings I'd harbored about us. Now I never would. I typed severely on my keyboard: "I hated myself for not loving you, but I tried. You hated yourself for not loving me, but you never tried, did you? Did you!!!!!!!!"

Uncleansable shame enveloped me—a spreading stain that

was the pretense that I'd made my peace with him. I sat up. My truncated breaths quickened. A dissonant metronome that ticked inside me accelerated. I loathe my father, always have, I realized, and then I thought: His life has ceased, but he is not dead.

I escaped my room, dismantled. Until yesterday, I believed that a sanctuary in my soul, in everyone's, existed: a purifying oasis that permits acknowledgment of the other's humanity, no matter who they are or what they've done. It's a location not easily recognized or cultivated, but I searched my soul and found it, and it was to be the permanent resting place where my liberated memory of him—free of agony and sorrow, rancor and pain—would reside.

As I shut my door, I thought, I am his self-loathing puppet on a string, condemned by him to revile him, forever.

I completed the obit the following afternoon. After a phone call from hospice, I sent it to my editor, the only nonfamily member I've ever confided in about my father:

From: kbrennan@nytimes.com
To: jmarsh@nytimes.com
Date: Thurs., Dec. 30, 2010
Subject: FYI, Obit

Hey Jack:
Attached will follow next week's piece. Just wanting your nod of approval. About to email Terry for his. In advance, Herr Word-Count Sentry, I'll shorten the column to compensate for the obit's length and resend tomorrow.
Talk soon,
Ken

engagement connects,
acknowledgment binds

4

I slept fitfully that night. I summoned the float—my palliating routine that finally transformed 15 drug-reliant years—increased doses of Valium, Lunesta, Ambien—into reliance on me. On my back, one palm over the other, I placed both hands on my chest. Mouth closed, willing my fingers to tingle, I sailed above myself, rhythmically breathing, in and out—small, simple breaths—while listening to my heart, my soothing friend, beat pleasure and trust and acquiescence and the float. But my eyes remained open, my brain on. I persuaded myself that the dissonant metronome was like a phantom limb, and that closure—the healing act of letting my father go—was already occurring and would finally occur so long as I acknowledged him. I hazily pictured Jack's knotty index finger clicking open the attachment and wincing over its length and barely getting through the opening:

Bing: 1918-2010

My father, Lawrence Crosby Brennan (a.k.a. Bing to intimates and his legion of fanatically loyal readers) succumbed to lung cancer on December 29th, 2010. A day later this newspaper's official obit acknowledged Bing's passing as well as his best-selling novels and enormous popularity. Though several of my father's earlier novels (which had longer titles) outsold his one-word *Peacekeeper Series,* he often told my brother and me that these gratified him the most. Each story's protagonist, as Bing once wrote us, "embodies the courage to do what is right." Among those he expressed the most pride in were: *Payback, Respect, Cheetah, Patriot, Southie, Linebacker, Minister, Townie,* and *Phoenix.*

At 4 a.m. I eased out of bed and noticed my wife's eyelids flutter, then still. I opened the door to my home office and shouted silently in the dark at a child, me: *Get over it.* I slumped in front of the computer, scrolled down my emails, and clicked open Jack's:

To: kbrennan@nytimes.com
From: jmarsh@nytimes.com
Date: Thurs., Dec. 30, 2010
Subject: Obit

Ken:

The obit is fair and accurate. Given what you've shared with me over the years, it is also charitable. You're a good son, Ken.

J

A good son. I'd steadfastly refused every opportunity to publicly excoriate Bing for his outrageous and humiliating treatment of my family and me. I was a good son. I'd always wanted to be. Ken knows what "good son" means to me, so his characterization was especially gratifying.

I printed out my obit. I moved to the couch. Tugging at the floor lamp's two chains for maximum illumination, I read it over. My words, meticulously chosen and arranged, had fulfilled their promise: accurate reportage, no fanfare or hyperbole.

As I read the obit, I imagined the words as a tightly sewn dispassion-quilt that cloaked their inner malice. I lowered the paper to my lap and saw myself, the angry, intolerant son, drunk on duplicitousness. I thought: My unyielding commitment—glibly proffered in professional journals, educational forums, and *The New Yorker,* and at cocktail parties—is to insist that acknowledgment of the other's humanity is the only way that we can locate our own. I thought of "Family Connections," conceived on this immutable "acknowledgment ethic" that was conspicuously missing from Bing's obit.

I stared at each word—as cold as the light's glare—and grimaced, then snorted, thinking how this obit would have confirmed my father's unspoken sense of who he ultimately was to me: a dead star, flickering pretense.

Anxiety tugged Jack's "fair and accurate" reassurance from me. "Fair and accurate" was, I thought, my escape route from a lie, not about Bing, but me.

I emailed the obit to Terry, then went back to sleep. Disgrace slogged through me all night. Apparently, I had fallen asleep. WQXR startled me at 6:15. I jumped from bed, went to my computer, and opened my brother's email: "LET'S MEET SOMEWHERE—TER."

We'd decided on Gee Whiz—my old neighborhood's first-choice untrendy diner. A block south of Chambers, Gee Whiz was a significant chapter in my history: sponsor of my son's soccer team; a familiar comfort nestled among Tribeca's increasingly upscale residential and commercial establishments, where I sometimes wrote or contemplated—cocooned by its ambient hubbub—in solitary.

I waited for Terry. Seated alone in a booth by the window, looking west across Greenwich Street, I recalled, as if it were yesterday, the coffee, the oatmeal and raisins, scattered packets of Equal, empty half-and-half mini-containers, reading the *Times*, and boom! And then rushing to the street to witness the billowing fireball from one of the Twin Towers. My God, what a horrific accident, I'd thought.

I blinked as the winter sun poked through blackish clouds and illuminated the cityscape. It was already making good on the forecast's promise of a seasonal reprieve: sunny and a high of 58.

* * *

"Great obit," said Terry, "if you're writing it for Wikipedia."

"Meaning?"

"You know, generic, like you never knew him. Perfecto!"

"What should I say?"

"Try how you feel," he said.

"And how do I feel?"

"The wicked witch is dead!" he replied, as he slid out of his parka, then removed his ridiculous-looking Elmer Fudd sheepskin hat.

"Ter, it's practically summer out. You look like a fuckin' Eskimo."

Terry raised his hand to signal the waitress.

"Did I ask you?"

Terry signaled with what he calls my motivating three-ring sign: arm extended and three obnoxious fingers wiggling their alert. Personally, I'd be motivated to slice them off.

I caught Elena's eye—the ageless lifer whose enchanting Nuyorican was sometimes indecipherable, but who cares—and waved my lowered hand, subtly. She smiled back and nodded. I hoped my nicety would somehow compensate for Terry's brutishness.

"Obviously it's devoid of sentiment about him," I said.

"Aaaaaaand?" he replied, his hand still in the air. That patronizing, elongated vowel splattered in my face like a toilet paper spitball. "Should there be something good to say about a motherfucker?"

"Terry! Elena sees you!"

"I'll let you know when she sees me, okay?" Terry lowered his hand. He drank the apple juice I'd ordered in advance for him.

"Thanks," he said, after his first sip.

I smiled. *Asshole.*

Terry never bought that his in-your-face hostility to Bing was useless. But it was indicative of Terry's overall emotional

M.O.: self-defeat. Eviscerate Bing, you eviscerate yourself, I regularly admonished him, especially after he mounted his Tourette's-like ire. To which Terry responded by cursing Bing again—and me, if I pushed him. That said, our experience of Bing as children and adults was identical: no Rashomon, no disparate perceptions.

Elena stood over us, scrawling feverishly. Terry ordered his usual He-Man Special: short stack, sunny-side-up egg on top, links, fried potatoes, toast. She turned to me.

"Y usted, baby?"

Terry interrupted. "Oh, make it whole wheat, butter on the side."

What a joke, like whole wheat is gonna spare your arteries; you're gonna slop butter on it anyway. Pig.

I ordered oatmeal, skim milk, and whole wheat toast. "Dry, Elena."

"Más café coming up pronto." She winked at me and was gone.

"What kind of sons are we?" I said.

"You speak for you! Don't speak for me!" Terry shot back.

"I appreciate the reminder," I answered. *Jackass.* "So, what kind of son am I? How do I recall Bing?"

"Goddammit. So what does this make me now?"

"I just want your opinion."

"No you don't, because I just gave it!" he said.

"Really? Maybe I don't understand."

"What about 'don't speak for me, goddammit' don't you get?" he said, in a quiet burst.

"I'm speaking for me," I replied.

"Bullshit. I'm here to make you feel better, not help you," said Terry, louder.

"Now you're a mind reader."

"Remember, I don't have your ball and chain, Ken, your

hidden agendas. I don't have to get up every morning and impress readers—"

"What?"

"With my moral superiority!"

"Fuck you, you dumb fuck!" I leaned into him and then poured forth from a sutured wound only Bing and Terry could rip open. "Do not analyze me! Do not criticize what I do as if you had a fucking clue!"

My breathing evened. *Wow! Big step backward.* I couldn't recall the last time we'd gotten into it like this. I'd thought we were past it. Terry didn't retaliate, or storm out, as he's prone to do. We sat till our food arrived, then ate. Occasionally, we glanced at each other.

Five years ago, Terry and I had quit speaking. We couldn't finish a conversation without one of us mentioning Bing. Invoking his name was instant Whac-A-Mole time that launched Terry into "unload mode." Since he rarely saw Bing, Terry's harangues were usually over their latest phone nonconversation. "Had another one-way idiot-logue," he'd begin, and then he'd rail about Bing not giving a shit, much less listening, and then, when he finally did get asked to talk about himself, how seconds into it, Bing would obsequiously—my word—drown him during a mid-sentence breath with "May I modestly change the subject?" Terry's revenge fantasy generally concluded his rant: "I'm in his writing room, and I ram the phone up his ass and cauterize the motherfucker's hole shut." I'd second his enduring rage but instruct him: "Just like Bing's diatribes subjugate me, yours do, too. You have to stop—"

He'd interrupt. "Well, you subjugate me with your turn-the-tables intellectual bullshit. Bing!"

"Do not ever call me him!" I'd scream.

Kaboom! We were Bing to each other, spewing the toxic repercussions of life with father as if venting our enmity might requite our yearning for his attention. We'd go weeks, then months without talking. Eventually we quit trying. We'd succumbed to the impossibility of acknowledging one another.

After Bing was diagnosed in 2009, Terry and I met at the hospital. Like reunited cellmates, we rehashed our jailer's psychic assaults. It was then that Terry and I determined that we would not pick up where we left off.

We left Gee Whiz that day forcing ourselves to connect, trying so hard, I thought. On the way out, I asked myself again, does he always leave a 25 percent tip to prove he's better than me?

We meandered west on Chambers, crossed the West Side Highway.

"Up or down?" asked Terry.

"Up," I said, and we headed north along the bike path. The grand Hudson and plain Jersey shoreline to our left, fast traffic shimmying against Manhattan's muscular urban backdrop to the right released a pleasure pheromone in me.

"My version of you?" I said. "Can I?" It was our post-conflict venting procedure. No rebuttals allowed. Terry nodded. "Tell it like it is. Straight shooting equals self-righteousness. How do you think I feel when it's shot at me?"

"My version of you." Terry said. "You swallow your anger, deny it, like it's not there. You swallow it about Bing. About me. You think I don't notice? Think again."

We walked more or less a mile in silence. I looked across the highway. We'd reached Bank Street. I leaned over the iron railing and stared at the river. Terry stood by me. I thought about the silence. We'd resolved to create a silence pact that day in 2009 at the hospital, a space we'd carve between ourselves the moment one brother's intrusion upon the other became intolerable.

"Sorry, Ken."

"It's okay." "I should have apologized for turning my problem into yours," I said.

"Sorry for the column remark," said Terry.

"Okay," I said.

"Okay?" he said, hesitantly. His hesitation particularized "okay." A plea for my unequivocal forgiveness, I thought; it was a recognition of my older brother leverage, a reminder, too, that his fear of sibling dissolution exceeded mine.

"I meant to ask you," Terry said. "Oh, and just to say, no withheld feelings. Um, anyway, there's an opening for a copywriter at my agency."

I squinted at the water's reflection of the sun: rippling in perpetuity, like us brothers, I thought. Terry was no Bing: Why could I never recall that in the midst of our arguments?

"I know some people," I replied.

The unseasonable temperature brought out a shirtless jogger, cyclists, a nubile rollerblader's taut thighs, bare midriff, and, as I glanced back, undulating tush, hmm, luscious—all passing us brothers as we strolled anonymously up the path. Between warm silences, the ebb and flow of our small talk—about the Jets' playoff chances, bouncy breasts robbing our concentration, Obama, Bloomberg, the city—moved us closer to each other.

"Staying home tonight?" Terry asked.

"Oh yeah. You?"

"Fo' sho', " he said. His bonding smile confirmed our mutual disdain for the New Year's Eve silliness.

"I'm gonna email my editor," I said. I couldn't withhold the big talk I longed to have with Terry.

"Yeah."

"You have to head to the office?" I asked.

"I have time. So? What?" said Terry, halting like a soldier.

I stared into his prepped-for-melodrama face, the Fudd hat, the no longer friendly Hudson and Jersey shore behind him.

"Ken. You don't have to mine for the good in Bing," he said, having read my thought, as only my brother can.

"Goodness," I interrupted.

"Am I speaking here?"

"Yes."

"Goodness. Whatever."

"Not whatever," I insisted. "Goodness, meaning his humanity, even if he didn't show it."

"All right, all right, you've told me ..."

Silence.

I felt chilled and zipped my jacket.

"Will you just tell me for chrissakes what is on your mind?"

"You have to approve my obit," I said.

"I approve it."

"No, I'm writing a new one."

"Whatever."

"Not whatever, goddammit."

"I'm sure I'll ..." Terry inhaled, and his squeezed mouth closed tight. Reeking condescension, an impatient puff of exhaled air caused his upper lip to flutter. "Approve," he said. His habit is so Bing, the over-the-top, mannered commentary that makes another's simple declaration suddenly all about him. *Listen up, asshole*, I felt like replying. I said, "My obit must not contradict your experience of Bing, okay?"

"Why?"

"Because it's the same as mine, can I just finish my sentence?"

"Finish," said Terry. "I'm listening."

"Look," I said, "the animus—"

"Speak English."

"Anger, okay. It still drives me, even posthumously, to want to annihilate him. Will I ever let it go? Will you?"

"Fuck Bing, Ken."

"Really?"

The distinct hum of propellers alerted my ears. Terry and I both looked up. A small plane was scurrying north above the Hudson.

"I need to acknowledge Bing, his humanity—"

"You don't *neeeed* to *explain* yourself," he stage-whispered.

God, you are sooo Bing! I said, "Look, you don't possess a public venue like me to express your side of things. I will not write anything about him you don't approve of. Period."

"I'll approve."

"Well, could you maybe read it first?"

In the ensuing silence I thought that sometimes I, too, must really piss Terry off to the core.

"That's fair, Ken."

"So, it's okay for me to email you the finished version?"

"Sounds fair."

I left Terry and briskly walked south along the bike path, and was agitated by his use of the word *fair*. Didn't get past me. It was a slight, albeit proffered respectfully. Terry often reminds me that I use *fair* as a weapon to sabotage his ability to argue. He should have been a shrink.

I crossed the highway onto Chambers and headed to City Hall, where I'd catch the uptown R for the east side. We'd maintained our civility pact, somehow, and I was relieved.

Invigorated by a renewed commitment to uphold my integrity and that of "Family Connections," while respectfully prioritizing Terry's feelings, I planned to wrap up this *acknowledgment* obit on New Year's Day.

From: kbrennan@nytimes.com
To: jmarsh@nytimes.com
Date: Sat., Jan. 1, 2011
Subject: Obit

Hey Jack:
Please pull the obit. Revise coming shortly.
Ken

engagement connects,
acknowledgment binds

From: kbrennan@nytimes.com
To: jmarsh@nytimes.com
Date: Sat., Jan. 1, 2011
Subject: re: Obit

When can I expect it? Happy new year!
J

That night, I stared at the computer screen: nothing. I could more easily have retrieved a redemptive sliver from Pol Pot's life than Bing's. With every reach for Bing's humanity, I recoiled at a lifetime of him seething and screaming over infractions I neither understood nor could have anticipated. *No thanks for the memories,* I sang to myself, after recalling one of Bing's greatest hits: a long-ago dinner hour—Mother, Terry, and I cackling over something frivolous that had occurred between us earlier in the day. And Bing, not privy to our intimacy, suddenly exploding, slamming his fist on the table, line-driving his fork into the wall and bellowing something about us three never giving him one goddamned second's worth of peace, which, if he told us once he told us a thousand times, meant "lowering the fucking decibels." Then, following a burst of invective unintelligible to me, he turned to Mother, his sneer icily precise: "You take better care of mama's tittie-sucks." Then he vanished.

I thought about two years ago, almost to the day, when the *Times* announced my Sunday column. I remembered how I couldn't wait "to honor the familial connections that inextricably bind us," as I wrote in my inaugural installment, "despite the vicissitudes that too often turn blood relatives into intimate enemies." Bing's emotional gutting of my brother and me was the source of my calling to celebrate family: fathers and sons, mothers and daughters, brothers, sisters, cousins, aunts and uncles who are particularly connected, forever.

Now I noticed the time: 10:17 p.m. *C'mon, already.* I deleted unfinishable sentiments for what seemed the hundredth time. I could not locate the courage to acknowledge Bing's humanity, to connect it to mine, to refer to him as other than Bing. I was mama's boy, I thought. She tried her best to shield Terry and me. She coddled us. Coddling her tittie-sucks enraged Bing, but soothed me. Terry and I quaked when Bing's presence erupted—frightened weaklings subdued by his tempest—and we whimpered helplessly as mama titty-fucked her worthless little boys. I wanted to wail to the world: He was a scumbag. I wanted to crush him and pulverize his legacy. *You're right, Terry: Fuck Bing.*

I went online.

My eyes panned aimlessly over unopened emails—among them, dozens of condolences awaiting my response. *Who cares.* My thoughts migrated to the letters, not to mention the packages and manila envelopes—stuffed with God-only-knows—that had been piling up in our lobby's mailroom. Bing's international celebrity ensured that tons more would come.

Yesterday, the *Times* dutifully messengered mail addressed to their office over to my East 69th Street high-rise. Sooner or later I'd have to sort through this shit. I'd ignored the super's terse knocking at my door that afternoon. I'd snickered after surreptitiously nudging the latch and squinting through the peephole. The wide-angle lens had distended his grumpy expression like taffy. *Incinerate them,* I'd growled silently. He knew I was home. I lowered the latch. *No thanks for the memories,* I'd hummed to myself as I slinked away from the door.

I clicked the Apple icon and scrolled down the menu to *Sleep.* Before raising my index finger from the mouse, I noticed— sequestered among the fans, celebrity colleagues, other notables— an email from a Flo Pines. *U.S. Representative Pines? I'd always admired her. She knew Bing?*

I opened the email.

It *was* Congresswoman Pines. I read her remembrance. I thought: My God. Leaning forward, I read it again, then a third time. I sat back in my chair. I tried to fathom a father I never knew.

As if it had always been in me, but cloaked somehow, my "Family Connections" obit poured forth, uncoaxed:

The Father I'd Known, and Didn't

Bing: 1918-2010

My father, Lawrence Crosby Brennan (a.k.a. Bing to intimates and his legion of fanatically loyal readers) succumbed to lung cancer on December 29th, 2010.

A day later, this newspaper's official obit acknowledged Dad's death as well as his enormous popularity. Ironically, *The New York Times* never reviewed one of his books, whose aggregate worldwide sales topped those of his peers, including his best friend and critically acclaimed drinking buddy, Evan Hunter (a.k.a. Ed McBain). Ironically, Dad's *Times* obit was 300 words longer than that of the "dago workaholic motherf*****", as he often called Evan.

Bing was once asked by Larry King—whose show he appeared on nine times—how he felt about the *Times's* perpetual snub. "I'll answer it this way, Larry. See, why Bing is so popular with the workingman, is that reading Bing makes him proud to *be* the workingman. Let the *Times* reify intellectualism, Larry. F them."

Publishers Weekly, my father's true nemesis, never awarded one of his books a starred review. I'm told they'll "star" his oeuvre, and life, in a forthcoming cover story, titled *Bing: Chronicler of the Red, White, and Blue.*

Though Dad's earlier works had longer titles, the most popular of his 23 unabashedly chauvinistic *Peacekeeper Series* novels were one word, reflecting, as he often said, "the purity of his protagonist's nature." The best-selling were: *Payback, Phoenix, Patriot,* and *Resurrector.*

Lawrence Crosby Brennan was born in Sheepshead Bay, Brooklyn, in 1918. His parents nicknamed him Bing. They never called him Lawrence or Larry. They insisted that everyone call him Bing. Between his middle name and nickname, he would always remind his parents of the singer "we idolize," they told him. Dad despised his parents. And yet he embraced their sobriquet. He once told me that his enmity for them filled his pen with "bile," presumably making him a better writer. I gathered that that explained his preference for Bing.

Dad is survived by: his two sons (Terry and me); his first wife, and our mother, Grace Neal; Inez Carrera, wife two; his third wife, Rashika Jones-Brennan, from whom he was never legally divorced; and his last partner, supermodel Irena Lukova.

Dad received a BA (business) and MA (American literature) from City College, in New York.

I cannot recall my father fondly. It's no secret to readers of my mother's best-selling memoir, *Bing! Bang! Boom!,* that while Dad was a saint to his fans, he was a tyrant to his family.

He repeatedly threatened my mother with physical abuse. Occasionally he acted out his threat—usually in the form of an open-handed whack or multiple pushes.

Bing's rage erupted from a darkness that was as frightening to my mother, Terry, and me as it was incomprehensible. If we confronted him, separately or as a family, about the toll that his outbursts took on us, Bing would turn mute; he would look away docilely. Days after an explosion, on his terms, Bing's standard mea culpa—summarily presented to us at the dinner table or before we went to sleep—would seek to eradicate our pain by invoking his. "If I knew why I did what I did, I wouldn't do it."

Bing terrorized us.

I remember when Terry and I accidentally-on-purpose entered Dad's writing room—verboten, as he'd always made clear. No matter. Damn the torpedoes! His 7-year-old and 5-year-old couldn't help bursting in unannounced to tell him about the backyard swing-set that our mother had finally purchased after we'd all pinky-promised to never swing without her present.

His chair swiveled. This gigantic ogre grabbed the toy I had in my hand and plopped it on his desk.

"Goddammit!" he bellowed. He leaned into my brother's face.

"Out!" His scream was ferocious.

Terry rubbed his eyes furiously, but he could not defend them against the invasive spray of saliva.

"Out!" Fear paralyzed us. We couldn't move. Bubbling tears flowed down Terry's cheeks.

"You fucking deaf?" he growled at me. His face touched mine. His breath burned my nostrils. I was suddenly choking as my shirt pressed into my throat. Lift-off. He had Terry and me by the back of our pants. Airborne, we sailed out the door and crumpled to the ground.

Terry wailed uncontrollably. I was dry-eyed.

Mother had had enough. She called a lawyer.

Days later, sitting at the dinner table: "If I knew why I did what I did, I wouldn't do it." Shortly thereafter came another predictable, post-meltdown ritual—the thought of its familiarity as disquieting as the act itself. It followed particularly harsh abuses: like after the time I watched him spit in Mother's face for some unfathomable transgression, then grab her shoulders and force her chin up, then push her to a mirror so she could watch him watch the snot drip from her nose; or the day after he slapped Mother on the back, the impact so stunning that her knees buckled as she tried silently to inhale the pain away while digging her fingers into my shoulders in an effort to keep from falling.

The ritual: He'd mumble plaintively, again, during mealtime (guaranteeing my loss of appetite), that he would help himself, if it weren't for his dysfunctional childhood. The memories perpetually tortured him. He'd remind us—at times, eyes watery—that his childhood was the cause of his unacceptable behavior and his lasting regret as a parent. Understanding him should be the impetus for our forgiveness and love. Our unequivocal acceptance of his trauma, he often said, made him smile during private moments.

And that was that. All better. For Bing.

The psychic scars my father bequeathed to Terry and me are indelible. As adults, our bewilderment over how to locate the emotional tools necessary to create a healing process is an indicator of why it is so difficult for us to manage the wounds that fester beneath these scars. We brothers are equally enslaved by bitterness and anger. We rarely preside over our feelings as adults when we discuss Bing. At best, we ruminate impotently. Bing thrives permanently in us. He is The Terminator in relentless pursuit of empathy. When we argue, he neutralizes our capacity to feel for the other. Conflict between Terry and me ensues and metastasizes to rancor that short-circuits our emotional compass, and frantically turns its needle from resolution to dissolution.

It seems that during so many of my conversations with Terry, there's a moment that we no longer see the brother but instead, the father, who never acknowledged our God-given right to be heard. One brother becomes the other's worst nightmare: his enemy; his Bing. We rabidly defend ourselves against The Terminator. We are powerless to halt this destructive juggernaut that seizes our better judgment and commands us to inhabit Bing instead of each other. Devoid of empathy, we spin out of control in anger's black hole. Kaboom! Then, we disengage. We emotionally retreat to our separate spheres: wounded, angry, and dehumanized. Maybe we'll try again. Maybe we won't.

Because of Bing, Terry and I are defective grown-ups.

Yes, Dad behaved badly. He left his sons emotionally inept. He left me unforgiving, without compassion—hating him, I imagine, almost as much as he must have hated himself. Along with his fiction he produced a traumatized former wife, whose public outburst, luridly colorful, assured its position among the recent spate of "life-with-a-raving-narcissist" memoirs.

So, now you know how I've always felt about Bing—the elephant in the room, the ignored truth that, because I haven't been forthcoming with my readers, assures my place among an undistinguished list of sanctimonious hypocrites. Now you know that my mantra—engagement connects, acknowledgment binds—applies to everyone except me.

Following is an excerpt from an obit I'd seriously

considered for this column: "Bing's passion for his work, his super-human ability to rise above his detractors, to never abandon his commitment to his readers, and to verbalize what others silently fumed over, is what particularized Bing. He was brave; he was fearless; he arrived from no mold and left none upon his departure. All this achievement from a child who suffered at the hands of a father whose acidic words, as he often reminded his family, 'vaccinated my sister, twin brother, and me against the scourge of empathy.' "

My conscience recoils as I read it: *Are you kidding me! These accolades mean nothing to me! Well, that's not totally true. They demonstrate that I can manufacture sentiment that transforms a narcissistic, self-serving maniac into a Hallmark card.*

Even in death, I could not dislodge the malignant tumor that was my father. The best I could do was never face it. I could not muster the courage to seek a pathway to acknowledging Bing's humanity. Until an email I received from U.S. Representative Florence Pines interrupted my loathing:

From: Flo C. Pines flocp@optonline.net
To: kbrennan@nytimes.com
Sent: Thurs., Dec. 30, 2010
Subject: My Lawrence

Dear Ken:

I've not had the pleasure of making your acquaintance, though I will introduce myself at your father's memorial service. May I express my most heartfelt condolences to you and your family for your loss.

It is late and I am somewhat enervated from a grueling day of haggling with several of my good Republican friends from across the aisle. Retiring before midnight was my 84th birthday resolution. It's a good thing I believe in compromise.

Ken, I am aware of Bing's reputation as a less than admirable parent and father. But I hope you will permit me, by reading further, to reveal in death what Lawrence asked me not to disclose during his life.

On August 17, 1945, I was forcibly dragged from a gas station's Colored-Only bathroom. We were in rural Mississippi, near the Columbus army base. Of all things, Ken, I was daydreaming and accidentally walked into the Colored men's room. Well, bad as that was, I saw three *white* soldiers standing over the urinal, in the midst of their business. When they turned to me, I closed my eyes, frozen in shock.

The flesh on my knees tore as they dragged me out of the door. "Grab her jigaboo hair," I remember one of them saying, his country drawl reminding me who I was in the deepest South. They took me to a wooded area behind the gas station. I lay on my back and kept my eyes shut tight. I knew better than to scream. Not in Mississippi. They were going to rape me. I was going to submit. I would not, however, look at them, even if they threatened to kill me.

Pairs of hands began to destroy my soul. I fought not to grimace from the grotesquely foul smell of a whiskey-voiced soldier yelping in my face. Something about celebrating VJ Day with "nigger-poon."

And then, quickly, the hands were gone.

"You had your fun!" a voice threatened.

I heard a fierce scuffle: cussing, shouting, someone gasping in pain, threats of extreme violence. My eyes shut tight, I lay there, imagining they were fighting over who was to get me first. The vileness of their anger at one another scared me more than their hatred of me. I was surely going to die.

The silent minutes that followed were an eternity. I felt

my heartbeat return to normal. And then the most powerful urge to cry, as I realized that not only was I alive, I had not lost my soul.

"Open your eyes. Please?" said a voice. It was somewhat breathless but compassionate and full of sorrow. Had I been rescued from these soldiers?

"You're okay," said the voice. "I'm going to take you home."

I shook my head no.

"Please," asked the voice. "I'm not leaving till you let me," the voice said. "And it's getting dark. And, ya know, I'm kind of afraid of the dark."

I shook my head no. Two fingers gently touched my eyelids. Not to force them open. "Please," the voice said. The fingers departed.

I opened my eyes slowly. A soldier's lips tried to smile.

"Are you all right?" he asked.

I was shocked and frightened again when I recognized him as one of the three soldiers. I turned away.

"May I accompany you home?" he asked. Accompany me home, I thought? How that honest-sounding formality from this white solder-boy tampered with my fear by making me feel respected. I was scared to look at him. But I nodded, yes.

On the way home he told me that I had changed his life. Forever. He wanted to meet my family, I remember him suddenly saying. When we arrived at my house—a small wooden shanty, mangled by the elements, dilapidated from a lifetime of disrepair—I remember him looking around, his eyes searching and searching. No electricity, he said. I nodded. He pointed.

"Outhouse?"

I nodded.

We shaded ourselves under the red maple tree in front of my house (what I later dubbed The Faulkner Tree. But I'm ahead of myself). The soldier—young, and, like me, less innocent now—stood nervously, at attention. I saw in his gaze a determination. I averted my eyes, demurely.

"I do not have the words, ma'am, to say what I feel," he said.

I remember, still looking away and then, of all things, thanking him for saving me. I felt stupid and angry at myself for being a nigger.

"No, ma'am," he said. "You saved me."

Moments later he walked away.

He returned the following morning. Before dawn, I supposed, because I always left at daybreak for my job as our church secretary. I smiled but could not possibly undo my conditioning: Was he here to hurt me? Though I kept my eyes from contacting his, when I glimpsed his hat tucked underneath one arm, I felt less threatened. He pulled an envelope from inside his pocket. I noticed how clean his pressed uniform was. The sun, inching above the horizon, seemed to direct its first light to the small gold bar on each shoulder.

He handed me the envelope. I saw the words "Stars and Stripes" printed on the upper left hand corner. I looked at him. I tried to hide my surprise at the dark purple under his left eye, and the emerging scab over his thick lower lip. He nodded slightly, maybe in recognition of my raised brow.

And, there I went again: "I *can* read, you know."

He smiled. "Yes, ma'am."

He asked me to read it while he waited.

And so I did.

"Ma'am, my name is Lawrence Brennan. Yesterday, I stood by and pretended that you were not a woman, much less a human being. Though I finally stopped the others before they could further hurt you, my actions till then spoke for me. My

25

inaction, actually, hurt you every bit as much as their actions. Standing there, everything I believed about myself, morally and ethically, vanished. I became those men.

"I neither expect nor deserve your forgiveness.

"I have searched for words that can adequately express the sorrow I will live with forever for the pain and humiliation that I have caused you. I cannot find them.

"You are human. You are a woman. I understand better what that means now than I did a day ago. I can only say that, for the future, if I am ever witness to one person's hatred for another, I promise you, I will become the hated, and I will react instantly, no matter what physical jeopardy awaits me.

"I hope, in the future, I will have the honor of knowing your name, and if I am fortunate, of hearing it from you.

"With your permission, I ask that you will allow my future actions to speak for me.

"Sincerely,

"Second Lieutenant Lawrence C. Brennan, U.S. Army."

I can hear him admonishing me, Ken, as I write this. *That's enough, Flo.* But may I describe the inner being, that place where our spirit encounters God's, whom I will recall when Lawrence Brennan appears before my mind's eye?

He sent my mother $50 a month till she died in 1970. He helped me with tuition to a private Negro secondary academy. He came to Mississippi with the express purpose of not leaving until I shouted back at him, "Okay, you're right, I am smart enough to go to Bennett College for Women." He persuaded me I'd receive a full scholarship to NYU Law "if you'll just apply, dammit." He worked tirelessly, and anonymously, on my behalf when I first ran for Congress in '92.

These were such profound kindnesses that I shall never forget them. But it was our encounter on election night, in

1992, that I will always recall with the most sublime fondness. For it was in those moments your father's spirit embraced mine, and God's.

Already a celebrity, Lawrence snuck into the back storage room of my Bronx office, to congratulate me, of course. Hatless, as always, he was damp and shivering from the cold November drizzle.

"Congratulations, Congresswoman Pines," he said. He extended his hand. As I clasped his, I looked up at him.

"Congresswoman Pines thanks you," I said. "And so does Florence Charlotte Pines."

I placed my other hand over his. He reciprocated.

He looked, it felt, inside my eyes, as if he'd finally spotted something he'd been searching for. He pressed his lips together and let them relax into a smile.

"So that's what the C stands for," he said. I nodded.

Still holding my hand, he squeezed it gently. "I'm honored to hear it from you, Florence Charlotte Pines."

May God bless Lawrence. And may God bless you and your family, Ken.

Yours truly,

Flo

So now I saw Bing as Representative Pines did. I sat and tried to visualize the man she knew. I thought of my father as Dad.

I read her email again. But from a new venue, a sightline that permitted me to reach out, even in death, and to connect my yearning for him to his humanity. *Hey, Dad, it's me, your son.* I tried to live inside her words and wondered, what if—even had I never discovered these or other acts of kindness—I had assumed that, like all of us, Dad had his story. And that his story was, in its most essential form, an expression of his yearning, his desires, hopes, dreams, successes, disappointments: his humanity. Would that insight have permitted me to say, once and for all, what I now feel: *I forgive you, Dad.*

I will meet Representative Pines at Dad's memorial. I will thank her for the remembrance of a father I wish I'd known. I will thank her for teaching me that I can celebrate what I preach—a fundamental goodness, a shared humanity that binds my father to me. I will tell her: You have saved me from being destroyed by the thought of him.

I typed my obit's concluding paragraph:

> Dad, in recognizing Congresswoman Pines's tribute to you, this obit represents my first step toward dislodging my fear that I will never succeed in tranquilly navigating the ties that bind us, much less honoring them. I am determined to keep trying, Dad. At 53, I am still angry, unforgiving, and afraid. I have a long journey ahead of me.

I sent my obit to Terry. I hoped he'd approve, which meant I suspected he wouldn't. I leaned back in my swivel chair, cocooned in the night's salutary blackness. A gusting wind rattled my office window and comforted me.

I raised my head and gazed at the photos on the wall to my right. Above the couch, framed memories stretched from one end to the other. *Generations,* I called it: early 20th-century individual and family portraits of my grandparents and Trish's, as children and adults. My favorites: a post-war UPI shot of Ike with his arm around a surprised, rugged-faced war correspondent—the only time I'd ever seen Bing look flustered. To the left, Ensign Neal (my mother), saluting an aircraft carrier as it departed her Navy base in San Diego. Her eyes, as if they saw from her heart, always softened her stolid expression. I imagined her wondering, as she often told me she had, whatever became of the sailors she'd attended to—who'd returned, who hadn't. "C'est la vie," she'd say, and I heard the four sentient notes that were the music in her voice play: melancholy, sorrow, hope, stoicism.

Mother did not possess the mental or physical strength to challenge Bing, much less defend us from his assaults. Her volitional ability surfaced post-conflagration, when she would hug our violated souls, wipe our tears, and listen patiently to our endless complaints. Mother's compassion and unconditional love for her sons couldn't protect Terry and me. C'est la vie. I loved my mother, unconditionally. I always will.

My focus shifted to a photo of Bing standing among his twin brother (whom he despised from birth), older sister (whom he despised from birth), future sister-in-law (whom he despised the second they met) and mother's parents ("Morons," to quote Dad). It was his twin brother's wedding day. My revulsion over Bing's petulant smirk, the disengaged eyes averting the camera's lens, surfaced like a missile. I shook my head, resigned only to perplexity over what drove Bing to be *such* an asshole.

I thought about the final six months of Bing's life. Terry and I saw him more than in the previous six years. I remembered Terry spoon-feeding him strawberry sherbet near the end (Bing's favorite), then dabbing his lower lip with a Kleenex, and, speaking softly, asking if he wanted more. Bing barely nodded. Terry gently pushed two small spoonfuls between his parched lips.

Leaving hospice that day, I complimented Terry for his delicate compassion, and he reiterated his major concerns: probate, and the disposition of our seven-figure inheritance.

My eyes drifted from the photo gallery, to my desk, to a crooked row of several pennies, nickels, a dime. He's actually dead, I thought, and in his absence, I wasn't so much angry with Bing as bewildered by him. I curled fetally on my office couch, reached up, tugged the lamp's two chains, and in the blessed, silent dark, willed myself to float, maybe just an hour or so.

I awoke with a start at 7 a.m., and raced to read Terry's email: "MEET ME SOMEWHERE."

Elbows on the table, Terry's fists cradled his chin. He was wearing his black-and-red flannel shirt, and yellow tie— emblazoned with multihued letters spelling "Peace Out"— indicative of a forthcoming meeting with his agency's "creative." The tip of his tie dangled precipitously over a gooey brown smudge blemishing our otherwise spotless table. We eyed each other: empathetically, I prayed. He sipped his apple juice.

"Speak to me," he said.

Elena quietly placed our food on the table, smiled, and left, wordless—her sixth sense, I guessed.

"Your omelet's getting a chill," I said, thinking how foolish he looked in that getup and that I loved him. I glanced out the window and watched the powdery snow stick to Greenwich Street. The plain-gray sky was ominously flat. I was determined to win Terry over, respectfully.

"No matter how you slice it, Kenny, good outweighs bad. It's what people are wired to hear."

"I thought I was the one explaining," I said.

"Sorry."

"It's not about Flo's anecdote, Terry. It's about allowing the goodness it reveals in Bing, *Dad*, to connect me to his humanity. Okay."

Terry's voice murmured, like he was suffering a low-grade fever. His chin was tucked in his palms, hands pressed against his cheeks. "Like I wrote, Kenny, even if it's one good deed to 50 bad ones, all people will hear is the good. It's like Foreman losing on points and then, one punch. Boom! Down goes Frazier! No one remembers how well Frazier did. It's the obituary's nature, what it does, it sanitizes the shit."

Whatever. I said: "Acknowledging his inherent goodness is practicing my faith, Terry, in our inherent humanity, my belief that we must, we must recognize that what we all share matters. If we don't, who are we, Terry? Our remembrance of Dad—"

"Bing to me."

"Okay. Terry, this obit isn't about Bing, it's not about good versus bad," I insisted. "The obit is about how I choose to remember him and what that says about me, the son, and you. If you approve."

"How about Hitler?"

"What?"

"You don't find Bing's version of humanity ... a problem," Terry said.

"I'm not talking about Adolf," I said.

Terry lowered his hands. He leaned in to me and whispered, "I am. And Bingo was his name-o."

Mr. Melodrama. I should have known better, I thought.

"In plain words, you're telling me what?" I asked.

"Plain words *are* my specialty! They were my major at City College, remember," he said.

In the silence, Terry's banal glibness was all the more annoying because it churlishly discredited my discourse, my Philosophy of Religion PhD from Cornell, and my choice to unpack life's purpose the way I prefer. I listened to myself breathe.

"Can I be me? Pretentious asshole that I am," I said. Terry sliced through the middle of his omelet. I noticed the tomato, melted cheddar, and bacon bits oozing from each half. Bite, chew, coffee, swallow—that's how he always eats his omelet. So annoying. He lowered his fork, then knife.

"Yes," he said.

"I'm talking about our highest calling—where I find god— lower-case g, okay. I encounter god—what I think of as our essential goodness—when I bravely acknowledge the humanity of others, even those I hate, as if they were me."

"He never, never, never acknowledged me," said Terry. "Or you."

"Let it go," I replied.

"I'm stuck on Adolf, and Saddam and Pol fuckin' Pot, and," he whispered, "Bingo was his name-o!"

Jesus, what a hard-ass.

"His life wasted us," he said.

"I know," I said.

"That cold fact does not need your asterisk, Sister Mary!"

Silence.

"Sorry," he said.

"I'm acknowledging his humanity. That's all," I said.

"Your obit is shit with whipped cream."

"Oh, my God."

"Don't mock me!" he said. "Fuck yourself."

My heart beat faster. "You fuck yourself," I said.

Terry lowered his fork and knife and looked at me. His eyes intuited what was in mine. He gently bit his lower lip, nodded. "I know. Bing won't come between us, Ken, will he?"

"Never," I said.

"Count me out of the celebration," said Terry.

"Meaning?"

His voice was faint, garbled. I realized his mouth was full.

"I already told you. Down goes Frazier."

"What?"

"You let Flo Pines turn him into hearts and flowers—"

"That's not the point."

"It is." His deliberate calm drew me to lean in to him. "Everyone who reads this is gonna weigh her experience against ours. She wins. It's human nature."

"If he was a piece of shit, then so am I. You see that."

"No."

"What do you see?"

"An irresponsible motherfucker. You want my obit? 'Here lies an irresponsible motherfucker. Drive home safely!' "

"Terry, it's a slippery slope. First I vilify him. Then I marginalize him. Then he no longer means anything, to me, to you, to anyone. Then there's a place for no meaning in this world, Terry, and that's bullshit, because when there's a place for no meaning in this world, you can snuff out a life or half the population, just like Pol fucking Pot, and what would it matter?"

He licked his lips.

"There's still egg there. Gross."

The napkin muffling his voice, he said: "You and this congresswoman are letting him off the hook. Not me."

Terry scraped congealed cheese with his fork, then tongued it, like an anteater.

"What if there was no Flo Pines, Ken?"

"What if, Terry? Then maybe I'd be one unsalvaged, angry motherfucker forever."

"He was an irresponsible father."

"All right! All right! He was nuts. I'll just say that!"

"Ken, I can't make the memorial."

"Okay."

"I read it all, Kenny. Word for word. I stand by what I said in my email."

"And?"

"You need to explain yourself. Your way. I get that. I respect you, Ken. And what you believe. So, we're good."

"We are good," I said.

"I mean it, Kenny, publish the obit."

I emailed Jack.

From: kbrennan@nytimes.com
To: jmarsh@nytimes.com
Date: Tue., Jan. 4, 2011
Subject: Obit

Hey Jack:

Attached is obit to replace next week's column. Sorry it's so last-minute. And waaaay long. Could it run in 2 parts? If this doesn't work, forget the obit. I don't want to embarrass you/compromise the *Times*. Jack, if the obit can't be printed as is, I'll ask to resign as "Family Connections" editor as soon as is convenient for everyone.

Thanx for letting me give this a go. Oh, and Terry approved it.

Ken

engagement connects,
acknowledgment binds

A MINOR ADJUSTMENT

TRENT SITS on the middle edge of his bed exactly as he sits each night for several minutes before retiring at precisely 11 p.m., and stares at his blue silk pajamas while straightening his spine's incipient curve. And exactly as he does each night, he discerns time itself as tangible—alive and menacing, and time itself seems to intuit his vulnerability, and stalks him like a boxer sighting blood, and catches his certitude (so implacable during the day) off guard with stupefying blows, and he is defenseless, and cannot deflect time, whose impugning fists pummel his belief that his sin —callous, unconscionable, and without justification—is redeemable, and that he is.

Trent squints, and clutches his legs, and endures what feel like sinew-tearing blows to his body, each degrading his resistance to doubt, each bullying him into questioning his purpose, each castigating his mission: to rise up like a man, a real man—for the first time in his 71 years—and initiate a healing process by presenting his child with all it will take, on both their parts, to gather their relationship's shattered pieces, and collectively recreate father and son, one small step at a time, each small step, he reminds himself, *a minor adjustment.*

He is on his back, and cannot subdue his panic, nor parry his shame, and so he reaffirms his fealty to *minor adjustment,* a small-steps solution that he recalls emerging from within him a year ago —like a phoenix—from the residue of his failure: as a parent, a father, a human being; and he recalls himself at the nadir of his existence, when suicide seemed the only honorable antidote to disgrace.

No, he cannot imagine the depth of his son's anger, nor his son's excruciating pain, nor the herculean effort it will take for his son to surmount his rancor and finally speak to him. No matter! Reentering his son's life is no longer an option. As a father, it is his moral obligation to leave no stone unturned, morally right— right in the way *do unto others as you would have them do unto you* is right. And this A-B-C simple, absurdly mundane, minor adjustment-solution he has in mind—once accepted by his son— will, absolutely will, germinate into an authentic connection between them for the remainder of their time on this earth!

Trent reaches over and watches the King James Bible vanish as he shuts the drawer to his night table.

He pulls the covers beneath his chin, and surveys the bedroom's bare, off-white walls, and sparse furnishings—*like a cell for crackpots like me,* he thinks. Self-doubt immolates efficacy, and he is at least secure in the knowledge that, regardless of this ludicrous plan's outcome, his son could not possibly despise him more than he already does.

A distant fire engine siren—the only external sound, he thinks, that penetrates his rented brownstone's otherwise graveyard-quiet, ground-floor garden apartment—invites his momentary displeasure. The wailing disintegrates, and he reconciles himself to the judgment he has made his peace with, whether or not his son repudiates him: He is no hero, but merely undaunted like one—like Gandhi, or King, or Mother Teresa, or America's most decorated marine, Lewis "Chesty" Puller, and his personal role model. So, no matter how his son rebuffs him, no matter how many times he's rebuffed, he's not leaving Park Slope. He's in Brooklyn to be near his son, forever.

He rehearses the initial small-steps words he will say to his son. Again. Again. Again. And again. His heavy eyelids finally sink.

In the pre-dawn, Park Slope is desolate, and he feels indefatigable. First light brightens high clouds singed orangey-red: *Sailor take warning*, he thinks. *No matter, the time is now; not another day's delay.* He approaches the northwest corner of Fifteenth Street, tottering, focusing, imagining he's navigating a mine field, and he extends his neck like a pigeon, and peers down Seventh Avenue, and he is fazed by the sound of his shoe's sole scraping against the concrete, as if this misstep exposes him to the world as clumsy and incapable.

Anxiety enfeebles him; he waits it out. He tugs at his shirtsleeve, and looks at his watch. Below *Citizen*, he gazes left: JUN. Then right: *1*. He cannot constrain the gnashing in his gut.

Shortly, his son will emerge from the distance—unless maybe he is sick, or away—and he will watch him walking up Seventh Avenue—on the opposite side of the street—from Twelfth, where he lives, and, the result of no contact with him in nearly three decades, he will, he knows, ruminate over all he's missed, fantasize about meeting his son's wife, and infant boy, imagine entering his condo's interior, unlike, he hopes, the exterior of the drab, block-long complex, a converted dull-red brick factory that is architecturally more reminiscent of old Soviet proletariat than gentrified Brooklyn.

The instant his son is recognizable to him, he will retreat, crouch against the brick wall of the Japanese restaurant, his view partially obscured by the extended brown wooden fence that encloses the establishment's garbage hoppers. He will peek through its slats, the width of his thumb, and, when his son has turned on Fifteenth, and heads east to the Armory YMCA health club in the middle of the block, he will, like a cautious prairie dog, stand on his arthritic toes, raise his head and rehearse—as he has each Monday, Tuesday, Thursday, Saturday, and Sunday morning for the past five months—this final time.

His throat is dry. He swallows, and fusses with the knot of his yellow tie, and jiggles it up until it is tight against his Adam's apple. *Too tight.* Or maybe it's just the constricting humidity—first sticky day of the year, he realizes. He worms his index finger inside his collar for relief. *No.* He will not loosen the knot. He will remain buttoned up! He wipes pasty sweat on his neck. "Too fuckin' much starch," he mutters. *Goddammit!* He recalls before leaving Feng Cleaners, specifically and *slooowly* instructing Evelyn, who nodded like she was brain-dead. *Light! Right?* Yes, he was clear. *Fuckin' chinks! Never admit they don't understand you.*

He pats his birch-white hair to ensure that it's combed straight back. He brushes and brushes the jacket of his black pin-striped suit though he knows there is no reason to; it's immaculate. He's being overly fastidious: So what! He's just nervous. Why wouldn't he be? *This is it: Amends Day.* In 90 minutes, having left the Y, and having stopped off at the Green Olive deli on the corner of Fourteenth Street and Seventh before heading home, his son will exit with a green apple in one hand, and a bottle of peach-flavored Vitamin Water in the other. And the father who abandoned his infant and wife—whose perfunctory Western Union telegram issued from Honolulu stated, *Have fallen in love with someone. Won't be returning to Chicago*—will stand before his adult son. His explicating words will mean to beg reconciliation, initiate a healing journey, and express his resolve to right a wrong decision that bore intractable estrangement into his son's heart, and unspeakable sorrow into his.

If only, Trent thinks, he was seated on the wobbly counter stool by the kitchen in the Little Purity diner—where he's a 5:30 a.m. regular—drinking black coffee, munching a buttered bialy, and kibitzing with Edna, the ancient, smoky-voiced waitress whom he congenially recalls laughing like an old whore at a teenage boy's premature mess the day he honestly revealed that "just shooting the shit" with her was an elixir for his travails, and then Edna welcoming him to her world: "Honey, pardon the Midwest-goyim correction, but in Brooklyn, we don't *shoot shit* to relax. We kibitz. That's relaxing."

If only he was at the Purity now, getting an earful of Edna's comforting Jewish slang, which immediately enamored him of her, and bizarrely made it possible for him to open up, to share with her all his son's habits, preferences, and predispositions he'd learned about and memorized this past year, and also his most intimate fears, as he imagined he would to a shrink, and when he turned sour and reticent, being seduced, really, to speak, by her standard entreaty: "As an honorary inductee, the kibitz-commandment must be obeyed: 'When a member of the tribe says, 'Nu?' You speak!' So, nu?" Opened him up like a shucked oyster.

He yearns: for Edna's unequivocal dismissal of his flagging courage: "No, you *embody* courage"; for her affirming contradictions: "You are *not* naive or meddling or crazy"; for her persistent encouragement: "Brave as a Maccabee, you are!" to stand solitary vigil for as long as it takes until he is absolutely confident that the time is right to engage this 33-year-old man he last saw on his third birthday.

Is that him leaving the Y? Kerin's figure enlarges against the blurry landscape. *Kerry!* He cautions himself: His son permitted only his mother, and now only his wife and aunt, to use the diminutive.

Kerin nears Seventh Avenue. Trent cowers, and the inner Chesty Puller buckles; his heart pounds; he is perspiring like a pig; who is he kidding? As if this 12-word preamble to reconciliation will obviate his three no-show decades, his betrayal, and miraculously convene upon him a second chance he does not deserve.

No more procrastinating. It's June 1st. No more rehearsing, no more bullshitting.

Breathless, Trent murmurs his 12 words, and his jabbered monotone reminds him of those bearded Hasidim he sees on the F train, demented-looking aliens, staring into their prayer book, and double-time jabbering, like him. *Jesus!*

Kerin's image sharpens. He *is* handsome. *Wow.* Mussed tufts of coal-black hair—like tumbleweed—push from beneath his red cap. Trent can make out the white *N* above the bill. Kerin's 6-foot-3 frame, his muscles—defined, angular—really are a replica of him 30 years ago. *My God!* Is he jealous?

He recognizes the white-lettered *Nebraska HUSKERS* on his son's red wifebeater T, and he remembers the confidential call to his ex-wife's sister, his groveling: "Anything, any detail, please tell me." He is unnerved, as he was then, by her parting broadside just before she hung up: "It is enough that Kerry will say I violated his trust if he discovers this. If you do anything, Trent, say anything to upset him—and you damn well better remember you're talking to the *responsible* person who raised him after Janet's death—I will pray to God that you die like her, in agony. And don't think for a minute that my throwing you tidbits about his life means I give a fuck about yours."

Trent stands on his toes before Green Olive's window, craning his neck, spying, to get a glimpse over rows of stacked

Perrier of his happy-as-a-lark son kibitzing with the animated, middle-aged Arab owner behind the counter, and he realizes he is no parent, just a sweat-drenched, delusional fool.

Coins silently plunk in Kerin's open palm, and the two men laugh like comrades, confidants, he thinks. Kerin opens the door, broadly smiling.

"Excuse me."

Kerin about-faces. They are the same height. *Exactly.* And Trent sees his own sorrel-colored eyes; his own chin's delicate, oval cleft; his former pencil-thin black brows.

"I'm your father."

"I know."

"Really?"

"My aunt told me."

"Oh."

Silence. He is falling! *C'mon.* He reaches for his son's shoulder.

Kerin leans back. "No need to touch me."

Trent straightens like a berated soldier. "Did she tell you why I—"

"No need to know."

"I'm—"

"To know what you want—"

"Sorry."

"I don't need to—"

"Are you—"

"Goodbye."

"Busy? This weekend?"

Trent follows Kerin: not too close. "Or next weekend? Or next—"

Kerin stops. Trent stops, and squints against the sun. Kerin turns, and squints, as if the sun is in his eyes.

"Would you like to go fishing over the weekend—you and me?"

"What?"

"A chance to—"

"You had your chance. Chances."

"Please let me talk to you."

"No need to."

"But I'd, I want to know you—"

"No need to."

Trent ignores a mosquito on his knuckle. "You purchase an apple, green, and Vitamin Water—peach—after you work out Monday, Tuesday, Thursday, Saturday, Sunday morning at 6:20 a.m. for an hour and a half. You ... you." His memory flees. "You, oh, you had a football scholarship at Nebraska—cornerback. You suffered a traumatic ACL injury. Couldn't play full bore afterward." He steps a foot closer. "You graduated Fordham Law School. Met your wife, Patti, there—a year ahead of you. She's currently a clerk for a judge; you're a charter school principal. You guys married in '09, have a son, Damon, who is 2, 3 July 6th, and who will never know your stepfather, who passed away this last December 31st, who you loved. And you admired. Like a real father. I've learned about you, so many things, and I want you to learn about me, while we fish, because I know how much you love fishing and I can't alter, or change, or deny the past, but I can plead for reconciliation, to begin again; I can beg." Trent curls his lips inward, and presses on them, hard.

The acrid stench of a rumbling garbage truck coincides with its cacophonous halt right in front of them. Trent's wince has failed to break the ice. "Hey, remember to move the '09 Toyota Corolla in front of your condo before 8:30 for street cleaning— that Patti's folks got you for graduation. It's a Monday."

The garbage truck trundles forward. "Some stink. I've moved here."

"Oh?"

"Since January."

"To the Slope?"

"Yes. I rented a studio—three blocks from the Barnes and Noble."

Kerin is dumbfounded, Trent thinks, but he is still standing here, and he makes haste, and fumbles inside his coat pocket, and removes a folded square of lined yellow paper that includes the date, details of where they're going, and his email.

"For you." Trent extends his hand, and says he will park in front of his son's condo at 6 p.m. in two weeks. "Two Fridays from this coming. We'll stay in a motel Friday night—separate rooms—fish Saturday, then return that night, or Sunday."

"No need to—"

"Can I be your father for a weekend?"

He'll only call attention to the paper shimmying in his extended hand if he attempts to control it. "Here's my application." He slips the paper between the sweating plastic bottle and Kerin's palm, and is aware that he has touched the flesh of his boy for the first time in 30 years.

"If you insist I move—"

His son's shrug is limp.

"I will. Otherwise, I left you once. I will never leave you again."

Trent shuffles, head down, along Seventh Avenue, past the Barnes and Noble, and wonders if God witnessed this encounter, and he prays silently for an answer, and is distracted by a sandal-clattering caravan of three approaching black nannies—two of them top-heavy globs stuffed in spandex pants and V-shaped blouses, and the other one morbidly obese, sporting a loose-fit, sleeveless smock that accommodates her swaying slabs of gelatinous arm-fat and clings like cellophane to her medicine-ball rump—pushing four white babies in strollers. This typical urban scene—the dark and unprivileged attending to their white and privileged employers' offspring, especially the two puckish cherubs fussing at each other in the double stroller—repels him.

He affably smiles at the passing nannies, and continues praying; he frets that he's praying like a Christian, and stops. Prayer, he reminds himself, is consistent with his incremental departure the past year from lifelong agnosticism to God—albeit his personal deity, one unencumbered by idiotic denominational affiliation. He reminds himself that he's soliciting his prescient, empathetic associate, not an omniscient, controlling boss. Guided by suspicious optimism, he resumes walking, and praying, and he implores God to neither absolve nor understand, nor even love him, but to—in this life—pardon him.

He meanders through the morning's viscous air, and nears Fourth Avenue, and respite, and he asks God if his son might somehow sense his prayer.

Having heard nothing from Kerin three days later, Trent abandons hope, and he retreats to the outside patio.

He sits at the card table he'd purchased at Staples, and detests himself. The breeze is crispy. He sips Equal-sweetened, milky coffee, and opens the cover of his iPad. He'll check his Schwab account, then his emails.

He peruses his holdings, and reassures himself that tithing a tranche of his net worth to have-not charities qualifies him as a selfless person, despite the fact that it has no deleterious impact on his $6 million portfolio. Before making a move, he thinks again about his meticulous estimation of what it would take for him to outlive his money, and how much he'll require for the worst-case scenario: a prolonged death at his Hawaii home beside a private attendant who calls him Mr. Woodson. Having flirted with, and since abandoned, an oath of poverty—he remains unconvinced that dying in a nursing home on Medicaid could be rationally construed as a worthy act—he transfers another $5,000 to Doctors Without Borders.

Kerin's email appears: *This weekend, then you leave Park Slope.*

The frenetic chirping of a gray and brown bird in the crabapple tree near the corner of the high fence that encloses the modest patch of unmowed grass and weedy flower garden that —*only in New York*—counts as a yard catches his attention. *A starling?* The bird flies off, and Trent stares at the oscillating branch, and then up into the china-blue sky, where he follows a wandering cloud patch, as if carefree, overhead. *Fuck me. You did it.* Yes: He botched his presentation to Kerin, came off like a flustered ninny; five solitary months of preparation—for what! But it's all good, because from the get-go he had equated the chances of seamlessly executing his last-stand battle plan with Custer's. Still, he knew enough of battle—mindful of being denied that patriotic duty by his father, a coward, whose sniveling beseeching of the longtime family doctor ended in overruling his protestations, and saw to his IV-F in '67—to realize that after the first round is fired, everything goes *kablooey,* so you hang in, which he did, *goddammit,* especially when—*Wow!*—was he blindsided by his son's recognition of him, and advance knowledge of his arrival, and so he is forewarned: Expect the unexpected. But no matter! He is undaunted; his strategy is fixed: He'll hold himself accountable on this trip: his irreversible past that includes all his pathetic, stupid, selfish choices; his disgrace; his permanently disfigured soul! And he will finally have *his* say. Not Kerin's mother's, or aunt's, or Kerin's friends, or in-laws, or some psychiatrist's, but his say, Trent's say! After three decades it is his turn, his opportunity to provide context, to set the record straight, and then his son will know of him *from him,* and can fairly judge him. "Finally!"

From his Mazda SUV parked by the opposite curb, Trent can't help staring at Kerin, who appears from his building's glass double doors, turns, and looks up. Leaning out the second-story open bay window, a delicately attractive, sandy blonde woman holds her toddler's hand, and they wave as one. Trent averts his gaze. An intrusion. He hasn't earned the right to be privy to his son's intimacies.

The knock on the passenger window is jolting. Trent reaches over, and opens the door. "Oh, hey. I didn't even see you."

Kerin sits like a wary adversary. What else, thinks Trent, and he observes that they are both dressed in tan cargo pants, maybe not a coincidence, but he won't mention it; perhaps later, after he changes from his leaf-print short-sleeved shirt into the Big Red T he'd purchased online to match the one Kerin is wearing.

"Wanna heave your bag in the back with the gear?"

The wary adversary complies, and in a current of tremulous words that rush like rapids, Trent apologizes for his callous, deaf ear: to the stunned pleas of his disconsolate wife the week following his leaving her; and years later, to her calls as she lay succumbing to metastatic breast cancer; and to his heroic adolescent's dry-eyed, truncated pleas left daily on his answering machine; deaf to the gulps, and choking, deaf to his frantic bargaining for financial help. " 'On my knees, Dad,' you said. You were willing to quit high school and repay every penny. I wasn't deaf. I heard you." He does not dare extend his hand. "I have some explaining to do."

"Not to me."

It is as if a pin has been jabbed beneath his nail. "Ya know, I've never suffered impudence, Kerin, even when lighthearted, harmless, unintentional. The day I announced my company's IPO at a senior staff meeting—the corporate jet rental business I owned. Anyway, there was still some useless griping over the company's new name, which I'd already approved: *Fat Banana.* My CFO—he was 58—I remember catching him snigger, maybe a millisecond, and mumbling, 'Fat *chance* banana.' Twenty-seven years, loyal years—terminated by me, on the spot, in front of everyone. I managed the corporate—insincere—smile, and said, 'Take care.' I made certain the players in our industry knew he was fired." Trent twists the ignition key. "I've treated work, and people, like a war: Kill. Or be killed. It's a reaction I am working to rid myself of."

The empty street appears in Trent's side-view mirror. He eases the car forward. "My past imprisoned me. I still wear it— like an orange jumpsuit—each day, and night. I can't remove it, can't discard it, deny it; can't pretend my past isn't part of me now."

"I have no need to hear this—"

"I have a need to tell you!"

Kerin looks at him—for the first time, Trent thinks. "I agreed to this trip to reassure myself I feel nothing for you; so far, so good."

At the intersection where the red light turned green several seconds ago, Trent can now believe that his son is lost to him. There is a honk. He rounds the corner, and contemplates jumping. "I was thinking." He pauses. How long can he tolerate this one-way conversation? "That we can eat together when we get to Woodstock. Meet outside the motel tomorrow morning, 5:30, I know you're an early guy, and when I checked out Cooper Lake—"

His son nods. *You've said enough, Trent. Slow steps. Rome was decimated the day you abandoned him. You have a lifetime to rebuild it.*

Trent drives north through the Hudson Valley on the spindly Taconic, what feels more a predatory viper than a two-lane highway: twisting, shoulder-less stretches; must be deathly slippery when wet; too few lights; ramp-less entrances; and severely angled exits that seem purposefully designed to maximize hazard. But he knows that the Taconic—more scenic than the New York State Thruway, and *relatively* safe in daylight hours—would have been his son's choice, despite its being on the wrong side of the Hudson for Woodstock.

Trent approaches Highway 55. He detects a smiling scar that extends half an inch from the side of his son's mouth. *Football-related?* Kerin's vacant stare out his window dissuades him: Maybe someday he'll ask him about it.

"We'll hang a Louie west, head up by Poughkeepsie, cross the Hudson, and make our way to Woodstock," says Trent. How? How does he illuminate a dead star? "Your aunt; she's a live wire, huh. Anyhow, she described your love affair with the Hudson Valley—'totally primal!' She told me, 'His blood's Type B, but when Kerry's in the Valley, the B stands for *bucolic.*' How's the country house outside Kingston? Still spend two weeks each summer with the lesbian couple—"

"Patti and I consider them family."

"They're Damon's godparents."

"You know."

"I do."

"You know all about me."

"Your aunt—"

"You know all about me, huh Trent."

Trent cannot reply to a door slammed in his face: He entreats God for guidance.

Heading west on 55, Trent slows behind a herky-jerky, top-down Land Rover jeep belching oily, black exhaust. The edges of the ratty SUNY New Paltz sticker flap drunkenly on the bumper. A distant semi is approaching from the opposite lane. He depresses the pedal. As he passes the clearly adolescent driver, he wags his index finger at the pimply, peeved face, and in return is proffered a peevish middle finger. He speeds ahead, and imagines Kerin's slap-happy assessment—*Goofball, huh Pop!*—and his voluble, jocular snort. He casts a furtive glance at his son, whose restive glare out his window crushes him.

Silent minutes pass; he has assiduously not called his son by name. Dare he? No. He recalls occasionally murmuring the *West Side Story* song and substituting his son's name for Maria while waiting on Fifteenth Street: *Kerin. Say it soft and it's almost like praying.* He recalls cajoling Kerin's assistant principal at Stand Out and Succeed Prep, Catherine, whose initial suspicions were dispelled after he solemnly swore that what he begged from her was all he sought from his son: a chance. He knew the risk: She was Kerin's confidant, and when she agreed, despite her obvious prejudice, and loyalty, to treat him as if he deserved this inside information, he promised that his deeds—irrespective of Kerin's response—would never disappoint her, and he silently reaffirms his pledge to Catherine, and it is as if a trumpet—he hears it!—summons his son's habits and traits and quirks and predispositions that he'd surreptitiously learned about the past year from Kerin's aunt, from the confidential calls and visits to Kerin's friends and colleagues, and beckons them all to shout their approval for him to speak his son's name, now!

"Commodore Kerin," Trent says, and he prattles effusively: about Kerin's Nebraska clique; about its members' endearing pet name for their high-octane, overachiever star; about Commodore Kerin's conscientious professionalism, his rhetorical acuity, his fanatical devotion to Penn—where he and Catherine met while he was earning a Leadership MBA—and to his Penn classmates, who awarded Kerin a plaque honoring his consensus-building genius that read *Perfection Is The Enemy of Good*; and about Kerin's present role as SOS Prep's principal, and innovative guiding light, and the school's 3Ps-For-Success mandate:

"Purpose Plus Power. Succinct, and brilliantly conceived!" Trent is intrepid, awash in pride, and he quotes an education journal lauding Kerin's charter as " 'the model for America's most challenged urban neighborhoods.' Well, if anyone needs proof of nature over nurture," he says, "your 3Ps-For-Success mandate is exactly how I'd have phrased it. Exactly!"

Trent's eyes drift past his son's opaque demeanor, and he observes through Kerin's window a passing copse of clone-like trees before a verdant field, then a farmhouse, and cows by a fence. Does he fight on for his dignity, or capitulate? He concentrates on the road, and mocks his waffling fortitude. *So, Kerin. So. Kerin.* "So, Kerry."

"Kerin!"

"Of course. I meant—"

"Kerin."

"I meant to say, Kerin."

"What, then?"

"So, country roads, huh. All the way to Woodstock." Kerin's silence screams. He will see his plan through; he will honor his son's judgment—leave Park Slope, if that's his wish. What will be, will be.

They near Woodstock, and Trent endures the screaming silence.

A few miles from their destination, while following a flashing yellow highway maintenance arrow over a rutted stretch of blacktop to the opposite lane, he petulantly abrogates his experiment with God, with prayer: *Fucking pointless!* He will locate faith in his own agency, or die trying.

At the Red Lobster near Kingston, Trent sits across from Kerin on the faux leather seat of a cavernous booth that could easily accommodate six. Each sequesters his face behind a jumbo, multihued plastic menu.

"Hello, gentlemen!"

Trent looks up, and is startled by the young, curvaceous black waitress with a big, dome-shaped Afro that covers her ears, and borders her eyebrows—she's a dead ringer for Angela Davis. Her congenial smile matches her salutation, and the alluring gap between her front teeth just can't be coincidental.

"I'm Keisha, your server."

Her solicitous manner evinces a guileless charm that so belies her incendiary look-alike, and Trent revisits his impression of the strident black animus that defined the '60s. He might mention the uncanny resemblance.

"Can I start you two off with something to drink?"

Each immaculately articulated word is a pearl. She sounds British without the accent.

"You're, I'll guess, 18," Trent says.

"Twenty. I'm a junior at Bard."

"Congratulations." Keisha's pen is steady, and poised on her writing pad, as if Trent was her only customer in the packed, bustling restaurant.

"Majoring in?"

Keisha's head turns in a blur. Behind her, two toddlers are standing on their seats spitting at each other. She is harried, he realizes.

"Your table?" asks Trent.

She nods demurely—like one who assumes responsibility for what isn't their fault, he thinks—and he must take his eyes off Keisha's fetching eggshell-brown cheeks, and their enticing dimples.

"Sorry. Um, to start?"

"Wine. Chardonnay for me, Keisha. Merlot for my son."

"Right back for your order." She vanishes. The crack of a bat and the frenzied cheer from the men sitting at the square bar distract Trent, and he watches the TV as if he cares, and when he turns, and leans in to Kerin, about to speak, his elbow lands on the end of his fork, which somersaults as it shoots up, and sails over the end of the table.

They laugh.

"Nice!" says Kerin.

"Couldn't do that if I tried a hundred times."

"No, I don't think so."

"I'm sorry, um," says Keisha, "who gets—"

"White here. Red for my son."

"You need more time?"

"Nope. Broiled flounder for me. House salad. Balsamic vinaigrette," says Trent.

"Sir?"

"The same," says Kerin.

Keisha departs. Trent raises his wine glass, and moves his hand forward a fraction, and then looks away, and sips, and then pretends to examine his nondescript goblet's two defective bubbles, while pronouncing himself a fool. He lowers his glass to the table.

"Beautiful waitress," says Trent.

"Hmm."

"Reminds me of ..."

Silence. They sip their wine.

"I learned something since I arrived. Meant to tell you earlier. About how one word, an expression—never heard it before—just made me feel like I belong, like a real *New Yawkah*. Well, not a native, but, like an honorary one. Anyway, kibitz. The waitress at Little Purity, Edna. You know her. She taught me. She said you've kibitzed with her, and by the way, she never fails to sing your praises—how you always make her feel important, asking her about her kids, her life. 'Kerin's so giving. Such a mensch.' Oh, that expression I did know—"

While their salad plates are set before them, Trent stops speaking, and Keisha's quick departure without a word appears discreet, and he believes she respectfully intuited that his barely discernible nods were not meant to offend.

"So, Edna says mensch, and—"

"You're kidding!"

"No—"

"Is this why I'm here? To get a synopsis of what you know about me?"

"No—"

"What you *think* you've learned—"

"No, you see, son—"

"Don't *ever* call me that again!"

"I'm sorry."

"Don't call me son!"

"Kerin—"

"That's better."

"Kerin." He is vanquished. "Our salads. They'll get cold if we don't eat them." Kerin's quiet screams.

Keisha arrives and sets down their entrées, and disappears. Trent eats in time to Kerin, thinking that way they'll finish the meal together.

"I brought the letters you sent me as a child. I saved them all. With your permission, I'll open them. In the boat. Tomorrow. Read each aloud. Before you. Before God. Read what I never read until a year ago. But ever since, have read a thousand times. And then, with your permission, I'll explain who I was then. Why I chose another woman's raging jealousy, as if there was some, I dunno, hierarchy that placed her demand before your letters—"

"No need to know—"

"Kerin!"

"No need to know—"

"Goddammit! Becca loved me, touched me, acknowledged my feelings your mother rejected from the day you were born as if they didn't matter, and when I'm finished reading your hopes, desires, prayers, pleas—all these things that I was wrong to ignore, wrong!—I will own my past before you, own a failed parent, and father. Kerin. I am not a monster."

Trent refuses to look away. "I never intended to tell you about me, my demons, much less in a ... in a restaurant. I'm sorry."

Trent extends his tight fist across the table. He opens his fingers, and studies his weathered palm, its puffy hillocks, its leathery skin etched with crisscrossed spokes that remind him of arid riverbeds. "Nothing we say ever comes out right, huh."

Keisha clears the plates from the table. "Excellent fish," says Trent, and waves off her dessert inquiry, and while he is tendering his credit card, her colluding gaze caresses his.

"I know how you enjoy fishing. We can talk. About us. Get to know us; that's all I want."

"You already know about me, from—"

"Things, but not the real—"

"From practically everyone I've ever met—down to my school janitor."

"I thought, if we fish, it—"

"What?"

"It's a new begin—oh, God; forgive me, Kerin."

"You want forgiveness? From me? Is that what waiting on Fifteenth Street was all about?"

"No—"

"You just said—"

"No—"

"Then what? So we can start over? Start over, Trent? What does that mean? My childhood is fixable? Or, never happened! How's that? Your good intentions wipe out, what? How you destroyed Mother. Destroyed me."

"I can't make up 30 absent years—"

"*Absent* years, Trent?" Kerin stabs his chest with his

forefinger. "No, you reside in me. Permanently. Like a tumor. Festering, but manageable."

"I just thought that, if we could ... get to know each oth—"

"No need to."

"Look, I don't want you to forgive me—"

"No need to know what you want."

"Then how do I—"

" *I.* I, I, I! *I.* Do you get it, Trent? That's what this trip is about."

"No."

"Yes. *I* want to explain; *I* want forgiveness; *I* want to start over; *I* want Kerin to know me, so *I* will plan a little fishing trip."

"I want you to talk to me, but you never do."

"Okay, Trent. So, ask me to."

Trent lowers his head, shuts his eyes, and wishes to vanish.

"Look at me, Trent."

He is alone, and abandoned. And terrified—by what, he doesn't know.

"Ask me to speak! About *me.* Trent? Trent? C'mon, it's a minor adjustment."

TERMS OF ENGAGEMENT

FREDDIE'S GRIMACE catches the corner of Ted's eye. A test of his resolve, he thinks. She clutches her pocket makeup mirror and thrusts it to her lap and expels what strikes him as a wit's-end huff.

What now? He will conceal his displeasure. He is flat-faced. He focuses on the road ahead.

Freddie raises the mirror to her chin. Ted predicts the scowl. *The scowl.* The *white-flag* scowl that precedes Freddie's predictable reluctance to embrace nature's perfection in lieu of flaws that the corporate pulchritude-machine has bamboozled her into believing are eradicated by a commodity—theirs. Freddie's lips constrict and appear to him as a lesion. She inhales like an asthmatic. She huffs and groans. You would think the pink-framed, rectangular glass was a demon. Poised to wreak scorn and ridicule. Poised to render her despair unsalvageable.

"I really can't take looking at myself!"

"Don't, then." He will not play the foil for yet another drama-queen episode. He will not take the bait. Will not console her with the right words. With Freddie, he has learned, rationality merely exacerbates the drama.

Freddie coughs, and there is a seriousness to it, he thinks. She wipes the Volvo's faux leather dashboard with her fingertips. He is concerned. He is burdened by remorse.

"I'm okay." She hacks. "I'm okay," she says, and hacks.

He stops at a light. "Are you okay?"

Freddie's composure reappears. The reddish tip of her nose and watery eyes unveil his fiancée's particular beauty and fragility and lack of guile, and remind him why he loves her, what he loves about her, and if could he take back his earlier rejoinder, *Don't, then*, he would, and though she didn't recognize his passive-aggressiveness, it was not okay to react that way. He is too close to the car ahead of him and imagines stepping on the gas and jamming the brake before hitting its fender, and will he ever, he wonders, consider her feelings *before* the fact, *before* acting like a dipshit.

Driving down Devon, Ted slows, stops at the yellow light before it turns red and looks in his rearview mirror at the driver behind him pounding his horn: *Asshole*. He stares at the intersection's midpoint. The vehicles whooshing across Western appear surreal, and the certainty that possessed him, the logic that felt airtight when he turned off Lake Shore Drive, unravels.

Freddie flips open her makeup mirror and appears to zero in on her chin.

"I have to."

"What?"

She picks at something with her thumbnail.

"Get this puppy," she mutters.

"Go for it."

"I'm obsessed and you hate me."

She squints like a diamond jeweler. She positions her index finger opposite her thumb. Her nails, like pincers, connect and secure the interloper that Ted assumes is a hair. She is as still as a corpse. Her hand jerks forward. "Yahtzee!"

Ted depresses the gas pedal. "You're meeting my parents, Freddie, not royalty."

"I thought we agreed they should know me as Frederika."

"Okay."

"I thought we weren't calling me Freddie for now. You won't call me that in front of them, okay?"

"Okay. Frederika, I don't hate you, I—"

"You love me?"

"Yes!"

Ted cruises through Rogers Park. He implores himself: *Stay the course.* He turns on Ravenswood Avenue.

"This is it," he says, and stops by the curb in front of a prewar, five-story apartment building. "Where I grew up." He murmurs, "Or didn't."

"You won't call me—"

"Do you need to see your chin again?"

"Was that sarcastic?"

Ted reaches for the mirror that rests atop Freddie's bare knees. "Here," he says. He was sincere this time, he thinks. Her pout simmers and though it appears to be boiling into a glower, he experiences a pleasure in his equanimity.

"Why? Why am I wearing this skirt? It's too short, too red, I look like a slut! Dammit!"

Freddie's husky voice, which is reminiscent of honey with a hint of crunch, and its alluring melody infatuate him, and he recalls her bounding home last month, giddy, having signed with Imagine Artists and parroting her homosexual agent's unbridled prophecy: *Darlin', you will work all the time!!* He is making his peace, he thinks, with whatever propels him to respond to her voice as if it were an aphrodisiac, to a cadence that is intoxicating and even induces sympathy for her. How powerfully form influences feeling and belief, he thinks, especially when she is in full drama-queen mode, where he feels trapped, as if in a spider web. He remains susceptible, he thinks, to her effusive display of emotion, a vulnerability he hopes to someday conquer.

Freddie clutches the mirror. "I'm calm," she says. She sighs. "I don't look like a slut."

Ted gazes out his window. His certainty has collapsed.

Freddie says, "I know this is difficult."

"Stay the course," he replies. Her hand massages his neck. It is gentle. Her solace comforts him.

"You're doing what you believe is right."

With luck, things between him and his father will go as he has planned, Ted thinks.

Freddie removes her hand. "Are you okay?"

Ted nods. His resolve warrants recapitulation: Following this introduction to his parents, he and Freddie will return to their two-bedroom, third-floor walk-up on 113th between Riverside and Broadway, to her voice-acting career and to the halfway mark of his Comparative Lit PhD program at Columbia. Maybe they will see his father again. Maybe not.

"Can you give me the letter?" Ted says.

Freddie hesitates and then removes a white envelope from the glove compartment. "The glove *department*, you called it, right?" she says.

"Who told you?"

"Your mom. On the phone. She gave me the lowdown on all your malapropisms when you were a little boy."

Ted musters a smile and feels loss.

Freddie places the envelope on her lap and squints at it. She deflects his extended hand with hers and hunches down, as if examining some sudden, inexplicable problem.

"What?" Ted says.

"I dunno. It's the depression under the capital letters D-A-D."

"What are you talking about?"

"It just looks like you're *not* okay, Teddy."

"What?"

"By the way you pressed down on the letters."

His anxiety is fueling Freddie's, Ted thinks. He is matter-of-fact. He slips his hand between the envelope and her knee, and raises it up. His self-possession should reassure her. "I'm okay," he says.

"Oh, I know."

"Really."

She is unconvinced, he thinks, or she wouldn't avert her eyes. "I can't just acquiesce, Freddie. I can't *not* act!" He leans his head against his seat's backrest. His eyes wander across the car's roof. "I can't be around someone in a perpetual state of never being me." He inhales through his nose and exhales as if blowing smoke rings.

"Does that mean you have to give this to him?"

"Yes." He wills his emotional gears to quit shifting between his resolve and Freddie's doubts.

Freddie opens her door. Ted steps from the car, and the explicit consequences of Freddie's admonitions in New York yaw like a wrecking ball and smash through his conviction: *When in doubt, leave it out. You can't un-draw a line in the sand.* He vacillates. She is right, he thinks, and notices that the stoop to his former building's entrance has been replaced by a ramp. The tap of Freddie's high-heeled footsteps as she approaches reminds Ted that he is on *his* mission, not Freddie's.

"I'm Frederika, Mrs.—"

"Ruth. And Phil."

Next to Freddie, Ted's mother seems petite and, even in her black heels, is several inches shorter than Freddie. He is shaken. His mother extends both arms and embraces Freddie, and Ted is aware, for the first time, of a vibrancy that has abandoned her. His mother's dimpled cheeks seem softened by age, a neck no longer taut, crow's-feet that have deepened since he last saw her, that extend further out from the corner of her eyes; and her short hair, no longer springy, is white, an elderly person's white. He cannot abide the thought that she will die someday.

Freddie returns his mother's ingratiating squeeze as he imagined she would. She rests her chin on his mother's shoulder and turns to him and enunciates in grand and silent slow motion: *Oh my God, she is so beautiful!*

Ted's father seems to have appeared from nowhere. He is more portly than the last time Ted saw him. The top of his father's bald head and the unkempt thicket of black and gray hair on the sides that curls over the top of his ears disconcert him.

His father's right hand extends sort of halfway, and the tentative gesture conjures an image of him slicing through his father's wrist with a cleaver, and he, the implacable observer of a geyser of blood spewing from the stump as his father blubbers while he extends his hand fully: *You wanna shake my hand? Okay, let's shake!*

Ted offers his hand: So much easier, he tells himself, to defer to what is, to be compliant and accept that his father does not do hugs, not with him, not ever, that the world is arbitrated by *Phil's comfort level, period.* Ted's clasp betrays who he is. He raises his left hand and places its palm over his father's right shoulder and observes it hovering, and upon making contact with the sports jacket's burgundy corduroy, Ted's fingers stiffen. His father half-steps closer to him, and his left arm rings Ted's waist. Ted maneuvers his head until his ear is opposite his father's. Their ears touch. He recoils. His father's patting the small of his back, the sudden touch of his father's arm against his waist nettles him. He peers off to the side at nothing. He imagines a snapshot of this pose, perfect, he thinks, for this month's cover of *Spastic Quarterly*.

They decouple, Ted thinks, like ill-fitting puzzle pieces.

"How you doin'?"

In the midst of flicking lint from between his sleeve's brown buttons, his father says, "Lousy!"

Lousy snags Ted. Like a grappling hook. He cannot stand his father. So much for thinking that this rejoinder he has heard since childhood would no longer addle him, that he was over the revulsion that its utterance induces in him, that his age and education and maturity would by now have immunized him from the hemorrhaging he feels. *Lousy* has torn open a wound that has not healed, and that he cannot stanch. He feels neutered. "Sorry to hear that," he says.

"So," his father says.

His father's continued flicking at lint nettles Ted. He resists the urge to flee. This is likely to be their final encounter. He will endure his father, say everything he has come here to say. And then he and Freddie will go.

"I should lie?"

Oh no, not you. Ted retreats a step.

"Sit, please, everyone," says Ruth.

Ted is uneasy in the leather brown chair. Freddie's stride to the vinyl sofa across from him is too airy and cheerful. She eases herself down, opposite his mother, and tugs at her skirt and wiggles like a caterpillar and cannot seem to get her skirt close enough to her knees. She looks up, and her smile appears to enchant his mother. Not Ted. Something is up. Freddie is squinting. She is panicked. The sound, like masking tape torn from a package, directs his attention to her bare thighs separating from the vinyl. Freddie clasps her knees with both hands, appears okay, and he is proud of her. His mother is still enchanted. His father is checking his coat pocket and oblivious to this drama, he thinks, and wanders in his direction and is hovering inches from him and pinching the top of his nose. He endures the urge to flee.

"Sinus infection," his father says, apparently to everyone.

"Really," says Ted. His father places a hand on the back of his chair, and this transgression of his space galls him.

"Right here. Goddamned persistent, these sinus infections, exacerbated, I should add, by my ENT's feigned conviviality and utter, utter lack of wit."

A diatribe is imminent, Ted thinks.

"Wish you could see my ENT," says Freddie. "He's a hoot."

His father steps away, and Ted feels released from a cell.

"Well," his father says, "mine graduated with top honors from the College of Medical Dibbles and has since became the *ne plus ultra* of sinusitis practitioners."

His father has inched closer to the middle of the living room, aiming his effusion at Freddie like a laser, and Ted cannot quite capture her attention and—in vain, he frets—overenunciates in silence the golden rule she is about to violate: *Don't egg him on.*

"Dibbles?" asks Freddie.

"What?" says his father. "You don't know from a dibble?"

She shakes her head.

"Oy! So take notes, young lady! Pop quiz tomorrow."

Freddie blooms. She is his. Buccaneer Phil has swung from the yardarm and boarded her ship, thinks Ted.

"Definition. *Medical Dibbles*: That inbred cadre of pseudo-intellectual Jewish physicians whose haughty paternalism, *they think*, disguises the blatant faker that lurks beneath their disingenuous demeanor: a monosyllabic, no-nothing boor with attitude! Drag my ENT away from his sinus cavity/inner ear expertise and meet: Sheldon Abramowitz, a.k.a. Dr. Dibble, whose witless gray matter—when you poke beneath the pretense and the pandering and the paternalism—reveals a vacuousness unequaled in the annals of upper-income, contemporary Jewish American life."

His father's pause is for oxygen only, Ted knows.

"Why? How? Wherefore? Because, you see, unless it's about the hottest discount fares to Israel, evincing a scintilla of interest and compassion for humanity is ..." His father whispers: "Anathema to the plutocratic ethos of professional Jews!"

Oxygen. His father is not done.

"All of 'em! Contemptuous boors!"

"I never thought of it that way," says Freddie. "Wow."

His father mutters something to Freddie while pushing the sand-brown, square ottoman adjacent to the couch until he is situated a foot from her. "I kibitz about current events with all my doctors. Because, frankly, at my age, dwelling on what makes me ill makes me sick."

Anything to short-circuit the diatribe, Ted thinks, and says, "So, how are you feeling, now?"

"I'm in goddamn pain, like my sinuses are in a constant state of expansion, despite the Neti pots, the—look, it's a virus, maybe it was an infection. I've had the antibiotic, nothing, relentless discomfort, pain is what it is, constantly, so what the hell do I do? I can't concentrate. I'm enervated, but this too shall pass. No use complaining."

Freddie says, "You have a right to be upset, and these infections, especially if you're older—"

"Older I am."

"No!"

"It's okay. And how do I know I'm old? At my age, if I died tomorrow, it wouldn't be untimely."

"You are so funny. Mr. Weintraub, seriously, maybe try another doctor."

"Oy!" Phil stands and then meanders. To where, Ted

wonders? His father turns to Freddie. "What's really troubling about my age is, is my fear this wonderful fighting machine is mellowing. I've begun to notice, my fail-safe antidote to this increasing fatigue I feel used to be contempt for the terminally inane with whom I interact on a daily basis. I'm just not as pissed off as I used to be."

"Phil," his mother says to Freddie.

"Enough about me!" his father snaps.

"I was telling Frederika to call you Phil."

"Oh! Oh! Please, please, young lady. Phil."

In the quiet, Ted frets. He observes Freddie steal an inquisitive glance at the framed painting opposite her. *Don't get him started on Impressionism.*

Freddie looks up at his father. "Phil."

"Be right back." His father's gait is brisk. He nears the hallway. "Carry on without me! I just realized ..." He vanishes. "Keeeeeep talking!" His father's distant holler is gregarious. "Keeeeep talking." The knife ceases impaling him.

Ted and his mother gaze at one of multiple prints along with several original pieces that decorate all four vanilla-white living room walls. He notices Freddie standing on her toes inches from what appears to be roughly a 24" x 24" print that hangs adjacent to the vanilla-white French-style window frames.

"Monet's *Water Lilies,*" says his mother.

"Oh my God," says Freddie.

His mother whispers to him. "She is adorable."

Freddie peers at a smaller print on the wall to the left of the French-style wrought-iron front door, and he feels at peace in the presence of his mother and Freddie.

"Monet's *Garden,* Frederika," says his mother.

"I'd swear it's the original!"

His mother laughs, and he feels sheltered.

"Don't I wish, honey."

"I love Impressionism, Mrs.—Ruth."

"It's our passion."

"Teddy says, if you can't go to Provence, there's always Mom's kitchen."

"We just redid it. Oodles of sunflower yellow, lavender. I'll give you a tour in a bit."

"That would be awesome, Ruth." Freddie approaches another print.

"So, how's school, Teddy?"

"It's good, Mom."

"Let's sit. Frederika, come sit with us."

His mother is nestled on the couch between them and nudges closer to Freddie.

"In your last email, you mentioned your teacher ... from India? Um ... Professor Gayatri, did I pronounce that right?"

"You did. Gayatri Chakravorty Spivak."

"Still rocking your world?"

"Oh, yeah. She's tough. Still shoots me down when I have the nerve to disagree with her. But she gave my Lahiri paper an A. I think I've earned her respect."

"Then you're doing well—"

"I am, but, believe me, Mom, you do not wanna open your mouth unless your act is like, airtight. I make her laugh because, you know, my hand's waving before she finishes her question, and she'll sort of play-wrestle it down and say, 'Mr. Weintraub, one can't possibly speak to what one hasn't fully heard yet, but you'll try.' "

"And you admire her?"

"Definitely! Gayatri is no joke, Mom. Very big in theory. I'm super-influenced. I mean, she's only taught me how to read a novel!"

"I'm loving *Unaccustomed Earth*."

"I'm almost done," says Freddie.

66

"I think I understand you, the way she treats her South Asians," says Ruth. "Maybe?"

"Right. Look, Mom, at *how* we know Lahiri's characters."

"The South Asian ones?"

"Right. Remember the key word?"

"Habits."

"That's it, Mom. Now think habits, as opposed to essences, meaning we only know Lahiri's characters are South Asian by what they do, or wear, not who they are! And this is profound, Mom, and contrary, you know, to all this fetishizing of identity we see in much of contemporary literature, which, if you think of it, once you dispense with identity, which reifies difference, right, which creates a you-aren't-me, I'm-not-you binary, suddenly readers are liberated, ethically, able to engage Lahiri's characters as if they were engaging themselves."

"I see."

"It's crazy, right, Mom?"

"Truth, Teddy, it's a little above my pay grade—"

"Mom, when I sent you *Crossing the Brooklyn Ferry*—the way you analyzed it. Believe me, your poetry minor puts you in the game."

"So long ago. Oh, I wish I'd majored in theory at Holy Cross."

"Not important. You're enjoying Lahiri's stories."

"I love them."

"That's what matters."

"So you asked Professor Spivak to be on your dissertation committee?"

"Yes."

"And?"

"I might get blown away, but she's the best."

"He's all about ..." Freddie's quotation-mark fingers bend with each word. "The ... best! As we know."

His mother turns to Freddie.

"That was a compliment, Mrs.—"

"Your voice on that Lifetime special was mesmerizing. The way you explained the history of contraception and the pill. Mesmerizing."

"I told you she was impressed, Freddie!"

Her smile is cruel. He mouths: *My bad.*

"Oh, well, Mrs.—"

"Ruth."

"Ruth."

"And that is you on the Lysol commercial?"

"It is."

His father is in the center of the living room, as if he'd been teleported, Ted thinks, and shuffling several pieces of paper.

"Excuse me. Ah, Frederika, may I, just a second."

"Of course." She jumps up, as if on a pogo stick.

"No, no, sit." She sits, and his father plants himself between her and Ted.

"Excuse me. Teddy?" His father leans down, and Ted endures the paper undulating before his nose.

"This is our updated will. The latest; I keep forgetting about it; you need an updated copy. The original's in the vault, you have a key. Just in case, put it someplace safe—"

"Can we discuss the will later?"

"Please, take it. Humor me."

"Could you sit—"

"I'll sit, I'll sit."

As if his request were rhetorical, he thinks.

"So, whom may I say is imbibing?" His father speaks to the room while ambling in the direction of *his* art deco walnut cocktail cabinet. He opens the bottom pair of doors and selects a red wine and then the top doors and grabs brandy and vodka. He cradles the bottles in his arms, and one shifts precipitously. "Oy, oy vey ist mir!" He secures his grip and closes a top door with his elbow and then the other door with his elbow, and a bottom door with his foot and the other door with his foot, and then shuffles in the direction of *his* rectangular coffee table.

"I love your coffee table," says Freddie.

"Solid mahogany, Mukabwa," says his father while ushering down the bottles.

"Beautiful."

"Indeed, and at 70 percent off its inflated-by-70-percent sticker price, a steal, I thought, and assumed Ruthie would, too, but she vetoed it without consultation, as if by fiat, and when I pleaded, at least hear my case, oh she tore me asunder in a fit, and when what remained of me pointed out this so un-Ruthie anomaly, this abrogation of the *mutuality pact* upon which our relationship is predicated, she was gracious and nothing but magnanimous in reappraising her intransigence, and voilà."

There is nothing he would not do for his mother, Ted thinks.

"Though I still suspect, Ruthie, this is Phil's table."

"It's ours," replies his mother. "You said so yourself."

"Touché, my dear." He aligns the bottles from smallest to tallest. "As is our wont, we compromised." He says to Freddie, "Mukabwa means big."

"How fascinating."

"It's an East African dialect."

"For sure this table is a conversation piece, Mr.— "

"Phiiiil, young lady." He straightens the row of bottles. "So, preferences?"

"Wine," says Freddie. "White if you—"

"My heavens, the white is in the fridge—"

"Red," says Ted.

"Red is good," says Freddie.

"Good isn't perfect, I'll be right—"

"No, perfect, I love red."

His father steps lively to the cabinet. "Okay, but—"

"I want red. Perfect."

He returns cradling four wine glasses and stands them in pairs on the table. "The fridge is a heartbeat away, young lady."

"Red is perfect," says Freddie.

His father fills each glass. "Voilà!"

"Wonderful," says Freddie. "What's the wine, Phil?"

"To Frederika." His father raises his glass. Everyone follows. "A sublime name," he says. "A beautiful bride-to-be. À votre santé."

"Merci," says Freddie.

"CLC's new Communication Arts dean is named Frederika."

Freddie's gaze is quizzical.

Ted murmurs, "College of Lake County."

"Like you in name only, no doubt," says his father.

"Oh, right," says Freddie.

"To the far right of the far right."

"I'm pretty liberal—"

"To Dean Frederika Cannavaro, celebrating diversity means owning different caliber handguns. Is she vengeful? Does the pope shit anachronisms in the woods! Don't applaud loud enough, and you can forget tenure. I really think she studied in North Korea. I do, however, credit her with extensive knowledge of current events, if you stop at the 11th century. At least she's ahead of my students. And to think, she's a dean. And she votes! All to suggest, young lady, having now been introduced to you, I can happily imagine this exquisite pulchritude before me whenever I encounter your hideous namesake."

Freddie smiles and flicks back her hair.

"My God, when your hair falls back that way, you are Mary Travers. Incarnate."

"I've been told—"

"Mary was the soul. Peter and Paul? They may have grasped

the import of a lyric. But Mary. You could feel it in the way she swayed."

"People say I have her eyes, too."

"Enchanting."

"Thank you, Phil."

They sip their wine in the silence.

"This is Cabernet?" asks Freddie.

"Indeed. Colombia, like Teddy's school, but with an o. Crest Reserve, aught-seven."

"We're Two-Buck Chuck peeps, Phil. We splurge on Yellow Tail."

"What occasion would it take for my son to surpass a single digit?" His father sniggers. "You'll convince Teddy to maybe live a little isn't a felony."

"Why would I ever spend more than $9 for wine?" Ted says.

"To liiiive a little!" says his father.

"That's my Teddy," says Freddie.

"And my enigmatic sophisticate," says Phil. "Ivy League meets bush league. Go figure."

An hour has passed. Ted's head feels swollen. He wards off the temptation to finish the third bottle of Cabernet that is all but empty. His father has feasted on Freddie's undivided attention more than he imagined. She is too much raw meat. It is graveyard quiet, he realizes, and his father is listing backward, eyes closed, mouth open, revealing the bottom of his Old Yeller front teeth, and is this a catnap, he wonders? Hopefully his father will stagger out and to the den to nod off on *his* French Provincial Fainting Couch. His mom and Freddie are conked out, and he envisions them as comrades.

"I hear there's a hotbed of anti-Israeli sentiment at Columbia," murmurs his father.

Fuck.

His father's index finger unfurls and he hoists himself up, and it is jabbing at him. "And who would give a good goddamn about those Zionist bastards—shoving settlements up the Palestinians' noses?"

"Yes, there's a lot of anti-Israel protest at Columbia," says Freddie.

Oh my God.

"Expanding these settlements is a canard," his father replies to her, and why is his father's finger still pointing at him? "The salient issue, young lady, is: *Threatened by definition!* You see, once Israel is *threatened ... by ... definition*, everyone's a threat! Now, do the Palestinians have the right to be *threatened ... by ... definition?* Oooh, no! That's only for God's chosen!" His father's arm collapses in his lap.

"This is an existential crisis," says Ted. "The diaspora—"

"A thunderous curse on diaspora!" says Phil. "These goddamned Zionists oughta be deported to Newark. Now there's a place that could use settlements. How many people in this country do you think, A, know where Israel is, and B, know what a Palestinian is? And, C, if they don't know, should we permit these citizens to vote? Actually, I don't give a good goddamn whether someone knows where Israel is, understands its history— none of my students do, because rigorous inquiry is anathema to texting, so that's their excuse—but there should be some fundamental, knowledge-based voting requirement—"

"Phil!" says Ruth. "We've heard this."

"You understand, Frederika?" his father says.

"Oh, yes. About?"

"I should probably ask you what's au courant at Columbia vis-à-vis Israel, Teddy. Whatever the latest, it'll induce far more compelling interchange than the anti-intellectual gobbledygook that passes for dialectic among CLC's faculty and admin: the few, the righteous, the middling, where 'courant' would be pronounced like a salad ingredient. My God, I am rambling. Please, someone speak."

Phil's head lolls. He slumps as if mortally wounded, and Ted guesses that even his reserve effusions have been depleted. "You won't be offended if I nod ..."

Ted sits on the couch close to his mother. "We may elope."

"Just a thought," interjects Freddie. "Probably not."

"Maybe," says Ted.

Like sentinels, Ted thinks, he and his mother assess the state of his father's repose.

"It's your decision, of course, dear."

His mother disguises her disappointment by feigning equanimity, and Ted is not surprised, nor unsatisfied. He is her emotional disciple. *Like mother, like son*, he thinks. The absence of a discordant ripple in his mother's tone is indicative of her acceptance and a cue that she endorses his wish without condition and consistent with her prioritizing his needs over hers, and he is relieved.

"Still way up in the air," says Freddie.

"We've had a long day, Mom," says Ted.

"Dad's been telling everyone about your wedding," his mother says. "My son the doctor. My daughter-in-law the actor. He brags about you. He's proud of you, Teddy."

Ted closes the door and is disconsolate. Why? He is, he thinks, a guest in the room that once belonged to him.

He and Freddie push the twin beds together and rearrange the blankets to cover them, and he recalls his alone time here as an adolescent. These four walls—his haunt, his womb, his rescuer— reconnect him to that teenage boy, released from the world upon entering, released from its uncertainty, its whimsy, free to shut it out, safe in his haven where he could yearn, contemplate, cocooned by tranquility, and silence. And though the room is no longer his, since its furnishings reflect his mother's aesthetic, it sort of belongs to him. He looks about, recalling his mom's email, describing each addition as if each were a child: the vintage ceiling fan's walnut blades, *just perfect, Teddy*; the carnation pink curtains, the two oval, 19th-century Giltwood English antique mirrors hanging to the left of one twin bed, to the right of the other, the plush, charcoal wall-to-wall carpeting, *I'm just so happy, wait till you see it, Teddy*. It is Mom's, he thinks, and in that sense, it belongs to him, too.

He tucks in his side of the blanket, and his mind replays the hours on the floor, on his back, imagining himself in a state of *free fall to China*. And how he'd stare at the ceiling without end and wish that the cohesion those moments engendered in him would last forever. He recalls the phone conversation when he asked his mother what *Dad thinks* and her nonaccusatory reply, *Ruthie's Roost he calls it*, and his father's decreeing before friends and strangers alike that this anomaly, the coffee table's twin anomaly, represents the only exceptions to their lifelong mutuality pact, and Ted knows that his mother interprets *Ruthie's Roost* as deprecating, knows it is a dismissal of *her*, and he understands, he does, that his mother would acquiesce if his father insisted on his input. His wrath unfurls.

Ted retrieves his large blue pajamas from his suitcase. The *Ruthie's Roost* pronouncement deserves at least severing his father's arm above the elbow. *Dick-face*.

Ted flops on the bed and slides into his pajamas and buttons the top over his undershirt and ties the waist knot tight over his boxer briefs. He stretches out on his back. Freddie is on her back next to him and wears only her panties. He thinks she can't really be serious. She wriggles like a worm. Her torso touches his, and her upward gaze confuses him.

"Is that your dad?" says Freddie.

From the adjacent bedroom, his father's shrill voice rises. "No, Ruth, I am not going to goddamn have you and Freddie—"

His father's voice drops. Silence. And rises. "Frederika!" And then something he cannot quite understand, and then, "Not eat dinner without us. Shopping, yes. But we're all of us eating together." Silence. His father's voice has faded to a murmur he cannot decipher, and rises. "You'll get to know her just as well with the four of us." Silence. He makes out, "Teddy couldn't care." Silence. Murmuring he cannot decipher, and then, "For chrissakes, humor me, Ruth, okay? I'm in no goddamn mood."

"He's nuts," Ted says.

Freddie is on her side and faces him. Her fingers scurry beneath his pajama top and tug at his undershirt, and he just can't see doing it here. Her hand reappears, and she snuggles closer. "I love you, Mr. PJ man." Her breath's warmth and scent maneuver his will. He caresses her breast and nipple, and she clasps his hand and presses it to her chest, and he is relieved.

"It just seems, I dunno," says Freddie. "Is this worth it, is what I mean?"

"Yes."

"I understand now. Why you don't like him."

"Don't like him?"

"Teddy, you can't hate him?"

"I don't."

"Yes, you do."

"No."

"Yes, or you wouldn't be so upset."

"I can learn indifference. Learn to not care about him. I'm getting there."

"He's your father."

"You know the people I read, that I admire most, they were brilliant, great artists, great at critique, but so many of them, they couldn't critique their lives, their existence suffocated them, they couldn't find a way out, a way to live an authentic life. I told you William James contemplated killing himself. Hard to believe."

"You did."

"I'm not gonna suffocate."

"Your dad's a little, self-centered—"

"Ya think!"

"But—"

"Did you notice his off switch?"

"No."

Freddie raises the blanket and covers them. The bed undulates. Maybe tonight he'll give sleeping in the nude a try. She grips his hand and leans over him. A kiss? Is this all she wants?

"Who is our wedding about, Freddie?"

She kisses him. "Us." She kisses him. "I love you."

"I love you."

"You're gonna be a wonderful dad."

"Just do the opposite."

"I see your soul. And don't say there's no such thing."

"Okay."

"So, Tedski?"

"Yeah." She is removing her panties.

"If we're quiet?"

Ted sits up and unbuttons his pajama top and then inches the bottoms down and then his underwear until the clump reaches his ankles, and with a fluttery kick, he is free of them.

He is atop Freddie's belly and raises his arms. She hoists his undershirt over his head and releases it to the floor.

"I love you, Mr. PJ man."

They are seated around the square solid-oak kitchen table that Ted assumes was his father's choice, or he would have heard the commentary by now. His parents and Freddie are drinking coffee and nibbling baguettes with butter and blueberry jam, and he squelches the temptation to mention his work at Columbia.

The antique Viennese wall clock chimes, 9 a.m., and he peers at his father, seated at the mini rolltop desk by the kitchen window and stabbing numbers on the phone's keypad with his index finger, and the clock, too, his father's choice, he'd bet. His father appears to listen, then grimaces, stabs a number, and then listens, grimaces, stabs a number, waits in a tizzy.

"For chrissakes!" his father murmurs. And waits. "Hel, hello … Phil … Weintraub … I'll hold."

Bits of his mother's chat with Freddie register. His father's mood blackens, and he thinks there is no inappropriate moment for his father to excoriate the world's imbeciles, especially when one of them is about to turn a simple transaction into *Nightmare on Elm Street*. He recalls his mother's complaint in a recent email that these harangues ramp up during summer vacation, when he's home with time on his hands, and for her, the mere mention means that she is at her wit's end. *Maybe she'll leave him.*

"Yes, cheery-voice Thomas, you may help me!" his father says.

If only she'd leave him.

"Yes, I have a problem this morning. Yes, I'll hold."

What makes him crazy, his father will say, *isn't the problem.* It's the *putz* on the other end. After the conversation, during the standard summation, his father will reiterate that his contempt is kindled, as always, not by the problem, but by the putz. If he has learned anything from his father about the nature of human discourse, it's that the root cause of what his father calls *communication conflagration* is the putz. The putz's raison d'être: *death by a thousand infuriations.* Putzes demand the filling out of forms whose questions they have no idea how to answer and could care less about, and you'd better answer the ones with an asterisk, or back to *go!* Putzes request that his father call back when he wants to talk n-o-w. Putzes seek assistance from another putz, but his father knows a putz by any other title is a putz, and despite his damnedest to ensure that he won't have to reiterate to another putz what the current putz doesn't get, well, the putzes have you, and if it's worth saying once, it's worth saying again that what makes him *madder than hell* isn't the problem—shit happens, and his father knows that—it's these putzes who don't have the decency to take responsibility nor the brains to help him solve the problem. Stupid, stupid people who should *only be allowed to vote if it won't change the outcome.* Ted senses that this putz can't figure out how his father was billed for—

"A *Guess* handbag!" says his father.

Something he never ordered, Ted thinks.

"Sir, you'll *credit* me? For what—something else I don't want. Listen, sonny—"

His father has gone on nonstop since he returned to the table, and Ted determines that to excuse himself and leave will only discomfort his mother.

"I said I couldn't give a good goddamn about who you *think* charged my credit card," his father says. "And then the putz de grâce! 'Do me a favor,' I say, like a lamb. 'Yes, sir.' 'Give me ... no, I tell him, not your supervisor. Marshall Fields's president ... I know it's a Saturday,' I say. 'So, what, you can't look it up on the Sabbath?' "

His father checks his shirt pocket. "Christ!" He runs to the phone, grabs a scrap of paper, returns to the table, and shakes it. "Voilà! President Fields's email."

Ted is aware that he and his mother are looking in his father's general direction, their preferred location that suggests interest and avoids eye contact.

"You see, what this putz knew is that his supervisor—like every goddamn corporate, slash, government lemmings from right below the top on down—is programmed not so much to *ignore* you, but to *transfer* you. Follow, Frederika?"

She nods, Ted thinks, like a moth near a flame.

"Big difference. Biiiig difference!"

Freddie's bobbing head is the object of his father's affection: Freddie's head bobs up and down, bobs to the penetrating insight, bobs to the trenchant analysis, to his father's wit, and with each successive bob, Freddie-the-bobblehead is consumed, Grade-A prime. *Yum-yum, eat her up!*

"You can *fight* being ignored, but when you're transferred, placed somewhere to become someone else's burden, see, that's their game. Death by a thousand transfers! What can you do?"

"Go right to the top!" says Freddie.

"And that's because?"

"Um?"

"Theeeyyy," says his father.

As if leading the vowel with a leash, Ted thinks.

"Theeeyyy being the president, the CEO—*they* reply, they can't transfer you, they solve problems. Why? The Peon Dividend! Why should a department store president bother with a peon like me? Aha! Because, peons pay dividends!"

Freddie is silent.

"Let me connect the dots, young lady. Public relations. Think about it. The next shareholder meeting, or the CNBC interview with this otherwise inaccessible CEO who heard, who understood, who could and *did* move a mountain of putzes to satisfy one inconsequential peon, a.k.a. customer. Ah, the publicity. You see? Peons pay dividends."

"Cool."

Ted indicts himself for complicity, for allowing his father to believe that his silence means that he is impressed by his wit and by him. "So, Dad."

His father reaches in his shirt pocket for a pen and scribbles on his paper scrap.

"Dad?"

"Hang on. I'm listening."

"Dad."

"Bear with me."

"Can you look up a minute?"

His father raises his head.

"You know we're planning on getting married in New York. Mom's invited. Unless you agree to my terms, you won't be."

Ted gazes out the guest room window while Freddie sleeps. Dawn's glow illuminates tufts of mushroom-white clouds drifting over Chicago's north side. He strives to appreciate the resplendence. He cannot. His father hasn't completed a sentence since yesterday morning. Docile as a lamb. What to make of his father's response, *Your wish is mine to obey, and obey I will?* Doesn't matter. It did not surprise him that his father went to sleep at 6 last night. He does not care why. He recalls his mother's lifelong reiteration that Phil is who he is, the world's self-appointed scold, its indomitable, nonstop critic-mill, but when confronted by another's appeal for the simplest emotional acknowledgment, can appear rudderless, with an inexplicable suddenness, as if his inner world disintegrated, and he retreats within himself, taciturn and morose, and she long ago accepted this fact of life. *He is who he is, honey,* he can hear her say. He thinks, *I am who I am.*

Ted and Freddie pack their suitcases without speaking.

"We don't have to be at Midway till 3," says Freddie.

"I know!" His impatience with her screamed like a banshee, Ted thinks.

Freddie closes her bag, and the sweeping *zip* irritates him. He reminds her that since waking they've had free rein of the house, and isn't she grateful to be liberated from the gnawing sensation inside her head, ever-present when his father is prowling about, never knowing when pop-goes-the-weasel will appear?

"It doesn't bother me."

"Well, it fuckin' bothers me—"

"Stop it, Teddy!"

"Stop what—"

"Teddy. Tell him goodbye. At least say goodbye."

Ted stands beneath the shower, his preferred contemplation-habitat, where the water's steady cascade palliates stress, where he feels himself a more coherent thinker.

Ted steps over the tub and into the steam. He swipes the mirror above the sink. The squeak amuses him. Sounds silly, he thinks. There he is, speckled by the droplets. He flexes his bicep. His sporadic workouts have spawned an egg-shaped protuberance. Would that mental toughness was this simple. He contests the need to flee, to hide. At the very least, he will say, *I'll see you.* At the very least, no matter how his father reacts, he can endure him. He will have tried. He musters the misgivings, the guilt, the fear, the rage that shackle him, and trundles in the direction of a choice he wishes only to avoid and thinks, maybe seeing Phil one last time will somehow release the shackles.

Ted scowls at his thinning hairline. "Twenty-six," he murmurs, and this procrastination has lasted long enough. He will tell his father why he wrote what he wrote—calmly and with respect—as planned.

Ted steps into the kitchen. His mother is alone. He will say goodbye, he tells her.

His mother says that she doubts that his father will leave the bedroom until they have departed. "You may despise him—"

"That's not how I want it to be."

"I know. Neither does he. He doesn't want you to despise him."

"Does what Dad knows about me matter to him?"

His mother's hug comforts Ted. She retreats a step.

"How far you've come from that 17-year-old who barely passed English!"

"I'm getting there."

"Getting there? Let's see. From academic probation at Loyola, to U. of I., to Columbia PhD program. You *are* there. I'm proud of you."

"I'm proud of you. From secretary to human resources director for the city."

"And still a Democrat."

Ted clutches the envelope and wills fortitude and taps on his parents' bedroom door with his fingernails. He waits. Silence. He opens the door.

His father is seated in his French country-style chair at his antique cherrywood desk, hunched like *The Thinker*, dressed and unshaven and poking at his MacBook's keyboard. The screen's horizontal rows appear to be holdings and balances: his father's Fidelity account. His mom tells him what a savvy investor his father is.

Ted sits on the bed's edge and looks at his father's back. He feels threatened.

"Dad."

The poking ceases.

"Yeah, Teddy."

"Dad."

His father turns, as if unfamiliar with turning, and stares in the direction of his feet. He is lost. He is frightened. "I'm not okay with your coming to New York unless you agree to my terms."

Silence.

"Dad."

"Please. I can't. Please don't talk to me like this."

"Like what?"

Silence.

"Like what?" His inflection is as he practiced it in New York. He is heeding Freddie's admonitions. *Speak kindly. He's not the enemy. Be conciliatory.* "Don't talk to you what way?"

His father *can't* reply, he thinks. *Why can't he?* Doesn't matter. Because *Ted's in control,* in control so *Ted can cut Phil some slack,* lower his guard, cast a line of communication without fear of attack, fear of a verbal massacre, because those days are over, so if *Phil does blow, Ted won't fall like a row of dominoes.* Those days are over! Be kind, show deference, he reminds himself. *That's it.*

"Dad. If we don't engage one another—"

"Do you know, Ted, when my father *engaged* me? When he was angry? Know how? With a belt buckle. Retribution was his term of engagement, though, you know, I'll take his term to yours, Ted, to silence, silence, Ted, to Phil speaks and Ted sits there, to Phil displays his feelings and Ted displays nothing, nothing, except that he is withholding them, do you think I'm stupid, Ted, do you think I don't see silence as a weapon, a loaded gun pointed at me? So, do me a favor and don't tell me about engage—"

"You interrupted me."

"At least there was something to inter—"

"Do not interrupt me, motherfucker!" He is on his feet. "Do not fucking interrupt me! Do you fucking understand that?"

"You wanna scream at me?" his father howls. Is that the way you *engage* me? You wanna call me motherfucker, go ahead, go ahead!"

Ted sits on the bed. His mind catches sight of Teddy as a child, shouted down, hears the whine, the exaggerated simper shutting out his want, his desire, his need, hears the lecturing, its incessant drumming, hears his importuning interrupted by a fusillade of defenses, explanations, rationalizations for his father's side of things, while he sits mannequin-still and clutches passivity like a javelin and thrusts it at his father with all his might and endures, endures, endures while praying for him to leave, hoping, hoping for his father's standard, fait accompli exit line: *I know how you feel, Teddy, but this is a dictatorship, albeit a benevolent one.*

Silence.

"No. I don't wanna call you names."

"That quiet. You are so goddamn cruel."

Fuckin-A. "I'm sorry for yelling." He had entered on Ted's terms. How has Phil managed to wrest the wheel from him? "It's all in my letter, Dad."

"I don't need to read the condescension I live with."

"I'm willing to explain why—"

"You don't have to *explain* anything."

"I knew you wouldn't speak, so I wrote—"

"Get out of my room."

"I'm willing to talk to you—"

"Get out! Please." His father turns and murmurs something at his mutual funds.

"Or to never talk to you."

Silence.

"It's all in there," says Ted. "My feelings—"

"Your feelings—"

"My terms—"

"Your terms—"

"Don't interrupt me," he says.

"Please don't shout at me anymore, Teddy."

"I didn't shout. Do ... not ... interrupt—"

"You shouted earlier. Then I shouted. I shouldn't have shouted. But you can shout, Teddy."

"Dad! Take it or leave it."

"Have you ever uttered a sincere goddamn thing? To me? Not your mother. But to me? You know, the guy who put you through Loyola, then Illinois, the guy who said, yeah, sure, you wanna live off campus with your friends, in a nice apartment—conducive, you said, to studying. I haven't a bloody clue what you did off campus. But your mother does. You told her. Okay, that's self-serving, Ted. I feel self-serving right now, and I don't give a good goddamn if I do. Because, unlike you, Teddy, I can't hide my feelings. All I know is: I owe you. I'm your father. But I tell you, sincerely, I mean it: You don't owe me. No one does. You owe Frederika, Teddy. You owe your children. That's it."

Ted places the envelope on the bed.

Ted is several steps from his father's bedroom and thinks, despite things getting dicey, at least he was clear and explicit. He stops mid-step and wonders what his father heard, and he thinks, if his father opened his door and asked him to come back, he would. He takes a step and thinks, obligating his father to comply with his wishes was expressed with deference. What more could he have done? Guilt saps him, and he leans against the hallway wall. What possessed him to have addressed his father, *Dear Phil*, to have begun with *Understand that this wedding celebrates only two people: Frederika and Ted*. How pathetic. How lame. How *goddamn cruel. Dear Phil, Only two people*. How can his father consider the concept that his actions have consequences when he has so insulted him? He will be seen as little more than his father's father, and he recollects his adolescence when his father once finally left his room and that voice through his door, penetrating his skull, despite clasping his ears: He was not perfect, he had traumas and demons and were he able to conquer them, of course he would have, *for God's sake, Teddy, I'm not evil.* He should have asked his father to see a Cubs game with him. They both like the Cubs. How about their chances this year? His ultimatum could have waited until after the game, and Teddy the child crops up, splayed out on the floor, punching his mitt as if a pop-up might hurtle through the TV. And Dad, up and down, like his chair was programmed for electric shocks and always when the Cubs fell behind. *Right back, Teddy. Watch for two! No patience for losers,* then bombing out of the living room: *Life's short!* The disembodied echo: *Call me when they're ahead, Teddy.* Too bad he never knew his grandfather, and he wonders, what were Grandpa's side of things?

Standing by the adjacent kitchenette alcove, Ted observes Freddie fix her gaze and lean out of their third-story window, drawn by the police car siren, Ted assumes, that is racing down 113th Street.

His father drifts like a cloud along the five unpainted wooden bookshelves that extend across the living room's rear tea-green wall. His father pauses and attends to the top shelf. What has caught his attention, he wonders? His father appears to peruse a particular book and then glides backward and eyes the shelf below, and then drifts forward and pauses and curls his index finger and appears fixated on the stacked cinder blocks that separate the planks, and he flicks away a dust bunny from the middle one, and as he turns, it seems that the bowed fourth shelf has caught his eye, and Ted wonders if his father will actually look at a book of his.

Ted opens the fridge and removes a bottled water. "It's okay," he says to his father. "I need to turn over that board."

"Books, books, books," murmurs Freddie.

Her grumble is complimentary, Ted thinks. His mother sits on the tattered velvet sofa, and he is about to warn her—

"Whoops," she says, and sinks a bit and waves her arms in tight circles and hoists herself up. "Well!"

She laughs from the belly, he thinks.

His mother secures her rear on the front of the sofa's hard frame. "Your guys' apartment is so cozy, Frederika. Just like you described it."

Freddie turns to her. "You're okay?"

"Yes, honey."

Freddie points left and says, "That's the sturdy cushion."

Freddie hoists his mother like a crane, and the two sit close.

"So, I didn't mean, earlier, to, ya know, criticize Teddy's books—I love all the books, Mrs., Ruth."

"They go with the territory."

"Totally."

His father inspects a book's spine.

"I don't know why, I mean," Freddie says, "but I was raised to address elders as sir, ma'am, so—"

"You know, truthfully, Frederika—"

"Tell me."

"I prefer Ruthie."

"Oh ... my ... God! My family, my friends, all call me Freddie."

"And we are family."

"Yes."

"And friends."

They turn inward, their knees and hands conjoin.

"Okay, I'm glistening, Ruthie."

"How do you know *glistening?*"

"Teddy's expression for crying."

Ted sips his water, looks at Phil, and strains to hear.

"I'm the biggest crybaby Ted knows," says Freddie.

"I may have you beat on that one."

"Drop of a hat."

"Me too. Anything."

"TV commercials?"

"Are you kidding, Freddie?"

"It's outrageous."

He thinks Freddie should be glistening about now.

"Sometimes," says Freddie, "I look at the Sabrett guy on our corner and just bawl."

There's the sniffles.

"He's so old and sad-looking. And Teddy says, what, he's putting rancid mustard and sauerkraut on a hot dog whose only contents you can be sure of are nitrates and steroids."

His father is bored, Ted thinks, the way he is leaning against the bookshelf. His father walks to the black folding chair across from the couch, hands in both pockets of his corduroy sport jacket, and one of them is jiggling something. Keys? Change? *He's had it.*

Ted sits on a folding chair opposite his father and maybe, he thinks, if he sits, his father might, though his father is withdrawn, distant, pained. *Phil feels excluded* by the three of them, and this is *how Phil deals with that feeling,* like this, until someone wonders aloud if anything is wrong, is everything okay, to which *Phil replies* from a light year away that he's *fine* and now you know that he isn't! *Fucking 2-year old.*

"Glisten on," his mother says.

"Thank you."

They shake, they hug, they laugh and glisten and babble

something indecipherable to Ted, and it's official, he thinks, they've bonded. Will his father ever sit?

"You know any of those books, Dad?"

"Nope. Never was a theory guy, or philosophy guy. You know me, strictly European fiction and 19th-century poetry."

"Ton of fiction up there. And poetry. I know you have your students read—"

"We only matriculate the illiterate."

"What?"

"Open admissions, right?"

"I've got Baudelaire. You like him, right—"

"So, where's my collection, Teddy?"

"Your collection?"

"Book of Freudian haikus."

Can he endure his disgust? "Really?"

"Published my first year at CLC. Before your time."

"You published a book of poetry?"

"Seven hundred, first printing."

"Send it to me."

"Call the warehouse in Skokie. There's a sale. Buy one, get 699 free."

His father's gaze pokes willy-nilly about the living room. How long can he last? Ted thinks. A stream of propelled air whooshes through his father's pursed lips, and his eyebrows rise and cheeks swell. When will the dam burst? His father steps with purpose and nears the front door, jiggling the change in his jacket pocket. *Whatever.*

"You're leaving?" his mother asks.

"Quick jaunt. Take in Columbia's enlightenment-vibes. Good for what ails my discourse."

"Phil, we have to be at—"

"The bookstore, a stroll down Broadway, stop at Zabar's. Truthfully, I'm having a rugelach moment. Just one. Bring the rest to the rehearsal dinner. In case of an early exit before the meal."

His father is in the hallway. "I'm joking! I'll be right back."

"He's fine," says his mother.

"I hope I didn't do something—"

"Of course not, Freddie."

"Phil has two gears," Ted says. "Me and I'm outa here!"

"Teddy!"

"I'm sorry, Mom."

"I just wish you wouldn't, Teddy, especially now!"

"I'm okay."

"He is who he is. You know that."

"It's okay."

But he is not okay, and if the unconditional demands outlined in his letter are not respected and implemented by his father, no more last chances, he is done with him. *Forever!*

His mother returns from the card table with her purse and sits on the couch. She hands the envelope to Ted. "I have to live with him, Teddy."

It has been opened. He is positive that she has read it. "He didn't look at it."

"No, honey."

He wishes Freddie's arm was around his shoulder instead of his mother's.

His mother tells him that he "sat opposite her on their bed's edge," and said that if she read it, he would listen, but raised a hand after the first sentence, and she watched him get smaller. "He looked like a boy." He got the gist. Stupid he's not, his father said, and then "squeezed his nose and wiped beneath it. 'I'm a felon, Ruthie,' he told me. 'My life sentence, that letter.'"

A bubble appears from Freddie's nose. Does he expect her *not to feel sorry for Phil?*

" 'Teddy is a harsh judge. You know the irony, Ruthie, not as harsh on me as me.' "

"He needs to read it, Mom."

His mother folds her arms around his neck, and he hugs her, and memories of their post-immolation talks that stanched his doubt, his pain, his anger, his fears embrace him, and he cannot imagine that she will ever die.

"He loves you."

"It's not enough, Mom."

"He understands."

"What? What does he understand?"

"That this wedding is about you and Freddie."

Ted glances at both pages of his handwritten script. "You read it, Mom?"

"Every word."

"A lot of demands. All on my terms, huh." He places the letter in the envelope.

"Indeed."

"I'm gonna mail it to Dad."

"Teddy."

"He needs to read it. Will you tell me when it arrives?"

THE UNDERDOG

DAVID AWOKE, startled, out of sync. His limp hand wafted through the dark for the ringing phone on the nightstand by his side of the bed. "Hello."

"The Underdog here. I wake you, boyo?"

What time was it? David's fingertips contacted the top of the oblong digital alarm. His spreading appendages lightly tapped their separate ways to the clock's warm plastic sides and gripped. His twisting wrist burned as he turned the clock about-face. Squinting into the backlight's kiwi-green glow, he strained to focus on the jumbo red numbers: 4:56 a.m.

Sherri mumbled, "Who is it?" The extra soft mattress undulated as his wife strained to haul herself up in an awkward V. She belly-flopped, causing the bed to bounce like a trampoline. Her face was buried in her pillow; her flailing hand conked David's nose and retreated swiftly under her thigh. " 'Scuse me." Her muffled, contrite murmur was apology enough for him.

He glanced at her tousled hair and proffered a dispirited whisper: "Ralphie."

David stared into the receiver's indented oval and its tiny

portals packed tightly in a circle and endured his father's effervescent charm. "How ya' doin', boyo?"

Caution summoned David. "Me? Great, Dad. You?"

"Amazing!"

"Glad to hear that." David wasn't glad to hear that. *Amazing!* was a trapdoor. *Amazing!* summoned caution.

"I'm sorry. It's early," said his father.

"He's okay?" whispered Sherri.

"Hello?" said Ralphie.

"No," David said to Sherri, in a way that conveyed Ralphie was okay.

"You there, boyo?"

Sherri scuttled away from David.

"Boyo?"

"Dad, it's—"

"You know how long I've been up?"

"Three hours."

"And who says you aren't The Underdog's boyo? Been counting my blessings with my copilot and navigator: God and Tylenol. Got my arthritis under new management, boyo! Back to two-minute planks, half my age in diamond push-ups—"

"You're cured."

"Wanted to hear your voice."

"Really?"

"I can't make my Medicare payment his month."

"I see."

"Or my rent. Not this month, boyo."

"Why's that?"

"I'm gonna hang up—no biggie!"

David endured the trapping quiet.

"Still there, boyo?"

David glanced at Sherri for sympathy: asleep like a baby.

"Coffee with The Underdog, boyo?"

"How is next week? I have a pretty tragic case. A 16-year-old boy whose sister says she witnessed him wrestle a semi-automatic from their stepfather who was in the midst of battering their biological mother. The kid wastes him, then, apparently, as he falls backward into his sister, kid's still shooting and accidentally gets his mother in the head. Fuckin' mess."

"Can you help?"

"This is more than the Medicare?"

"I need 5,000."

David could not sleep. Curled like a fetus, he faced Sherri. The Underdog clawed him beneath his ribs. He'd deal with it tomorrow. He raised the airy comforter over his head. His sightless eyes blinked. His dank breath soured his nostrils as he surveyed his memory in search of bygone clues. He nudged the comforter just above his nose. With his crooked index finger, he brushed bubbles of moisture from his upper lip. He couldn't recall a time when his father wasn't known to him as The Underdog—a self-anointed moniker, as far as he knew. And he was his father's *boyo*, for as long as he could remember; and he felt now—it seemed for as long as he could remember—shackled by obligation. But that was life with The Underdog. And David accepted it: *That's life.*

Unruffled exhaled air whispered through Sherri's nose: useless to the world, he thought. David long ago forgave his father —the blithe spirit—for his ice-cream castle worldview. He is heavy, but he's still my father, David thought. No choice, he concluded, but to accept *that's life.*

Although lately, as if time deepened all wounds, David's acceptance mantra had begun to fester. Acceptance? Why? Pearling sweat trickled down his forehead and nose. Maybe, he deduced, because The Underdog was the wellspring of his melancholy. Or maybe he was just sapped by his father, tired of lowering, and then raising, a bucket of melancholy.

David lifted the cover from his head and, as if granted a reprieve from his breath's stench, inhaled without regret. He uncurled himself. He didn't want to get on with accepting anymore.

Slumber numbed David's fretting. He welcomed a recurring fantasy to linger in his mind like a trusted confidant: hard-hearted David's hands clasped against The Underdog's temples, rubbing his face in his own shit pile until he bleats repentance, "Okay, okay!"

"What's my name?"

"David. David! Are you happy?"

"No."

David laughed churlishly, in *amazing disgrace*, he thought, and then reminded himself that, no, he was insulated from disgrace: He was his father's loyal attendant. Always would be. David accepted—as is—what he couldn't loyally change: The Underdog, 76, going on 4!

"Look, I'm driving, Sher, so we take the bridge, right?"

"Ya know, your parsimony issue—"

"... comes from being surrounded by multiple Jewish attorneys."

"Do you listen? I'm in a *rush* this morning. I explicitly said Battery Tunnel—"

"I'm not paying $7.50—"

"Five thirty-three. We have E-ZPass."

"Just to save ten minutes!"

"It's not ten goddamn minutes!"

"Are you kidding me, Sher?"

"Why don't you pull over right now, give me the car, you take the train?"

"Isn't that why I'm driving so you can put your makeup on? Well, put it on!"

"All right, I will, because I have a closing with my buyers from central-fucking-casting-hell, and because this one commission, David, one commission, one!—you listening, boyo?— is gonna pay Zach's full tuition at McGill this year, despite the fact that you're gonna hand your father $5,000 we don't have right now. No, excuse me, correction: *I* don't have, because you sure as shit don't."

"You want Big Law, Sher, go fuck one." A final epithet hurtled up his mouth, unbridled. He knew it was overkill, knew not to say, "Bitch!"

Sherri pushed back her auburn side-swept bang, revealing her statuesque cheekbone. Her cream-brown Mediterranean skin turned pinkish. She sat stiff, as though her neck were in a brace. She stared ahead, squinting. Her eyes looked feral brown. David was relieved that she allowed him the final dagger—a pyrrhic slaying.

He loosened his skinny burgundy cotton-knit tie—a tad threadbare and veteran of dry-cleaner-resistant spills and spatters, but his sentimental favorite and now best friend—that he'd purchased the day before he graduated Cardozo, third in his class of '88, and most likely to succeed at never earning a real salary. He turned the wheel and inched onto Adams Street. The Brooklyn Bridge was in sight.

Oh, c'mon! He depressed the brake and idled behind a police car. Its whirring, pulsating red and white lights danced ignominy into his eyes.

"Are you fucking kidding?" he said. He turned to Sherri. She was already on her cell.

"So, Jen, we're stuck ... accident ... Oh yeah, an overturned

SUV will tend to gum things up ... Yeah, drop some Klonopin in the Birdwells' coffee ... Thanks, girlfriend. I owe ya."

Sherri looked up. She oozed stoicism. A good sign, David thought. She's pissed. But regretful, too.

"I'm sorry," said David. "And I'm not."

"Start over, mister?"

"Okay."

"If I say *I love you*, will that conquer all?"

"Oh, yeah."

"I still love you," she said.

"I love you."

David rolled down his window. He turned off the air conditioner. Moisture permeated their Kia. David preferred the humidity—he was one of those.

He called, "Officer, officer!"

They were going to be there a while—a half hour, said the cop, meaning forever. He'd missed the beginning of Sherri's Ralphie tirade. But time enough, thought David, for Sher to bloody him with *her* perceptions. Yes, it was the money. But far more serious, it was the nature of his relationship with Ralphie: He was the host; Ralphie was the parasite. This had to stop! "And I do love him. To death," Sherri said, after reiterating that his father was a pariah self-stoked on magical thinking. "He lives in a perennial state of happy hour—his happy hour, David, at the expense of ours!" Especially since Ralphie's last wife left him a dozen years ago. "And, sorry, I'm crass, but I can't ignore these things. He's been sucking us dry."

That was enough for David! Not because Sherri's harangue upset him; he was still livid over her jab at his income. He guessed that therapy hadn't quite resolved that one for her.

"Sher, enough," said David. He hoped "enough" was kindly taken by her, that "enough" meant *you're right.* By "enough" he meant *Shut the fuck up! He's my father, not yours!*

David pleaded assertively, straining to evince adult patience. "What do I say, Sher?" He wanted to rant petulantly: *I have to live with Ralphie when he's gone. You don't.* Facing Sherri, David's timbre softened. "He's my father, Sher. Once and for all, can I instill in you the larger implication?"

"Which is?"

"What I am sentenced to for abandoning Ralphie? Permanent regret."

"You're not abandoning him—"

"Sher! Who lives with Ralphie when he's gone? Me. Not you!"

David and Sherri simultaneously lurched forward, and like synchronized acrobats thrown off-kilter, they hoisted their opened palms—fingers splayed—made quick, hectic circles with them, then turned to peer at the car that had thwacked their bumper. David's reassuring gaze contacted the flummoxed woman directly behind them with a writhing toddler slung over her shoulder and mouthing *Sooorrrry!* He waved his cupped hand —fingers closed like a paw—at the distracted child, mimed smiling reassurance at the woman, and turned back to Sherri.

"You get what I mean, Sher?"

"Not really."

"Goddammit, Sher! Ralphie doesn't live in *Manhattan*. He lives in *David*. So, voilà! Gotta fuckin' deal with it, Sher. Why?" he pronounced. "Because as a son, David owes Ralphie his fidelity."

"Do not make me the bad guy!"

"Oh, for christ-fuckin' sake, Sher. Then, can we agree on this language? Sher? Because Ralphie does not possess an ill will bone in his Peter Pan body." And since "Peter Pan" was Sher's description, she couldn't refute him on that! "That's Ralphie, Sher." She slowly shook her head. Her foul visage assured David that he'd mollified himself, not her.

David ineptly adjusted the rearview mirror in their stalled car, determined to douse her smoldering opposition. "Do you know the meaning of *weasel*?"

"Hmm?" said Sher. "What?" He'd looked it up a few days ago. One definition in particular caught him like a grappling hook: "To evade an obligation, to *weasel* out of."

David saw the SUV being towed from the scene, and the traffic crawled like David imagined that the near-dead might. "Hallefuckin'lujah," muttered Sherri, whose cell emerged from her purse. David thought, later, when things were calm, he'd explain to Sher that *weasel* was his eureka moment, that maybe his lifelong devotion to not weaseling out of his obligation to Ralphie was an excuse for him to evade, to weasel out of, devotion to his primary responsibility—David.

They thumped over the bridge's rutted pavement, as yet unrepaired, toward lower Manhattan.

David said that he planned to visit Ralphie, without the 5K. "Enough is enough!"

"David."

"Yeah?"

"Remember. He's your father."

David skipped every other step to Ralphie's fourth-floor walk-up on 83rd, near East End. He wore white shorts, Nikes, a wifebeater, an unzipped cotton hoodie, flapping. He felt like a gazelle compared to this time last May, when Zach casually discredited his *shock* over being diagnosed as a type 2 diabetes suspect. "Dad, most fat people are pre-diabetic." So this was how his son regarded him: fat! A light bulb flashed ingloriously in David's head. It illuminated a 5-foot-7, 200-plus-pound "fat ass," and activated his will to get on the treadmill and off Lipitor.

Since then, David had shed what felt like a 50-pound

rucksack he'd been hauling around the previous eight years. He'd renounced ingredients he couldn't pronounce and embraced a dietary wellness mantra: low-fat, low-carb, high-fiber, more protein. He was a svelte gym rat, committed to his daily *care for the self* regimen. If only, he often wistfully thought, extra fiber or sit-ups could suppress the merciless thinning of his curly, silver-speckled black hair.

"Hi, Mr. Stanton."

David smiled. Wen Fēi smiled shyly. She bowed slightly. David ambled in, thinking that Wen was about as Chinese as chow mein. Twenty-two. Born in the U.S.A, nanny-reared, Beekman-prep-educated, HSBC VP daddy, arts philanthropist mommy, and, until Columbia—culturally, intellectually, and in fact—Wen had never migrated outside her 10065 zip code, except to *schlep* like the natives three stops on the Lex to prep school, and summer-home it in East Hampton with her third-generation Chinese 'rents, who, Ralphie said, were strict disciplinarians, so when Wen's high school chums routinely jetted off to Cannes or Corfu or wherever they went for winter break, Easter break, or all of July and August, she holed up in the Hamptons and read Brontë. And that discipline propelled Wen's numerous academic accomplishments, according to his father; the most impressive to Ralphie was when Wen won the senior rhetoric AP class debate: Resolved: PhDs make the best private school teachers.

Before Ralphie had hung up that morning, he'd reminded David, "Wen's gonna be here." So, David was prepared for, as Ralphie described her, "the caretaker for a vulnerable heart, her aging goat's sublime shepherd." Wen's presence was to be endured until she left and he could speak plainly to Ralphie.

"Hi there, boyo!"

"Hey, Pop."

"Wen graduates day after tomorrow."

David couldn't settle comfortably in the burgundy wicker chair. He scrunched down on the cushion's bulbous, hard lumps. He couldn't relax. Across from him, Ralphie and Wen sat up military-straight on his father's chintzy psychedelic couch, reupholstered in screaming rainbow-hued fabric, that, along with all the room's disparate, secondhand furnishings, had been transported by U-Haul 12 years ago from the Salvation Army on 46th Street.

Ralphie wore sandals, frayed white shorts, a peach-red, short-sleeve Hawaiian shirt festooned with red and white flying parrots. Wen was enchanting—a natural-earth, nubile creature: no makeup; pouty, China-doll lips; small breasts; dark and exotically delicate, oval eyes; coal-black, shoulder-length hair. Wen was seated close to Ralphie. In her skinny torn jeans, blue Columbia-lettered T, and black and white Converse sneakers—men's! he realized—she looked edible. He noticed: Her thigh *was* just touching Ralphie's. And he thought, how surreal: me, broke by moral calling; Ralphie, broke by amoral calling; and Wen, whose trust fund, even if it was taxed fairly by the government, would still save Medicare.

Ralphie reached for the stapled pages lying on the couch.

"Wen's winning thesis on Keats, boyo."

"I can't read it, Underdog," she said.

"If you'll indulge me, Wen Fēi, The Underdog will."

"Pop, my time is—"

"Oh, Mr. Stanton, I'm so selfish," said Wen. She blushed salmon-red. Wen gently plucked the pages from Ralphie. He clasped them and gently tugged back until they slid from Wen's hand. She demurred.

Wen pleaded, "For another time." Ralphie lifted her chin. He spoke, as if to her aura, "Wen is grace, boyo. In the bleakest weeks following disc surgery, an angel appeared before me daily. I recall that first afternoon when she announced downstairs, so puckish,

'I'm Wen, your body sustenance volunteer.' And then she stood before me, 'Meals On Wheels.' My heart rejoiced, and I replied, 'Oh, no, dear Wen, yours are meals that heal.' And when Wen bade me adieu each afternoon, could she have ever known that her beatific light had nurtured my fallow muse? After a lost decade, I compose, I create, I imagine again: life as verse, and vice versa."

Wen smiled pathos, and Ralphie whispered, "I'm ancient and silly." Wen clasped his hand and demurred. Ralphie spoke her name in a Chinese tone, "Wen Fēi." She nodded approvingly.

"The Underdog is a poet again, Mr. Stanton."

"So I gather. And you're the reason why."

"Oh, no."

"Oh, yes. I haven't told you this, boyo. May I, Wen?"

What now? They're fucking; she's pregnant; they're married.

Wen smiled. She bowed. She murmured, "All because of you."

"After Wen graduates, with *very great honor*, she will embark on her new life." Ralphie paused.

My God, you've stepped in heiress shit, huh, Ralphie, thought David.

"By seeking her spirit's authentic roots."

"I leave in a week for Kunming, my ancestors' home," said Wen.

"She'll compose verse and work for her cousin as a pineapple-on-a-stick vendor. Wen has renounced her parents' wealth. They have renounced Wen, boyo."

Wen stood and petted the hoary stubble covering Ralphie's cheek. Several days' growth at least, David thought.

Ralphie sighed: "If you're too busy to visit The Underdog before you depart."

The tip of Wen's index finger glided down Ralphie's nose

and gently hushed his quivering lips. Her smile blossomed. A tear swelled. "I love you, my Underdog."

Ralphie brushed it away. He looked up at her.

"And never forget my promise," Wen whispered between a sniffle, "I am paying you back, in full, from the day I sell my first pineapple."

How David had comported himself tranquilly in the face of his destitute father's act of gratuitous profligacy, regardless of Wen's presence, he did not know. How he failed to slap his father after Wen departed—when Ralphie asked him if he could *bump* the $5,000 a smidge to account for the $1,150 for Wen's plane fare, the $300 for a guest house until her cousin could finish the add-on he was building for her, and the $150 to get her to JFK and then to downtown from Kunming's airport—David couldn't fathom.

Wen had been gone maybe 20 seconds. David sat, immobile, as if his skeleton would collapse if he moved.

"It's a bridge loan," said Ralphie. "Ya know, temporary financing. Like they do in real estate."

David surveyed this bald man-child, still brawny; but it was his father's supplicating eyes that alluded to a feeble soul. He asked if Ralphie felt up to taking a walk to the park. They'd bring a blanket. They could sit under a tree near Gracie Mansion.

"I have indolent leukemia," said Ralphie. "Nothing serious. Sure, I can go. You can ask my oncologist if you don't believe me."

David clasped Ralphie's arm as they stepped gingerly down the four flights. By the time they reached the front door, Ralphie had optimistically regurgitated the gist of his latest "condition," leaving David with the oncologist's silver lining: "At your age, he says, the leukemia will feel cheated when you die of something unrelated, so buy green bananas."

The May sun felt like August's: sizzly.

They ambled up East End Avenue. Ralphie croaked on.

David listened, inured to the same old same old: his father's big three regrets: time, good intentions, can't say no.

"Time, boyo. Lettin' time slip through my fingers"—that was The Underdog's Achilles heel. Part-timin' it as night manager at the Albert Ellis Institute was supposed to be only until he landed a career job, "ya know, with a pension and all." Instead, indecision waylaid him; he got lulled, stuck, from 1970, "No, '71," said Ralphie, "until '06, no, no, '05, whenever Ellis bought it. Time-slippin', boyo. Pfft!" And then four part-time years at the New York State Psychiatric Institute, " 'cause it was 2010 when The Buddha called me to Myanmar—formally Burma, you know that—for a year, right, boyo?" Ralphie had asked his 26-year-old Burmese guide—"the bee's knees, boyo!"—to "shack up" with him, but "lucky she knew I was incense delusional," or it would have been doomed like his last marriage, the shotgun one that inexplicably ended eight months later in "the wife just up and skedaddling!" And did he ever tell boyo about his "luck of the Irish" with marriages one, two, and four? "No kids!" Until his beloved third wife, boyo's ma, entered heaven on Christmas day, leaving Ralphie to care for his 6-year-old boyo. How child-rearing had blindsided him! "Total mystification! The Underdog? A single parent?" Compared to raising a child alone, wives one, two, and four—who all falsely accused Ralphie of being a bounder and a philanderer—were a snap. "Can of corn!" Oh, and Ralphie unfaithful? "Not in The Underdog's DNA, boyo!"

As they started to cross 86th Street, David lurched and barely caught Ralphie's forearm and jerked him back before he walked, utterly unaware, in front of an oncoming bus.

"Oooh, close one, boyo!" And talking about raising his boyo alone, Ralphie was reminded—as David, now clutching his hand, slowly back-stepped Ralphie to the curb—of a lifelong secret that he knew he'd "tell boyo someday." David eased him up to the sidewalk. "See, something's been corralled in me, my whole life, like a caged tiger." He needed to confess, now, while the two stood, facing each other, why he had failed as a dad. "Just scared of it. Never had the *cojones* to really try."

David stood in the silence, stared at a filtered cigarette butt near his feet. He shook his head helplessly, and then the two walked, uneventfully, and Ralphie talked, until they reached the park's 88th Street entrance.

"The only beacon of hope," said Ralphie, "what shines a light of perspective on The Underdog's failings, is generosity—agape love. Generosity is what gives The Underdog the distinct feeling that he is needed in this world. Generosity is the spiritual purpose that fulfills The Underdog's needy soul. I have no grace to fall from, boyo. But you know that."

Ralphie's arm slid under David's. They trundled along a winding, tree-shaded sidewalk inside the park. David observed a young male couple holding hands—so *in place* in New York, he thought—and a bench with two distracted black nannies, each rhythmically bouncing a white baby on her knee, and an old man with a rickety cane and wearing a black cardigan sweater in the near distance, staring off and listing feebly.

David noticed Ralphie's unsteady gait and looked up at him. Another "ripe confession," long overdue, his father said: "Someone up there loves me, boyo. Because, you see, after all these nothing years, alone, with no fatherhood guidebook, I am finally in possession of the words—divinely given to me, boyo, and I believe that—to thank you. Thank you for becoming the father The Underdog never had." Ralphie stutter-stepped awkwardly and stopped, then looked down, as if purposefully, at the green lawn by the sidewalk: "Just never possessed those words till now."

David, who was standing a few inches behind Ralphie, caught up to him, gently pushed his back, and they continued their stroll, the shade and sun seeming to cooperatively warm and cool them. David was his savior, Ralphie told him. "The Underdog's father abandoned him at age 3." David never abandoned him. "And in my dreams sometimes, strange as it sounds, boyo, you become the husband to The Underdog's mama." And if Ralphie's father had been a caring husband, like his boyo, "mama would not have leaped from our eighth-story tenement fire escape on Catherine Street" while he watched from below at age 9. Ralphie would not have had to cradle her broken body and bleeding head and helplessly endure her groans until she died in his arms while he wailed. "There are so many things about me, boyo, you don't know that I could never tell you. But I'm an optimist. You know that. You are my optimism."

They both stood atop the gently sloped knoll, barefoot, beneath a cloudless sky. The sunbaked grass soothed David's feet like a thermal glove as he stared over the gray-blue water beyond the metal fence separating the promenade from the East River. Ralphie had pulled the checkered red-and-black blanket from under David's arm. He was clutching it nervously, David noticed, and then his gaze returned to the distant Triborough Bridge. David thought about his flawed hero, RFK, for whom the bridge was officially renamed in '08, and what the legacy of his emerging humanity might have told the world about itself had he lived.

Ralphie vigorously shook the blanket out and let it drift haphazardly on the lawn. They sat on opposite sides; half of David's rear was on the grass. Ralphie patted down the two corners near him. David leaned back, supporting himself with his hands, and looked above his father's head at a tree's fluttering leaves while Ralphie urgently confessed "one last thing" concerning his generosity: Ralphie was sure that, if he'd seen Dr. Ellis as a patient, as boyo had urged him to do virtually his entire life, and that was why he never did, he'd have been forced to admit that his loaning money—to friends, associates, strangers, whom were really dealt "a raw deal like The Underdog was"—

was a pathology. "And, see, sometimes, boyo, you need a pathology to get through life's traumas, and I'm sorry I need 5,000, and oh, the money for Wen, so if you could borrow me, 6, say 7. I'm sorry."

Borrow me. A fissure grew. *Borrow me* buttoned up every loan request. *Borrow me.* David looked over at the river's rippling water; it seemed to roil. *Borrow me.*

David sat up, crossed his legs, a hand on each knee. Enter the weasel, clawing, gnawing: Until he put up, David knew that Ralphie would not shut up. He courted patience.

"Boyo, borrow me, and I *will* reform." If David would borrow him this last time, Ralphie promised to see the shrink, but unlike the past, not quit, take his "happy meds," and henceforth, when boyo denied him his "generosities," he wouldn't allow the howling triumvirate inside his head—his lost childhood, lost adulthood, lost life—to order him to terminate The Underdog. Ralphie promised to "master impulse control" and to "engage the responsible life," like boyo had always told him! He swore that death at the end of The Underdog-less tunnel was not the solution to disgrace!

Ralphie scooted closer to David and sat, leaning over his crossed at the ankles legs. "The Underdog pleads, trust me!" Even though David's forcing him to see that shrink precipitated his last suicide attempt, "this time, The Underdog seeks your counsel! And you will not have to summon the police to tease him in from the window ledge and pump the stomach of a cornball geezer—sick from delusion and pills—who wishes only to eternally rest in peace." And to prove he had reformed, even if David refused him this time, Ralphie would not, he "categorically" insisted, resort to self-annihilation. "I'll try not to, boyo."

Ralphie was breathless. He sputtered, "The Underdog's heart is pure, boyo." And the motives of those whom The

Underdog had gifted this past quarter-century with $158,000 —"FYI," Ralphie had kept meticulous track of every "boyo loan" in case a "real" job came along and he could repay David—"they were pure, too."

David sat silently and clearly felt Ralphie's braying solicitations crawl beneath his skin.

"Borrow me, boyo?"

"This I cannot do," David told his father. He pined to hear his son's voice and thought to call Zach at school when he got home.

"You sound like The Godfather," said Ralphie.

David raised both legs, folded his arms around them, and squeezed his clasped hands. He pushed until his kneecaps nearly touched his chest, and stared at them. "I am," he said flatly.

"Boyo! I never told you who I lent—"

"Don't."

"I only need—"

"You *want*."

"Six thousand."

"You *want* 6,000."

"No, boyo, I need."

"You *want*."

"The Underdog has no wants—"

"Too bad."

"Only needs: people, love, and boyo."

"No money."

"I need you."

"Not ever."

Or death—"

"Fuck you!"

Ralphie pounded his fist on the blanket. "*I* want nothing! *You* want! Boyo wants! Boyo wants The Underdog to exist like him, to be what The Underdog cannot be, or die!"

"I'd hate your guts, if you had any."

David put on his white socks, then his running shoes, and knotted the laces.

"I understand. That's just the child in you talking, boyo." Ralphie lowered his eyes.

David stood. He brushed grass from one hand, gawking at nothing, and thought about how he would never tell his father what lazing in Carl Schurz Park and just staring at RFK Bridge had meant to him. David recalled being 5 when Bobby was killed, when he heard in a eulogy on TV, "Some men see things as they are, and say, 'Why?' I dream of things that never were, and say, 'Why not?' " Sharing intimacies with Ralphie—let alone this inspiration, the seed that germinated into his commitment to public interest law—was not part of their repertoire. If a genie would grant David one wish, he thought, it would be to be admired by his father.

David looked down at his father's mostly bare head—a few solitary, thin white hairs, pallid freckles, several blotches the color of potato skin—and wondered if he would succumb to what plagued him right now: I'm all he has.

David tapped Zach's cell number from his landline.

"Hey, Dad," his son whispered.

"Where are you?"

"Library. Can I call you back?"

"Sure, whenever."

"Dad, I'll go where I can talk."

David waited impatiently. He had never longed more than this moment to hear his son's voice, its music, its timbre, its pleasure. His son could not rescue him. He was sure of that.

"Wuz up, Pop?"

"Same old same old."

"Are you worried about something?"

"No, no. Hey, I'm gonna be in Montreal Saturday, a law conference thing."

"You are?"

"Wanna go to, what's that insane all-meat place?

"Le Milsa," said Zach. "On Bishop."

"That's it. Where you and your roommates swore I'd find a vegetable—"

"Hey, Dad, we don't have to—"

"So, you down with Le Milsa?"

"Oh, yeah. Totally!"

ADAM'S ROTTEN APPLE

NOTHING.

Nothing is going to deter Adam Fleisher from telling his son that he has to move out of the house.

Now!

Or, on a specific date. *One we can agree on. Mutually. Unless.*

Adam has already begun prevailing upon himself to mitigate his son's unacceptable behavior! That's what he always does. Did. But this ludicrous straw—his son's brazen, unconscionable response to the police—has finally broken the camel's back. He isn't caving. Not this time.

And no succumbing to Suzi's overflowing tear ducts either— those dissuading spigots that sully his will with guilt, deflate it, and then propel him to metaphorically grope for his spine and to feel himself a flatworm; a toady, pusillanimous invertebrate; a jellyfish minus the stinger.

Today there will be no second chance. Well, not second; more like second thousand. No more coddling his kid—stoned now, in his room, in front of his plasma TV—and patiently, rationally imploring him. *Fuck rational!* No pandering this time to Max's impenetrable wall of silence that follows his respectfully proffered dialogue. *Fuck respectful! And fuck this insipid kid's impenetrable wall of silence*: silence that screams disdain for him and repudiates him, immolating silence that mutates into worry, into wild paranoia over what he must have done to have deserved iceberg silence from this selfish, pathetic, indolent—now add to that, lawless—blob, whose once magnificent promise, so, so long ago, shone like a beacon on a hill.

Adam sits across from Suzi at the round antique table in their smallish Foursquare kitchen, sick of himself. Spiking ire reinforces his resolve.

"You're angry. Aren't you?" says Suzi.

"Ya think?"

The implication of her sulk antagonizes him. "Don't cry, please."

"I can't help it, Adam. I'm his mother." She rises.

He slumps, as if bowing, one hand on the table. He sees a napkin stuffed politely between his fingers, hears a creaky cabinet opening, then a ladle or spoon maybe, stirring a pan, and the metallic clank of the cover settling over it. He yields to the voluptuous aroma of sweet curry. The impending pleasure of savoring his favorite spice causes him to salivate. His appetite aroused, he impatiently awaits the ragout and its seductive blend of banana, granny apple, raisin, mango, dark-meat chicken, red pepper, onion, cashew, coconut milk.

"I'm not hungry," Adam mutters. He is.

Upon hearing the dull thud of his plate, he raises his eyes. One, two ragout helpings are placed before him, then a helping of rice. Peripherally, he watches Suzi's hands deliberately lower her plate across from his, and then they vanish. While marshaling his determination, he hears Suzi scurry to the fridge and then uncork the not inexpensive bottle of Hudson Valley Chardonnay he'd placed there yesterday for something celebratory, and her presumption steams him.

Adam eases his plate forward. Suzi's hand nudges it back. Then a small glass from his favorite winery slides into view, and when the red script *Baldwin Vineyards* appears, he could not care less.

Opposite him, Suzi lists. *The glum-mannequin tilt.* Adam gazes at shiny planks of the recently waxed table—created from 100 percent reclaimed wood that he and Suzi had purchased with 9-year-old Max. Adam taps the table with his index fingernail.

"Remember him telling us, 'I'm proud of you for saving the environment, Mom and Dad'?" says Adam. How had he failed as a father, a parent? When did the initial fissure occur? And why can't he mediate what is eating him alive now: revulsion for his son. And the haunting fear of retribution should his irrational feelings ever be revealed to Max: permanent dissolution of his son's love for him.

Suzi's whisper flutters: "Dinner's getting cold." Adam detects that melodramatic hitch in her breath, the one she had *meant* for him to detect.

They eat in an air of sobriety.

"This is his second offense," he says.

"He doesn't deal—"

"Are you fucking kidding me, Suzi?"

"Please, please don't shout—"

"I'm not saying he's a trafficker, for chrissakes, but he sells it. Where do you think he gets his video game money, his gadgets from? Unless *you're* giving it to him—"

"Oh, Adam!"

"So you know what the police told me—"

"He failed the Breathalyzer."

"No, he just squeaked below the limit. Gerry said he'll

handle it, but if the police had wanted to, Gerry said, they could have stuck him with a DWI."

"Thank God." Suzi shovels in two mixed forkfuls of ragout and rice, gulps her wine, and smiles crookedly.

She's useless, he thinks. He jabs his fork into a red pepper as if executing it, then drops the fork.

"Suzi, did you *hear* what I just said?"

"Why did Max call Gerry, and not us?"

"Maybe he thinks Gerry's his lawyer, too."

"But that's okay, Adam."

"Maybe it's fucking *not okay*! Maybe his sense of entitlement lubricates his choices so no matter how stupid, they never rub him the wrong way—just us."

"You're not helping me cope—"

"If you interrupt once more, I'm gonna throw my plate against the wall."

Suzi's somber demeanor withers. Adam watches the saline-swell. Tears careen from her eyes—as if from bomb bay doors—and pelt her plate. Her *tears of torture,* he would like to think aloud. Her red nostrils flare and bubble. She speaks in a capitulating monotone. "You don't have to hurt me, I'm just ..."

Gluey mucus migrates from Suzi's nose. Her tears of torture, and the implicit message that they should recuse her from responding to the trauma of decision-making, especially where Max is concerned, especially lately, repulse him; so, by default, prickly Max-decisions were, are, up to Adam. He would like to smack her. He feigns empathy.

Silence.

Adam-the-science-teacher zeroes in on Suzi's quivering upper lip, and he thinks of suggesting that maybe her lacrimal gland isn't just a source of tears, but also the existential source of her emotional paralysis. And he bets that if he could keep a straight face, she'd actually buy his *scientific* justification for her abstention from involvement, which to him is *never* justifiable, especially lately.

Adam swallows his petulance. He evinces calm and helplessly observes Suzi's rain-parade. He mentally switches channels and tunes in Cristina, this 23-year-old, Guatemalan hard-body in his physical science class whose irresistible ethnic allure propels him to strictly adhere to his only-three-quick-glances-per-lecture rule. His nose twitches from recollections of Cristina's undomesticated body fragrance: wicked and unpredictable. Maybe someday. Right, he should be so lucky. Suzi's whimper is voluble, and Adam groans to himself, and imagines licking Cristina's dimpled cleavage, envisions himself on his back, her mouth opening, closing in on him.

Between husky gasps, Suzi says, "He needs Gerry more than us, anyway."

"What?"

"And—"

"What are you talking about, Suzi?"

"I don't know, I don't know, I don't know."

"He lumps around like King Farouk. And we're afraid of him, and you know it, petrified he'll abandon us if we confront him, and you—the way he talks to you—the disrespect, the—"

"Stop it! Stop it! Maybe it's what I deserve for showering the pent-up affection I never had from my mother and father on him —and you never had it, so don't tell me it's just me!"

"So, what, if we don't *shower* him with affection, he'll end up like us?"

"Yes!"

Not the tears, c'mon. "Well fuck if I see him showering affection on you!"

"I can't control how he feels about me."

"You can't *deal* with it."

"Leave me out of this! Do you hear me?"

Suzi's palms are suddenly over her ears and pressed; *here we go*. Her head moves up and down like a seesaw, and she wails and wheezes. Adam recalls Max's terrible-twos tantrums, and how, in the face of his toddler's overwrought outbursts, he reacted to him the same way he is now reacting to Suzi: wounded, furious. Her wailing, like his toddler's, is an explicit rejection of his respectful engagement of her. *Bitch!* And now, he thinks, just as with his toddler, surging guilt over wishing to thrash Suzi for what he knows deep down has nothing to do with him palliates his unacceptable wrath.

"Stop making me weep." Suzi pokes at her food. The saline flow has abated. She raises her head. He stares into blight incarnate.

"Gerry told me Max said the cops beat him at the station," says Adam.

"Do we file a brutality suit?"

"You mean battery? No. Max provoked them—"

"So say the police," she says.

"Gerry believed them. Suzi, the welt on Max's back was a warning."

"But they can't just—"

"Cops told Gerry, in front of Max, 'Kid's been warned.' Okay?"

"What did Max say?"

"Nothing. He wouldn't answer their questions. Well, Max did tell Gerry that when they held up the half-empty bottle of Captain Morgan, he finally spoke, and I quote: 'Whatever.'"

"They hit him for that?"

"Oh, no. It was after they threatened him with DWI, to which he confessed, quote: 'Yeah, driving while *inured*, to the police state.' He told Gerry one of the 'retard' cops goes to the computer—Max can clearly see Dictionary.com—next thing, he's bent over clutching his stomach." *There goes the glum mannequin.*

Adam scrapes his mostly uneaten meal in the garbage below the sink and is aware that Suzi has departed. The fork grating against the plate agitates him. Scorn for himself crawls beneath his skin. He deposits his empty wine glass and plate in the sink, and trundles without purpose to the kitchen window, leans against the sill, and peers into the dusk and across Park Place. *He already hates me, what's the difference.* The car rushing by is a reminder that the speed bump will be put in after a fatality.

His Honda is parked on a Tuesday side of the street. *Isn't it?* He had reminded Suzi to move it before the 8:30 street cleaning as he was leaving at 6 for his 8 a.m. class tomorrow. *Didn't I?*

Intermittent flakes of snow fall, and Adam realizes it is already mid-December, nearly five years since the move—the day before Christmas—to Prospect Heights, Brooklyn, from Manhattan, with The Lump, after he had officially withdrawn from Vermont with three incompletes, one C, one F. From Vermont! *Fuckin' Mickey Mouse U.* And he quits on it.

Adam had hoped that by now his new neighborhood would fit like his Cardigan slippers. Not yet. He still pines for Tribeca, where he and Suzi had thrived from 1980 until '06, where Max was born, and where his son's intellectual promise soared from pre-K through Stuyvesant High School until the first semester of sophomore year, when, inexplicably—like that!—*promise implodes*, and nothing, nothing! *What happened that I never saw?*

Another car whooshing by. Adam leans back from the window, and it's a wonder that he doesn't already feel complicit in what will surely be an eventual fatality. Why is he dwelling on the time Cristina sidled up to him to ask some homework question, and why does the thought that she was flirting intrigue him? Maybe there was something there—

"Max loves you, Adam."

He is startled. When did Suzi come back? That is how out of it he is. He doesn't feel like answering her and continues to labor through looming fear and suffocating self-pity to locate confidence, the balls to terminate his glowering son's paralyzing grip over him.

By the time Adam turns to Suzi, the thought of what his father's take on Max would have been overcomes him. He squelches the irony in his laugh. "So, you know what my dad would have done—"

"Oh, c'mon, Adam, don't start on him—"

"No, I'm just saying this, okay. And I'm not *starting* on him, goddammit—"

"Let him rest in peace—"

"Why? He never let me rest. I should let him?"

"So now this is gonna be about your father—"

"No, it's not, but I'll tell you, it doesn't escape me that here I am—supported Max his whole life, encouraged him, talked *to* him, not *at* him, when he was sad, co-mun-i-cat-ed with him. An exact 180 from my own life. You know how often my father asked me about me? Exactly never. I ever tell you what he said—only thing that morning as I lifted up my duffel bag and went off to college—what he hoped I might *learn* to appreciate?"

She murmurs, "No.

"The value of money and sacrifice. His."

"He didn't know how to love you."

"Fuck, he knew. He never tried."

"Haven't we been through forgiving him—"

"Well, *I* have tried with Max."

"You're a good dad."

"So where does good get me? Huh? Kicking my son out."

Adam basks in his trenchant, state-of-things recap. Suzi is impressed, and her eyes are dry. *Hallelujah.* "Will you love me after I banish him?"

"I cannot go along—"

"I said, after *I* throw him out. Suzi!" A tear dribbles down one cheek.

Fucking shit.

"I'm his mother, Adam."

"What?"

"You're the father. You're responsible for what happens when he leaves."

"Don't worry, he'll find a real job."

"No, I mean emotionally."

"The next stop is Grand Army Plaza." The robotic female voice announcing his station might as well have said the next stop is Execution Plaza. The 2 train's sliding doors close, and Adam leans back against them, and the subway lurches forward. He feels lame, useless, and gapes at the notice opposite him warning passengers not to lean against the doors. He stands up and spreads his feet for balance. He grips the holiday-decorated Bloomie's bag that contains a Silvertone link bracelet, wrapped in shiny paper, that he'd purchased there for Suzi, a Brooklyn Nets hoodie he had picked up at the nearby NBA Store, and his World Community College ID card, just in case he forgets the bag and a Good Samaritan finds it. *You're lame, Adam.*

The train galumphs and lurches to a stop, and Adam shuffles along with the exiting mob through the one sliding door that opens. He arches his back and sidesteps within an inch of a scrumptious black-haired Asian in black short-shorts, black pumps, black stockings, and black fur jacket, careful to avoid contact, and inadvertently steps on her toe.

"Sorry, getting out," he says.

She mutters, "Dick."

The disembodied overhead voice intones, "We're being held

by the train's dispatcher. Thank you for your patience." Adam peeks through the open door, and the Asian's disgruntled eyes meet his, and she glowers, and he frowns like a sad clown. *Bitch.*

Anxiety over confronting his son chokes Adam, and explains, he thinks, his too frenetic pace as he heads home.

By the time he reaches Park Place, he is practically cantering, sweating inside his red Members Only Racer Jacket, as if the wind slapping his face is tropical rather than wintry.

Adam stands before the waist-high iron gate in front of his four-story, fin-de-siècle brownstone. Panic dizzies him. He fiddles with the tomato-red tag tied to one of the gate's blackish-gray fleur-de-lis spires. Its Do-Not-Use directive is an adequate deterrent to those faceless strangers who roll up and stuff Chinese restaurant menus and grocery store flyers into the spire's inviting curly cues, and yeah, he accepts that these ubiquitous tags degrade the aesthetic, that they are endemic to Brooklyn living, part of the trade-off. He is sick of trade-offs.

He unlatches the gate and pauses, as he does periodically, to meander through wonderment-images of what he fantasizes day-to-day life was like for this home's first owners—1896, according to the original deed. A simpler, magical era verging on modernity as he understands it today—if you were well-heeled.

He looks up at the light in his son's room. His heartbeat quickens. *This is theatre of the absurd,* he thinks. *Let him stay, rot here. It's his wasted life.* He saunters up the newly sandblasted stoop—to the tune of 3K, he remembers—opens the door, and the cornball line from the silly Miller Lite commercial that has, until now, triggered a guffaw barks contemptuously at him: *Man up!*

It is two flights to Max's room, two flights to D-Day. He lowers the holiday shopping bag. He unzips his jacket with a swoop. He stiffens: combat-ready. Adam fingers the bill of his orange UVA Cavaliers cap—his alma mater—removes it, stares a moment at the V over two crossed sabers emblazoned on its rounded crown, and envisions himself a conqueror. He cradles his upside-down cap in his palm and notices the off-white label sewn inside: *Made in Vietnam.* He thinks, *What a world!* Trade over ideology. Hard to hold a grudge when you can earn a dong from your former enemy, no matter the degree of their brutality. He is buoyed by his recognition of this irony. *Commerce über alles.* He is not stupid! He looks up and slumps foolishly inside, feeling not the paladin, but rather, his inglorious doppelgänger. Through the hazy light he stares at himself in the hallway mirror: 58, clueless, lame. "Off to meet the enemy," he murmurs, peering at his bulbous Yid schnoz, weedy eyebrows, mussed shock of thick, silver-white hair, and eyes, goofily enlarged by his thick-lensed Mr. Peepers glasses. "Me."

Adam hangs his jacket on the wooden coat hook, dons his UVA cap, removes his glasses, and slips them into his checkered black-and-green shirt pocket. He will not chance giving away his presence by flipping on the upper landing's ceiling light; there is just enough illumination from the outside porch lamp. Squinting, he looks up the stairs and through an unseemly, yellowish haze, brightened by the unseemly nightlight on the landing wall. He clutches the railing and trips over something on his first step. "Schlemiel!" A clenched fist in his chest trembles. He secures his footing, and climbs. He is sure Suzi is sequestered in their bedroom, ostensibly reading, or reviewing her sixth-graders' essays, or prepping for tomorrow's classes, but definitely hiding out, swathed in unadulterated denial that she confuses for maternal instinct. She bailed from responsible parenting years ago, but has that stopped her from tirelessly preaching to her students' parents those very guidelines she herself fails to practice with immaculate discipline! *The friggin' irony!* With each step he laments to his unresponsive God: *Never—not from day one—has Suzi allied herself with me when I correct Max. Ever! Instead, she criticizes me for trifling, as she always says, with*

his ego. As if I, Adam—who maybe yelled, what? five times at this
kid and never so much as gave him a potch on the rear, let alone a
whack—am a reprobate, callous, uncaring. What a fuckin' guilt
trip! You listening, useless Yahweh?

Adam halts on the small landing atop the first flight. He
panics. He rummages inside his jeans' back pocket. The torn
notepad paper was there! He breathes, relieved. He removes the
pad, unfolds it, and reads—as if he hasn't already checked it 50
times. He mouths without sound his bulleted, five-item agenda
for Max, noting the asterisk by the two demands he'd give ground
on. If forced to. But not the big three: Those are nonnegotiable!

He looks up and inhales the indisputably acrid odor of
marijuana, one of the asterisks. But now that he thinks of it—
trampled by fury over Max's insufferable arrogance and his own
endlessly timid indulgences—permitting Max's *homey* to
brazenly enter *his* house bearing *his* son's biweekly Mary Jane
stash! Fuck that asterisk! He races up the second flight.

Standing outside his son's door, it is as if a shiv has pierced
Adam's gut, and in a contained fury he rips away Max's Snoop
Dogg poster, reviling this misogynist chronicler of misogyny,
reviling rap, reviling all rappers whose lyrics violently disdain his
traditions, his culture, his world—he could wipe the floor with
Snoopy!

He regards the poster's ragged edges, the crease through
Snoopy's bandanna-covered head. He feels ridiculous and
ashamed for lashing out—like a child. He is no better than
Snoopy. He re-thumbtacks the poster. He will tell Max that he
tripped, accidentally, that he grabbed at it. He removes his UVA
cap. What did he think wearing it meant? He drops it.

While pressing in the final tack, he hears an unmistakable
female giggle, and the door swings open!

"Oh, wow!" says the naked girl facing him.

In the silence, Adam orders his gaze to flee, and in a split second he finds merciful refuge in peering through the sliver between her arm and waist at his son's bare toes wiggling in front of his laptop, and Adam puts two and two together: He has inadvertently crash-landed into too much information about his son. He wants out but remains, un-sure-footed, and endures his dread.

"I am, like, so okay with this, Mr. Fleisher. You're looking at nature." She smiles. Then grimaces. "I just gotta pee. 'Scuse me," and she scuttles like a snake between Adam and the door frame, and hippity-hops past him. "Oh, um!"

Adam turns to her without looking.

"You are Mr. Fleisher?"

"Yeah. Yeah."

"That's a relief."

He dares to contact the girl's face, and her sugar-white, wavy short hair with its fine cinnamon streaks captures him, and he peripherally catches sight of her small, milk-colored breasts and their teeny, pink nipples, and he smiles like a dummy.

"Max said you never come up here." She cups her mouth, giggles, and croaks devilishly while craning her long neck in his son's direction. "Like, wrooooong!"

She turns back to Adam and he surrenders to her lower lip—impish, puckered, and moist—and to the knoll-like swell of her cheekbones. She is tantalizing.

She looks at Max. "Um, I'm gonna dress first, and then —I'm off."

Her black pubic hair is *a Mohawk!* Shaved on either side. *Black!* Jesus! Adam raises his eyes as if sprung from a trampoline and he is busted, he thinks, when her face reappears. He is laser-focused on her *charcoal* eyebrows.

"Max says you know Keith Richards!"

"Hardly," Adam says. "I met him backstage at a concert. We

talked, commiserated about life. He sent me a, whatchya call it, thank-you note, I guess you'd say."

"Max told me you didn't save it."

"I did, actually, though exactly where, I can't recall."

"That is so awesome, Mr. F."

She disappears into a corner of Max's room. Adam steps back, as if it matters, he thinks.

"We'll chill tomorrow, okay?" she says.

Inside Adam, her unabashed nonchalance hurts. He could have been clothed, or not, could have been real, or an apparition. To her he is here, not here. No difference. He has never felt less effectual.

"Yeah, later," his son says, as if he is not here, and he thinks, their indifference exposes him to himself: *Yep*, ineffectual; innocuous debris orbiting his son's life. He hopes God will forgive his sins, though he really doesn't know what they were.

The girl reappears in the doorway, wearing lace panties, clutching her bunched clothes and jacket that cover her chest, and grips her long, tan boots. A flowered, brown pullover cap of some kind with embroidered red flowers covers her ears and half of her eyes, and Adam feigns interest in her hat's swaying braided topknot.

"Still haven't peed, Mr. Fleisher—"

"Oh, yeah."

"Thanks. I'll finish dressing in the bathroom, just vamoose when I'm done. Oh, I'm Dani. Reaaaaaally gotta pee!" She sprints past him. "Bye!"

Adam stands, hope drained from him, he thinks, and observes his son, who is stretching his hands across bended legs, straining, huffing a bit, struggling to put on white ankle socks. His hairy belly-rolls fold over his Adidas Nets shorts. The nipples of his cone-shaped man-tits graze his kneecaps.

Adam shuffles a few feet into the room, stops, and inventories the agglomeration of expensive audio electronics, the plasma TV, Grateful Dead and Snoop Dogg posters, the floor mattress. It stinks of pot mixed with half-empty glasses of Olde English 40s, all a testament, he thinks, to his son's embrace of narcissism. For which maybe there really is no antidote. Though, dammit, his hopes for Max matter, despite the feeling that hope is trickling from a spigot—him—whose source of empathy, sympathy is finite. When will he no longer care to jump-start his son's inert ambition?

Max will not break the silence.

How weird, Adam thinks, noticing that his heart is acting like a normal heart. He feels wicked-safe and okay, *detached?* Hmm. His earlier paranoia over the certainty of Max's disdain for his unsolicited interruption seems to have abated, as if his inexplicable detachment from Max has somehow arrested his insecurity. As if this detachment, gentle as a breeze, has ushered his son from inside of his heart, which doesn't so much beat but flail when he is around Max. Max is lacing his shoes, and Adam is aware of his passivity. He doesn't give two shits about his kid's life or what he does with it.

Max will never break the silence, he thinks, and his rage swells. *Look at him, semi-conscious sludge typing something inane on his laptop and ignoring me.* His anger whirs, as if the anesthesia has worn off. *I'm standing here, you grotesque yokel.*

The thought that poor Max just could be the fuck-up poster child for baby boomer parents squelches his ire. Like the parent of so many of his peers' aimless adult children who still live at home existing off mom and dad's un-tough love, Adam has, he is sure, pushed the pendulum of unlimited support and bottomless-pit concern for his unaccountable progeny so far left that it has reached its stupid-limit. And feeling okay, really okay, he entertains the impermissible heresy that, just because his 26-

year-old asshole kid is wasting away his life, the fault, dear asshole kid, is in your stars, not mine!

In the silence Adam's selfishness overcomes him, and gale-force anxiety erupts. He renounces himself as traitor to his sacrosanct oath to support and encourage Max no matter how tough the going. *My God!* Adam realizes he is staring, not at Max, but at what has become of Max. Yes, goddammit, his son is salvageable. The *encouragement imperative* that tethers Adam to his very conception of the moral father scolds him and demands that he reach out to Max, *Right now, you coward!* when Max is most at risk, and assure him that he is unconditionally loved, unconditionally supported by him and Suzi, unconditionally not alone, and that they would never, never, never, ever abandon their aspirations for and commitment to his happiness.

"That was a first."

"You're never here," says Max. "What's up?"

His son's impudent salutation infuriates Adam. But he will tolerate *What's up?*, which crouches with impunity behind a colloquial veil of pretend camaraderie, therefore, checkmate! He cannot accuse Max of disrespect.

"I wondered if we could talk—"

His son's cell phone *raps.*

"Lemme get this, Dad. Then I'll put it on vibrate."

"Maybe turn it off," Adam murmurs.

"Yo ... yeah, I was with Dani ... So, like you and me can chill Friday ... Yeah, I gotta put in my hours at the Cat Practice, so maybe after 6 ... Yeah, but, yo, my taxes are done supportin' capitalism. Tomorrow's my last day ... I'll tell you Friday ... yeah, supervisor followin' me around, observin' me clean, then disses my *work ethic* in front of the owner and I'm, like, yo bitch! Do I get the job done satisfactorily? Do I earn my paper, Brenda? Then it's like all tense the next two weeks. Fuck that. I couldn't cope ... Nah, I'm just gonna no-show Monday ... yeah, later."

Max tosses his cell to the nearby bare mattress, and then appears to scrutinize his laptop's screen.

Adam cauterizes his seething. "So, you had a problem at the job? Max?" He squats.

His son shrugs. Adam frets: *How will he pay his rent; maintain his part of the deal to live here; oh Jesus, now the kid's broke again!*

"I thought we agreed you wouldn't quit another job before we hashed it out," says Adam.

"I'll still pay you my rent."

"But you're unemployed."

"Trust me. I got the money."

Trust Max? Paranoia reigns: Where is his son's money coming from? Drugs? Is he dealing? "Oh, I trust you. I, it's not my business, but, I really just thought, I can help you with your savings, investments, like we discussed." Will Max ever turn from that screen and speak to him?

"Whenever."

"I've got," says Adam. "Hold on." He reaches in his back pocket and grapples with the crinkled paper, as if it might fly off. Just a peek—not that he has forgotten his points, just their ranking. And the ranking is crucial, as each point is ranked according to its do-ability: *easy* to *problematic* in order to maximize Max's motivation to successfully actualize them all. He unfolds the note, glances quickly, then stuffs it in his back pocket.

"Do you have a minute, guy? Maybe five, ten?"

Max turns a fraction to him.

"Up front. I'm a ... I'm uncomfortable with this conversation," he says.

"What's wrong?" says Max. "If it's about the police ..." Max lowers his head, arms thrust above his hunched shoulders, palms to the heavens. "I was lucky. I messed up. But *I'm* over it."

"We're happy to let you have the car—"

"It's your and Mom's car."

"But you really weren't responsible with it."

"I don't need the car."

"I know, but it's a question of driving responsibly when you do, like if there's an emergency—"

"No car, I said. Okay?"

Max's ridicule irritates Adam, but he nods as if unperturbed and strains to retrieve the order of things he plans to say.

"Was that Greg? On the phone?"

"Yeah."

"Do you have any other friends? I've never seen you with another friend, heard about one, and Greg's never here, hardly ever, and you think it's okay that he's, what, 36?"

"Forty-two."

"Oh, and married. I mean, you get where this is troubling, and see, this is what I meant to say earlier—I'm here, Max, because of me, my own insecurities, my own inability to, ya know, communicate what I need to, but hoping you and I and Mom can really turn a corner or else, well, lemme just, one thing at a time. So, it doesn't strike you as having friends your own age, is, ya know, functional, I mean, more appropriate."

"Haven't we been through this?"

Adam's back is killing him. He sits cross-legged a few feet in front of Max, who is *scrutinizing* the laptop between his outstretched legs. Adam hesitates and inches closer like a snail. His back, his legs, everything is sore. *What is he reading?* Adam inches closer. He cannot recall when he last hugged him.

"You are a loner, basically, with guys. I know you have girls here sometimes, like this one."

"Dad."

"Yes?"

"Could you? Move."

Adam shimmies a few inches back. His soul cries.

"Dad. What's the matter? What?"

"You relate better to girls," says Adam. "Huh?"

"I relate better to my life!"

Adam surreptitiously reclaims the lost ground until he is just close enough and extends his hands over the laptop and they are within inches of Max's shoulders. Max sits upright, and Adam's arms float in disgraced space.

He gets up with no self-respect and sits by Max's side. "How will you pay your rent?"

"You don't listen. I have money."

"You've saved it?"

"Yeah."

Max clicks open an email and reads it. So does Adam. *You were right. He does look like an older Napoleon Dynamite. Tee-hee. LOL—Dani.*

"Where did you meet her?" He imagines himself as a sponge, condemned to absorb his son's indignities, without end. He is no better than Suzi.

"Who?"

"The girl. Dawn."

"Dani. Naked chat lounge on Skype."

"That's where you? You met?"

"Online, yeah."

"Oh, that's an intimate way to get to know each other." Adam fakes a breezy chuckle and extends his neck to sneak a peek at his son's emails.

Max turns full-face to Adam, and he imagines himself a pigeon staring into the face of an owl.

"How's school going?"

"It's goin.' "

It's goin'. Another none-of-your-business rejoinder each time Adam inquires about school. *Jackass.* Still, Max swore at the start of the semester he'd complete it, so Adam is bound by principle to acknowledge Max's word, and he fears that being a noodge will only embolden Max to use that as an excuse to drop out.

Adam's anxiety approaches fever pitch! "Finals this week?" He implores himself: *Shut up.* But, goddammit, he isn't yielding to Max's self-destructive intransigence. He must and he will continue to fend off his son's recalcitrance for shards of information about his college attendance, because Adam is dead certain that if Max can just stick it out at Kingsland Community, the mantra that he has drummed into his son's noggin since preschool will germinate. Dare he say it aloud: *Education, education, education!* Dare he share with Max the formative years when he'd extol the virtues of learning to his wide-eyed toddler while they cuddled nightly, and, as if seeding a cloud, whisper before Sandman-time, *Every hero has a hero for a teacher.* And like that, the lack of influence *Adam-the-nonhero* exerts over his son shames him. He recalls a year ago revealing the meaning of *his* Judaism to Max: *His* Judaism spiritualized Adam and *essentialized* him, not as better, but as special, he had confided, to which Max, devoid of expression, said zilch. Never again will Adam reveal such precious intimacies. The permanent sorrow his son's abject disinterest injected into him is far too painful a reminder of his vulnerability for Adam to ever, ever open his soul to Max.

Adam is up, resolute, roused by his immutable conviction that all it would take for Max to turn himself around is a four-year degree, and that that college degree, that diploma—despite Max's moronic indifference—will certify him as a respected member of the tribe, not to mention be his pathway to white-collar employment.

Of course Max will not break the silence. Adam despises himself for being possessed by such a nonsensical, self-righteous conceit, but once formally educated, it would only be a matter of time before Max would respect himself, his heritage, and maybe,

maybe even beg Adam's forgiveness for refusing to even consider his multiple requests to say Kaddish with him the night his father passed. Adam recalls Max's glib pronunciation that he presumes sealed the deal: *If you think forcing me to get a Bar Mitzvah made me Jewish, think again.*

"I have two finals left," says Max.

Adam feels his angst burrowing. "Oh, you'll get straight A's." He congratulates himself for masking his anxiety.

"Community college is kind of a joke."

"Not really, see, you can transfer. Maybe a SUNY school, private college. And look, your SAT score proves you're smart."

"Proves I'm smart?"

"You are."

"According to a standardized test."

"I'm just saying—"

"Made up by white-flight suburbanites."

"With a little more effort—"

"The joke about college—"

"It's not a joke!"

"Is that it's for everyone."

"No, I'd, I beg to differ," says Adam, and he thinks, maybe, is this his chance to get through? "True, there are those ..."

His son's eyes are glazed. They bleat ridicule. Max's lips stretch open. His yellowish upper front teeth appear. He bites hard on his thumb's nail. He looks like a sedentary, half-demented orangutan too long in captivity. Adam trembles. "Could you look at me?"

Max gnashes his hangnail. "The real joke about community college is ..." His tongue slithers between his lips, and he spits the nail-sliver. "That it's even called a college."

"You are *out* of this house January 1st!" Adam's shrieking burns his throat. "You shiftless piece of arrogant shit, when I fucking talk to you, *look at me!*"

Adam's heart pounds. He stands before Max, livid. He flattens his words. "Look at me." He kneels and contests the Sphinx's vacant glare. "I'm your father, Max." He yells, "Look at me!" He screams, "Look ... at ... me!" He screams again and again, the same three words, like a banshee, louder and louder. He notices that Max's cheek is moist with his saliva.

The Sphinx stares. Adam stands. "I'll send your new address to your dealer, so don't worry."

Max shakes his head and smirks.

Adam self-administers *composure*. Like novocaine, it numbs his contempt for Max. He directs his *rational* mind to contextualize the contempt and discover sympathy. He *acted out*. His reproach of Max was juvenile, vicious, immature. Period. He defied a wisdom he understands as axiomatic truth: Anger breeds enmity, engagement breeds possibility. "Can we start this over?"

"Sure," says Max.

"Virginia plays N.C. State day after tomorrow. ESPN, 8 p.m. So, wanna watch?"

Silence.

"You home?" he says.

"Uh-huh," says Max.

"You can point out, or no, I'll tell you when I catch a moving pick. Also ah, oh, I explained to Mom, not as well as you could, that it's also called, oh God! Um?"

"An illegal screen," says Max.

His son's response feels like a lifeline: All is not lost. "Right! Hey, since we're getting into B-ball, ask me nicknames? C'mon?"

"Carmelo Anthony."

"Melo."

"Jordan."

"M. J., Air Jordan. Okay bro," says Adam, "now I will stump you: The Human Eraser!"

"Marvin Webster, played for the Sonics and Knicks in the '70s."

"Far out!" He peers at his son and prays that this banter is cleansing. "I watched a Nets game last week—alone. You were at the Cat Practice. So! I'm absolutely down with us goin' to Barclay Center, maybe January, ah—"

"*Barclays*, with an *s*."

"Right. Barclays."

"I'll go."

"I don't know the Nets' bench players yet. Anyway, we'll order from the Thai place when we watch on TV."

Max nods. Adam admonishes himself to leave while he is ahead. He thinks and chances, "The problem I have, Max, with your, our arrangement, here, is with me. And if you're open to it, we can all see Janet, the therapist I mentioned last month. Suss things out, um, casually. I'm sincere, I regard what's going on as mainly our problem, I mean Mom and me."

"Then maybe you both go."

"No, I think we should ... structure this, as a family."

"I'm sorry about the car."

Max is *full of shit*. "I know." Adam hustles himself through Max's door into hallway air that feels breathable. He looks at Max. "Um, Mom and I noticed you've been leaving the house around 11 sometimes. Just ... wondered?"

Max does not move. "Ah, the parties I attend don't start at 8 p.m. Okay?"

"I'll look into a roommate service. Investigate the cost. I'll help you. We can talk over our ideas during the game. Okay."

Adam distinctly hears Max murmur, "Fuckin' neurotic," and he smiles, as if Max said, love you, as if Max's dismissal hadn't disemboweled him.

With each uneven step down the stairs Adam thinks less of himself. He is neurotic. A fraud. A coward. He stops. *And such a nebbish.* Adam laughs in silence, as if he was Max laughing at Adam. *I'm incurable. The Incurable Nebbish.* The moniker bounces inside his head like a pinball. And it comes to Adam that he has lived, and is going to die, without honor.

Adam pauses on the ground floor landing, and he thinks of Max as his *bastard son,* bastardized by Adam—the cowering father—too cowardly, too anxious, too terrified to face his untoward feelings about his son, much less vent them to Max, or to himself: If I tried harder, maybe *I could give a flying fuck about basketball.* Though the thought of speaking from his gut mires him in incoherency, he has had enough, and he determines that there will be no retreat from *his* Waterloo: UVA vs. N.C. State. Max will know who he is dealing with. *And so will I.*

Connection-Central is how Suzi had conceived of the smallish, box-square library that is contiguous with their bedroom. She had designed it *quirky-snuggy,* she'd always said, so that they all felt *close-comfy,* and a sense of belonging in an environment that represented their *collective and personal taste.* She had chosen the room's mid-century decor with *meticulous amour:* taupe-brown couch, oatmeal wool armchairs, '60s Danish lamps and snack tables, along with her prized Russel Wright pitchers—granite gray, dark green, and coral pink—clustered in repose atop Adam's contribution: the '30s art deco walnut liquor bar.

Suzi reclines in *Suzi's* armchair. Adam sits scrunched against the far end of the couch, legs crossed, head buried in his laptop, poking through his Vanguard account and wary and anxious, unable to even know what he is looking at.

Teetering on the opposite edge of the couch, arm's length from Suzi, Max watches the Nets game on his signature addition that Adam and Suzi paid for: an ultra-wide-screen TV, half the size of the wall behind it. Adam deflects his intolerance for the unintelligible play-by-play—*grating fucking gibberish*—by keeping a bead on Suzi and how long she takes to turn her book's pages: about one every ten minutes.

Suzi has barely touched her plantains; Adam is warding off incipient diarrhea from too much mango-jerk salsa, and Max has already inhaled two portions of jerk chicken whose spices, Adam thinks, are hot enough to ignite kindling.

"Screen. Screen!" Max shouts at the TV. His hands rise as if launched.

Adam notices bits of food stuck to Max's fingers. *Gross.*

Max's arms collapse. "Dammit!"

"Now hush, baby, you'll ruin that player's concentration," says Suzi.

Suzi sounds to Adam like some gangster's brainless moll.

"Mom!" says Max. "What are you talking about?"

"Just joking, baby."

"She's just participating," says Adam.

"You have to know about something to participate in it," Max says.

"Well," says Suzi, "I have questioned you, sincerely, to demystify the game. So I can enjoy it with you, baby."

"Mom, you don't care about basketball."

"But you do."

"Brilliant. So can I enjoy it?" He stares at the TV.

"When the contest's over," says Suzi. "Max?"

He'd heard her, Adam thinks.

During a beer commercial, Suzi reaches below her chair and lifts her iPad. "Introducing Judy Collins. Ta-dah!" She extends it. "Max. It's halftime, right?"

Max nods, fixated on the commercial like it was the game, Adam thinks. *Dope.*

"A sublime Judy interlude? My favorite. Sixties music helped change the world."

"Oh, yeah." Max mumbles.

"What, baby?"

"You know what '60s music changed?"

"What, baby?"

"Well, it wasn't, *what, baby?*"

Adam observes Suzi in disgrace. It is halftime. He should have spoken up for her. But considering he is girding his psychic loins to banish his son during tomorrow's UVA game, holding Max accountable for his insolence isn't a battle he can afford now. Revulsion for him thickens his resolve.

"Bang-bang!" shouts Max.

Slang for a three-pointer; that much Adam knows.

Max shakes two raised fists. "Oh yeah!"

Another three. Max shakes two raised fists. "That right! You gotta *grind to shine!*"

Adam googles *grind to shine*. A rap critic's translation—*work hard, sell drugs to get rich.* So now he's a thug, Adam thinks, and his paranoia over Max's already moral-relativist descent into hedonistic nihilism—*or worse!*—is in overdrive.

Suzi stares inanimately at an unturned page for the remainder of the game, and Adam's panic flails. He methodically scrolls through his Vanguard accounts: pension and then taxable joint savings that are linked to Max's checking account for emergencies. It is doable. He'll tell Suzi, if Max moves out, matriculates at a four-year school, *not* two-year, they can subsidize him, up to $100,000. It's doable. He reconsiders. If —*big if*—Max keeps his grades up, abides by our rules, he *could* live here. Adam shuts his laptop! *No.* He wants Max out! Now!

Adam leans way back in his swivel chair, hands clasped behind his neck. He gazes about his World Community College office. His metal desk, the white walls, fluorescent overhead light remind him that he is an institutional cog, as unremarkable as his austere environment. Anxiety perforates his stomach. Feels like shrapnel. His dropout pothead son is nowhere man, headed nowhere, except maybe jail if he is involved in something illegal. Adam's inner torturer lashes him double-time, and he replays the fait accompli scenario that ceaselessly yanks decisiveness from his reach: The second his son leaves—*nope!*—is expelled by him from their home, he will, he knows, condemn himself to wrenching guilt. He will exist, subsumed by guilt in a permanent state of strangulation, with enough air to breathe, but never deservingly.

And then, wondering what has propelled this quite sudden, quite odd sense of self-confidence, of liberation, as if granted a stay of execution, it occurs to Adam that he has been gazing at the three groups of blue final exam booklets stacked neatly on his desk. He leans forward and feels safe and sheltered in his tiny office, his world. He smiles a little, caught off guard, he thinks, by this unanticipated reprieve.

Virtually none of his students will pick up their exam booklets, he knows that, yet he keeps them there as per his offer to do so. He is a bit of a laughingstock to other teachers for maintaining his holiday office hours just in case any of his students actually want to see their tests, review their answers— right or wrong—with him. Yeah, yeah, Intro to Science is of little or no interest to those for whom it is required, and the ones who register for it as an elective do so solely because of his online rating consensus as a *no-brainer B.* Show up, hand your required work in *promptly,* study minimally for *friendly* multiple-choice exams, participate in class discussions—be mindful of Prof. Fleisher's frequent imploring to never underestimate your valued contributions—and a B is a lock.

Adam knows that virtually none of his students will pursue science at a four-year school, let alone on a graduate level. Though some—mainly the eastern European ones—definitely possess the smarts to do so. But, no matter. Because, this instant, he is, he thinks, a difference-maker in an indifferent world, and pride rallies his spirits. For decades, he, Adam, has capably introduced an arcane world—science—to legions of minority students who, until the '70s, had near-zero access to college. *I am Cristina's teacher*, he thinks—even if she is incapable of surmising that noun's profound ethical implications and the lifelong reward this unique teacher-student relationship presents her.

Where's my self-deprecation torturer? Adam wonders. Maybe, when he entered the building, it was the vacant hallways' holiday-induced quiet that somehow gave him the space to reflect on his calling, to regard it as worthy and important. What happened to lack of fulfillment and sense of purpose as cornerstones of the urban, open admissions teaching experience? Where is Professor Adam, the underpaid assembly-line worker cranking out semi-literate graduates in a degree mill masquerading as an academic institution?

Maybe his healthy ego's controlling doppelgänger—that de-actualizing demon he'd capitulated to long ago and can't vanquish—is also on holiday. *Go with it.*

Adam surveys his own academic trajectory: self-possessed, intellectually gifted, graduating from Stuyvesant High School with honors, undergrad standout at UVA, and he wonders if his father's insistence that he return to New York to care for him and his mother—*you'll get your graduate degree at Lehman, like me*—had more to do with his shame and capitulation to lowering his sights than he realized. He despises his father.

The polite knocking on his door alerts Adam. No, a criminal wouldn't knock politely.

"Come," he says, as he fantasizes himself Captain Picard watching the sliding doors whoosh open.

Reality enters.

"Why you don't give me an A, professah?"

"I guess because I gave you a C-minus, Raoul."

"Then the C-minus you posted outside was for real? Oh, man. That's my final grade?"

"Yes."

"It's no error?"

Adam asks which section he was in. Raoul answers.

"On your way to work?" Adam says. He searches the stacks for Raoul's booklet.

"Yeah."

While searching, Adam detects Raoul fidgeting in his seat and licking a fat scab on his chapped lower lip. Raoul's crossed arms squeeze his backpack against his chest as if its contents are illicit.

"No worry, it's here," says Adam, smiling and searching and thinking Raoul's chances of professional upward mobility are nil, no, nonexistent. He shoots a patient grin at Raoul, and wonders, *Who the hell am I looking at?* Dressed in a tan blazer—*The Vandermeer* in red letters on the front pocket—white shirt, green tie, and tan slacks. Who is this brown face splotched with black freckles, this Latino, this byproduct of all the disadvantages his urban environment has to offer, who, the more he strains to "whiten" his discourse for the Caucasian teachers, the more he illuminates his ignorance of even basic rules of syntax and grammar? His current service profession—doorman—may be the pinnacle of what is realistically achievable for him, unless he gets lucky and makes branch manager, though he is planning on law school, Raoul once told him, straight-faced. And who does Raoul have to thank for this, this duping? Adam now feels the full fraud that he is. He locates Raoul's booklet.

Adam flips through it and looks up at him. *Who in God's name does Raoul think he's staring at?* He does not dare fathom it.

"So, did you grade wrong?"

"No. I don't think so, Raoul."

"You know, I worked my ass off for you, professah."

"I believe it," says Adam. "Here."

Raoul clasps the booklet reverently, *as if it were the Torah,* Adam thinks. He doesn't open it.

"Hard work, professah. You tell us is gonna pay off in life." He lowers the booklet to his lap.

"Always does."

"For everyone except me, huh, professah."

"How are your other courses?"

"They good, seriously, you can check. No C-minuses. Mostly B's. Man, like my grandmother is gonna go crazy."

Adam determines not to accept his entreaty until he senses that Raoul has palpably detected that his teacher is no pushover.

"Look, Raoul, you showed up regularly—"

"Was I ever absent? Never."

"But can you say—I want the truth—that you always paid attention in class?"

"I, um."

"The. Truth!!"

"A few times, professah," murmurs Raoul.

"A few times, what?"

"I would like, sleep a little. But—I swear to you—when I get home after work, and it's time to relax, have a beer, I don't! I study."

"How old are you?"

"Thirty."

Adam considers Raoul's contrition. Decades of these tough-love *Intro-to-consequences* confabs convince Adam that he has his supplicant's respectful attention. Raoul gets it. Adam can now switch gears from hard-ass to empathy to *deus ex machina.*

"I'm giving you a B-minus for the course."

"Thanks, professah."

"There could be a lesson here, my friend."

"You know, I try every day, man. Every day."

Adam smiles professorially at him. Raoul departs, happy as a lamb who'd dodged the wolf, he thinks, and as his door closes, he is unperturbed by this jaded, wizened, futuristic *Professor Fleisher* that materializes before his eyes, and has visited him unbidden more and more lately. *We did give a fuck, didn't we.*

Adam stares into the dim overhead buzzing fluorescent light and traces his commitment to pedagogy—his professional raison d'être—back to its existential roots: Woodstock, *Hair*, Tet, Rabbi Kahane, Godot, Reinhold Niebuhr (the Jew's gentile), Ringo—his Beatle. When he began teaching in '74, Adam was case-closed-positive about his pedagogic outcome, and he spread *the word* like a proselytizing missionary from the first day he passed through WCC's main entrance: *Knowledge is power; education powers success!* Goddammit, thinks Adam, this haiku-like commandment is still right, not *just* right, it is *Spielbergian*-right: panoramically universal, grand, pure and biblical.

Still as the dead, he cogitates: Knowledge-deficit is the lacerating, crushing success impediment that so particularizes this open admissions population. Only knowledge levels the playing field. Feed these nonwhite folks knowledge, and no matter their birthplace or ethnicity, once the playing field is leveled, the sky is the limit. So, it truly isn't *ethnicity* that condemns Raoul to a less privileged life than Adam. The truth is that Raoul's lower-class understanding of *educated* is, sadly, anathema to privilege.

Convinced that his singular responsibility is ministering to this academically underprivileged strata of society, Adam unapologetically accepts the non-politically-correct fact that he is middle class, Raoul isn't, and never the twain shall meet. So, really, what can he do beyond preach the knowledge gospel? Giddy—as if he had inhaled helium—Adam imagines himself trying to explain his definition of *educated* to Raoul, how it has emerged from his *Ashkenazic historicity*. Right! He muses, *I'd hire Raoul to supervise another Raoul, but never someone like me.* He lowers his head, and stares, unshaken, into his clasped hands, and congratulates himself for feeling only mildly chagrined by this unsympathetic and racist sentiment that he could never admit publicly. He fancies himself a kind of post-modern incarnation of Jefferson.

He looks up, at nothing. *Professor Fleisher* appears in his mind's eye. He does care. He does. And he wonders if there is any way, maybe, that if his son comes to know this, he will be loved by him.

Anxiety pilfers clarity. Adam grimaces, as if something has urinated on him. His utter ignorance about Raoul's experience, Raoul's being, and all those faceless minorities like Raoul, assault his certainty and violently castigate him for the presumptuous, regal gall to even think he understands them.

Adam leans back in his chair and congratulates himself for demonstrating to Raoul that ... this fatuous 58-year-old was somebody to be reckoned with. As if the world should be wowed by Adam Fleisher. He is just so, so tired of not measuring up, so sick of shame and fakery. He wants to go home.

Adam's eyelids balk as they flutter open in the blackness. He is exhausted from a restless sleep. He wills his pupils to grant entry to the smidgen of moonlight peeking through the open sliver above the valance covering the closed drapes. The dissonant noise that alerted him was definitely Max's feet, now trundling down the stairs. The trundling ceases. Suzi is on her side. Her breathing is rhythmic and he is reassured. *Zonked.*

The sound is faint, but distinct, he thinks. Rattling house keys. He is frantic. He turns his digital watch right-side-up on his wrist, and presses the side button to illuminate the time: 11:35. *Right on schedule.*

He has said nothing to Suzi the past few weeks, just crazy-hoping that whatever activity is stuffing his son's pockets with money is kosher or savory or harmless. But he has always known better. It has to be illegal, he thinks. *Has to.*

Repeating last night's third dry run, Adam slithers church-mouse-quiet from the covers, fully dressed, including his Reeboks. He leans over Suzi and is reassured by her baby-moans that she is still zonked. Slipping into bed after Suzi, who falls cadaver-like asleep in an instant, is *cake*, he thinks. He frets. She often wakes in the middle of the night, and getting caught by her would be humiliating. By his son? Who would care? Max never has regarded him as viably masculine.

Adam tiptoes on the double, reaches their bathroom, opens the door, tiptoes in, closes it, enough so the latch doesn't click. Then, hands searching in the pitch black, he opens the opposite door, and double-time tiptoes through their library, hyperaware that Max will vanish momentarily. *This is insane*, Adam thinks, and if his suspicion over Max's nefarious money-making activity is confirmed, his objective while watching tomorrow night's UVA game with him will be rendered pointless, and he and Suzi will have to adopt a plan B that, unfortunately, will insist that Max remain home, for his own welfare, or maybe live in a rehab, or halfway house or something. Bottom line: He has to prioritize rescuing Max!

Adam pushes open the library door to the second-story hallway, tiptoes in agony, peeks behind the wall, and peers down the stairs. He eyes the front door as it shuts. He hears the bolt-lock switch close, then tears ninja-quiet down the stairs to the landing, grabs his hooded coat from the wall rack, counts *one-one-thousand, two-one-thousand* as he had rehearsed, opens the door, sees his son's back disappearing down the block, and curses his suicidal resolve. *Insane!*

He follows at a distance; if he loses Max, then it is meant to be.

Adam crouches like an inebriated derelict in the 3 train's last car. At each stop he leans his head through the open doors while yanking the hood almost over his eyes, and fights to see all the way down the platform.

This time, he is sure Max has gotten off. *Finally.*

On the street, he passes by typical inner-city storefronts: *Check Cashing! Ruby's Natural Nail Salon, Amen Mission.* He intermittently weaves by people not like him: dispossessed types, all black or Hispanic. *Mother!* He follows Max, across the street and a solid block behind, to what appears to be some nondescript bodega—*has to be a front for criminals*—and his worst nightmare is fast blooming to fruition.

Adam crosses the street and stands, mouth agape, in front of the corner bodega his son has entered. Defending against an icy gust, he hunches his shoulders and peruses the garish blood-orange and yellow overhead canopy. He sniggers aloud at its asinine name written, no less, in pink script: *Paris GROCERY.* He reads the flapping canvas's come-on: *Cold Cuts Beer&Soda Organic.* He thinks, *Organic, right.* As if that didn't certify that this overpriced shithole's predominantly food-stamps clientele should somehow feel better about being ripped off by what was surely the only excuse for grocery shopping in this locale. Disgust oscillates in him. Probably all low-life druggies in there, he thinks. Maybe some street gang members. Or organized crime. The cold bites into him. His son has become a nothing. Nothing. Adam is all shame and fury.

Adam looks right and walks a few steps, and then down the

side street, where he stops in front of barred windows that, maybe, he hopes, will reveal the store's back room. He wanders by the window and grasps the brick ledge. He struggles to hoist himself up an inch or so and peeks through two of the thick metal window guards—there, he surmises, to protect the criminals inside from the criminals outside.

Adam grunts, wonders if the pinch in his neck is serious, and squints. The glass is smudged, but he can see. His chafed fingers whiten, his biceps burn, his lower back doesn't feel right, but he manages to inch himself up for a better look. He sees ten, 11 round tables. Each is covered with a dark-green cloth and bathed in dirty-white light from a cone-shaped lamp hanging from the ceiling. Pain shoots through his elbows. He searches the room.

There! Definitely Max, seated at a table with several other men—all white, ageless, unkempt, but not *dangerous*-looking. And an Asian. He scours the other tables for reassurance: mostly Caucasian; another Asian; a Hasid, black fedora, payos; and scruffy, white, middle-class looking … college kids? No blacks. Not one. Adam checks his son's table. He is less fearful. Less and less. No need to tolerate the pain anymore.

Adam lets himself drop. He realizes, is virtually positive, what this is. He sucks his bleeding pinky finger and endures the embrace of idiocy. *Poker.* Max is just gambling.

Adam has been standing still as a post for what feels like a century. Waves of relief pacify him. He yields to serenity. And in this moment, Adam feels blessed. He is not driven, not at all, he realizes, to understand his son, or himself.

SMILE LIKE SISYPHUS

GIL HELD OUT THE IPHONE. As if to no one, Davis thought.

"Here," said Gil.

Davis raised his crossed legs and swiped at the damp grass that irritated him. When will the sun dry the morning dew, he thought. He fretted while a drifting cloud dulled Gil's face.

"And the kid who took them?"

"What do you mean?" said Gil.

"He won't say anything?"

"He swore," Gil said. "Please, Davy!"

Davis lifted the iPhone, and Gil's hand retreated to his lap as if it had been stung.

"I have the cord," said Gil.

Davis's palm felt as if it was scrubbing his black buzz cut. *Chill.* He cupped the iPhone in both hands. He regarded the quad, and glanced at the administration building. He noticed two girls leaving Evans Hall: It all looked surreal, sad.

"And you're like, positive?"

"Well, yeah," said Gil.

"What do you mean, well?"

"What do you mean, what do I mean?"

"*Well* means I'm not positive, Gil."

"It isn't like there are close-ups, but—"

"No, no, no! I mean, *well* means you are *not* positive this kid won't tell someone."

"Okay, I don't know, okay! But he promised he wouldn't," said Gil, whose nervous fingers picked at the blond stubble on his square chin.

"And it's him?"

"Yes."

"It's not, like, photoshopped?"

"No. Okay?" said Gil.

"Okay what? What?"

"It's your dad."

"So you're positive—"

"I told you—"

"No, no, I mean positive they won't show up? Anywhere? On the net?"

"No."

"So what if they do? *What if they do?*"

"He doesn't want it back," said Gil.

"What?"

"His phone. Okay," said Gil.

"And the other one?"

"Other?"

"Person. Who was with my dad."

"Can't tell, Davy."

"For sure?"

"I told you!"

"So. You looked? At them?"

Gil lowered his head.

"You won't say anything?"

"Davy! C'mon, man!" said Gil.

Davis followed Gil's stare to a tree's fluttering leaves. Pretending he is distracted, Davis thought, by the wind gust.

"I'm, like, freakin' a little, man. I'm sorry," said Davis.

"Everyone loves your dad. Like, really admires how much he cares," said Gil, while twisting a wave of blond hair above his ear. "Including me. He was so inspiring from day one of class."

Oh yeah, thought Davis, and the familiar impossibility of ever getting through to his father, no matter the urgency, found him stammering within to put an end to his jealousy.

"So what do I do? What do I do?"

"I don't know, Davy."

"My life is so screwed."

Davis yanked his car door shut. He was cocooned, safe. The spinning in his head slowed. And though the unraveling initiated by Gil's panicked call last night had ceased, he was still *freaky numb*. But his *grip*, he sensed, was within reach.

Davis drove through the empty student parking lot and felt his hand gripping reason. This revelation was insane. No matter. He would reason out *the lie,* his father's lie, on the way home —methodically.

The campus exit gate fell behind him, and he sped away.

At 18—having received an A-plus in his *History of Truth: The Destroyer of Civilizations* senior AP anthropology seminar— Davis understood the power of truth and an equally powerful irony about truth. He had learned that without absolute fidelity to the truth, there can be no binding morality, or ethics, just chaos. But he was also taught: Beware of *The Truth.* When *The Truth* with a capital T is used to enforce ideological purity, to exclude and punish another's differing truth, then *The Truth* becomes a terrifying weapon, a subjugator, a destroyer of law, institutions, humanity. And when a people—a social group, state, or civilization—can no longer tolerate *enforced truth*, the inevitable outcome is rebellion, strife, and ultimately, destruction and dissolution of the subjugator's truth.

His sudden awareness that he was on the highway shocked Davis. He couldn't recall the entrance ramp. His chest tightened. He squeezed the wheel with both hands. *Chill, dude.*

Davis cogitated on truth's opposite. He had no AP class to assist him in unpacking the lie. Everyone lies, he told himself. It's wrong to lie. He had lied in his life, but if it was important enough, eventually he had recanted or forgotten about it. His ruminations swerved to people who *knowingly* live a lie. *Sick!* And living a lie daily, aware that everything you say and do is based on deception. That means your life is invalid, immoral, wrong. Your life is a lie. He murmured, "You become the lie."

He fantasized reprimanding his father: *It's the lie, the deception, Dad, that troubles me. Not this new truth.* He imagined his father's typical silence, typical dispassionate nod, and Davis saw his fist bashing him, saw his father's bloodied saliva on his hand, heard himself scream, *You lied to me!* Heard himself lambaste him, *Fucking explain yourself.* Davis felt himself grapple to locate the *sane-lever* inside his head, the off-switch he'd taught himself to access whenever panic and rage and fear ambushed him. He felt himself *unwilling* to retrieve it. *Fuck!* Davis fought to steady the steering wheel. He was in free fall. Wow. *Unwilling, unwilling!* Was he going to cave, to lose it, finally? He noticed the speedometer pass 80.

Davis sat in his parked car in front of the gas station's Quick Mart, hoping to marshal his concentration so he wouldn't crash and die, and gazed at a long-haired white kid his age wearing a ghetto blue-and-white Giants cap and filling his tank. *He's gonna leave us. So what. Mom never meant anything to him. I never have. Now everyone we know will know that.* He squeezed the key and meant to start his car, but couldn't. He would be deluded to even mention the iPhone to his father. What good would confronting him do? *Fuck it.* "I do *not* believe this." He pictured himself staring zombie-like at the moving banner beneath the jabbering *Eyewitness News* weatherman: *Flash! Husband, father, fag! Tenured associate professor of history at Lenape College in armpit-of-the-east Monroe Township, N.J., since 1995, caught on film with unidentified Lenape student.*

He groped for the sane-lever and envisioned the wobbly footbridge over a deep, rocky, uncrossable ravine, the bridge that Mr. Overholt had insisted was there each time Davis sat before him, crumpled, riven by failure and doubt after some traumatic encounter with his father and swore no, no, and Mr. Overholt replied yes, yes, the bridge that connected father and son did exist, was real, and must be acknowledged by him, or Davis would never make peace with his father, never believe that he was loved by him. *Maybe I can ask Dad why. Maybe this is my chance.*

To Davis, Ben—as he had come to call Mr. Overholt, his freshman English teacher, his mentor, role model, best adult friend—was his savior. Had their initial conversation about an upcoming exam not ended with Ben's praise of his intellect and class participation, had Ben not asked him about his academic and professional interests, had Ben not had half an hour to spend with him in the teachers' lounge, had Ben not said every few minutes, it seemed, tell me more, Davis, for sure, would never have survived his father in one piece. So, when Ben would remind him, *You must acknowledge the bridge. Even if your father cannot, you must! Or you will never believe it can be crossed,* he felt saved.

A bridge? To an enigma, who—when Davis spoke to him, especially his use of the 'D' word—*Dad; hey, Dad*—transformed into this inscrutable character from a play titled *Secrets*. How could he expect to fathom his secretive father's secret world, much less confront him about it?

Davis exhaled, exhausted, depressed but sane, he thought, able to concentrate on the road. He stretched for hip hop enlightenment, plucked a Kendrick Lamar CD from the glove compartment, and recalled Gil's text that morning: *Davy gotta c u now!* Davis wished that Gil—a year ahead of him, though older by just four months, and his best friend, confidant, and *big brother* since junior high—was in the passenger seat. *Need you, bro.*

Davis passed Friday's. Four miles to home. He obsessively scavenged his memory for recollections of his time with Gil this morning for an insight that would produce a sliver, an overlooked scrap he might have missed: He'd waited, shattered, on the tree-shaded knoll overlooking the college quad, and when Gil trotted to him, they greeted each other with a bear hug. Definitely *too intense*, their grip, *too intense*; their sympathetic back pats foreshadowed looming excruciation.

His fondness and esteem for Gil lightened Davis's black spirit, and his car seemed to float along the highway. He remembered how they used to meet atop that very knoll, that sacred, transformative *hilltop*, where, as adolescents, they had commiserated about life. Davis saw his goofy grin broaden in the rearview mirror, recalling what turned out to be their five-year, endless summer ritual: panning the quad for scantily clad or teeny-weeny-bikinied coeds with the high-powered binoculars Gil had liberated from one of his dad's camouflage-colored knapsacks, cleavage hunting. Whatever happened to the yellow-lined knob-pad they'd kept one summer? They had guffawed like hyenas over each Knob Scoreboard entry: 5 points for whoever spotted the biggest knobs, 10 points for the brown area, 15 for the nipple, and 2 points for gross-out specials, like acne. Bonus points for an oozing pus-pimple or a mole with titty hair sticking out of it. *Eeewww!*

A police car's distant whine unnerved Davis, and he fretted that the flashing red lights drawing closer in his side-view mirror were pursuing him. When the cruiser sped by, Davis's sadness reemerged. He felt imprisoned.

He recalled the awkward silences between friends who normally blabbed without taking a breath, how he and Gil sat cross-legged, facing each other, staring off, dumbfounded, how they stonewalled answering one another's *c'mon-speak* body language, how Gil kept faking distraction from the shade tree's oscillating lime-green leaves and how desperate he knew they were to laugh and joke and be 15 again: sharing the quad's hilltop —the magical oasis, the magical medicine man that cauterized all psycho wounds, whitewashed all insane paranoia each time the two best friends met there. But Davis wasn't 15, and the knoll wasn't magical enough to whitewash the helter-skelter nightmare rampaging through his head that morning.

The rutted edge of his lane jolted him, and he swerved to the center, and regret for the way that he'd just unloaded on Gil—*I'm freakin', man. What do I do? What do I do? My life is so screwed*— reddened him with embarrassment, or the rearview mirror lies.

Davis passed the exit preceding his. "Wow, I lost it," he murmured. But Gil was a staunch and proven friend who understood Davis and had put both hands on his shoulders and offered him what he needed most this morning, when he needed it: unequivocal support. *He was there for me.* Davis promised himself, if only for Gil and Ben, he *would* keep his shit together, *hand on the sane-lever, boy!*

Nearing Cranberry, Davis glanced at the red-lettered billboard on the semi-developed tract of land to his left: *Another Rite-Aid! Coming Soon.* The world goes on, he thought, oblivious to his life having just been nuked. He wondered, why him?

Davis drove along Main Street. He sidled up to a curb and stopped. He should look at the iPhone. He should. He rolled down his window, and *thankfully*, it was May, and in September, on to Brown and the start of his new, fantastic life and the end of *Why him?*

The breeze tickled his neck. Brown's summer immersion program in Paris couldn't come quick enough. Bring on July. For now, his sights would stay focused on daily workouts with Gil and their buddy Mark, who was going to start at right tackle for Rutgers! *Fuckin' awesome!* They always knew he'd make a D1 team.

He shoved the idling car's shift into drive. What to do with the iPhone? *Bust it up. Throw the pieces into five garbage cans.*

Davis entered his ranch house from the garage. He took off his shoes. He treaded quietly from the den. The place was dim as dusk. He listened, and listened. *No parental units. Thank you, Jesus.* But he was taking no chances.

iPhone in hand, Davis made it through the kitchen and down the hall. His room was in sight. *Chill, Davy.* His shoulder grazed a framed portrait of his dad and mom, and he reached for the frame. *Fuuuuuuck!* His heart raced. The picture was barely askew. *I'm okay.* While straightening the frame, something got to him: his parents' youth, the zest in their smiles, his dad's gemstone-blue floppy PhD cap and billowy gown, his mom's crooked head snuggled against his dad's shoulder. A torrent of fondness overcame him. He would give everything to have known them when.

Davis sat cross-legged in front of his pillow. He aligned the stack of four acceptance packets he kept beneath his bed before him—in a row, one over the other's edge, like a deck of cards. They were his four aces: Michigan, Penn, Duke, Brown.

Brown, Brown, Brown, he remembered his mom tooting like a choo choo, puffing conviction, puffing pride. *Brown! No contest,* she had declared, the omniscient mom, as if she was president of the Brown alumni boosters or something. But, no, that was just *Nancy obeying her gut,* which—as she routinely reminded him in that annoying third person—had a higher IQ than her brain.

Davis's fantastic future paled. *Fuck me. If she ever finds out about Dad.* He was teetering on the verge of insanity, again. He pictured his parents at his college graduation, each seated at opposite ends of the row. His mother—alone, smiling awkwardly, dry-eyed, blown away, betrayed—and his father, stoic, holding hands with his boyfriend and their adopted Afghan infant on the guy's lap, fussing, pulling at his toweled head. *Oh my friggin' God.*

He dug into the Brown packet and reread his acceptance letter, and his mind's torque eased. His mom had said that each university boasted a top cultural anthropology program. But Brown's smaller campus had an ingratiating feel to it. She was right. He liked the kids he'd met during his two visits, and the teachers too, especially the associate dean of the College for First-Year and Sophomore Studies. She was no-joke smart. But also, really sincere. His mom loved her. His father? He wouldn't have. No way. Too faux chummy, he would have said.

Davis gripped the packet tight, and he recalled his father's reaction after showing him his acceptances: *The school that works for you works for me.* His grip tightened.

Obey your gut, boy, like Mom. He plugged the charging cord into the wall outlet by his bed and left the iPhone on the floor. Obsessing over! Back to normal! After a two-hour nap he would drive to school, work out in the gym with Gil and Mark, shower there, come home, eat dinner alone, go to sleep, go to school tomorrow, figure out his father and the iPhone later.

Davis awoke to his mother's annoying door-tapping.

"What?"

"When did you get home?"

"Mom, I don't feel well." *That sounded believable.*

The door inched open. His mother's pink fingernails appeared, then her hand, then her nosy nose.

"Why are you coming in my room?"

"Because you're sick!"

"How many times do I have to tell you not to come in here unless I specifically—"

"What's wrong?"

"Nothing, okay?"

"You're not sick, then?"

He looked up. "I'm okay. I'm going to the gym."

"Well, we're eating. Your father's waiting."

"Could you not stand directly over me?"

"I could."

"I'm going to the gym."

"We're eating!"

"If you don't leave, I'm taking off all my clothes."

His mother ran her fingers through her short crop of auburn hair and patted the back of her head the way she did when her hair was long, Davis thought. She thrust both hands in her blue jeans pockets, bent forward, and hovered.

"Mom! You're like a whirlybird."

"You have two months left. Two months—"

"I just, I really don't want you in here anymore. It's my room. I need my privacy honored—"

She straightened as he imagined a Marine would. "Oh, really!"

All bark, Davis thought, no bite, not to him, though he was confident *she* believed that he was intimidated.

"I expect you to honor my privacy," he said. He smiled.

Silence.

"What's wrong with you?" said Davis.

"You think I give a damn about what you do in here?"

"Yes." He sat up. "You're still pissed about—"

"Listen to me." She sat next to him on the bed, and he thought to hug her.

"What?"

"The maid *will* clean your room this week."

"Oh, c'mon, haven't we been there, done this!"

"Just making sure that if you put a lock on this door again, I'll have it unlocked, again and again, and yes, I'm still pissed!"

"The maid is so annoying; she moves my shit."

"Tough. Oh, and I will come in here unannounced if I think you're hiding—"

"I don't hide my weed."

"Good, so when I find it, I'm pitching it, just like last time."

Davis can no longer stifle his smile.

"Laugh at me all you want."

"I'm not laughing at you."

"Whatever. House rules. You don't like them, you can tell me to go to hell, I'm not going."

"Mom, I would never, never do that."

"You've done it," she said.

"Only when I'm riled."

She stood, and leaned over him. "Dinner."

"All right, all right." Davis glanced at his *cool* mother as she neared his door.

"Yo, Mom?"

"What?"

"Why did you cut your hair?"

"Summer 'do. Thought I'd try it."

"Radical."

"It's retro. A little Twiggy."

"What?"

"Never mind. So, you hate it?"

"No. I dunno. It just looks a little dykey."

"Who asked you?"

She closed his door like a snot, he thought, and memories of his enamored teammates roused in him adoration for his mother and pleasure, and an intense sense of fealty overtook him. Not one could believe she was 52. He was, he thought, already thinking of her in the past tense, and he recalled, as if telling his college friends, how his mom attended every home game and team event in jeans, heels, low-cut sweaters or blouses, her shoulder-length ponytail swinging with jolly abandon as she joked with his teammates, razzed them—win or lose—about their play, and how they had always treated her with total respect, admiration even, because she was that dedicated a supporter. If she knew their nicknames for her—MILF, Tight End—she'd be so pissed! No, she'd be cool with it, flattered.

Davis texted Gil: *Yo! sup, beast. No go 2 nite. Later.*

In a moment his phone vibrated: *K. Me and my dad are watchin Crankees game anyway.*

Davis sat on his bed and shook his head as if to chastise the jealousy. Would he ever not envy the closeness Gil and his dad shared? Gil's dad wasn't perfect. They argued. But he was Gil's best friend. *Fucking unreal.* They did what best friends do together: watched sports, went camping every summer. When he went to Gil's, his dad always asked him, *What's shakin', dude?* And *yeah*, Gil always winced, and said: *Dad, you talk like a doof!* And his dad always winked at Davis, always offered him a *brewski*, always busted Gil with some whack putdown, and he recalled Gil's dad once cracking: *So Davy, can't kick him out, 'cause when I'm a geezer, Gil's promised to support me in the style he's become accustomed to.*

His jealousy was petty, Davis thought. "Get over it, mook!" he murmured.

Davis retrieved a book from his backpack: *Disgrace*, by J.M. Coetzee. He plopped on his bed and pulled Brown's summer reading list from the cover. *Insanely powerful novel,* Ben had said, as the two looked it over in the teachers' lounge. *You psyched?*

Davis was. His head fell like a rock into his pillow, and he stared at the white stucco ceiling, stared at Ben in the past tense, and stared at the loss he would encounter at Brown. The man who had introduced him to a surfeit of literary protagonists and their agonies and yearnings and angst and despair—so much like his—was fast becoming the object of his darkest melancholy. Guided by Ben's knowledge, Davis's festering uncertainties bore witness to the machinations of Holden Caulfield and Portnoy, the absurd universe inhabited by Camus's Meursault, the doomed existence of Kafka's K, and James's Catherine. And then Davis replayed *the moment,* when he had shocked Ben one afternoon his junior year, wrecked by despair, and confessed that those characters' destiny were his, followed in an instant by Ben's refusal to accept his surrender: *No, Davis!* And before Ben could continue, Davis had unloaded his doomed existence on him, reddening Ben's ears with his certainty of failure and his wild insistence that life was futile. How he had slumped on Ben's office couch, spineless, defeated, paralyzed by the terror that had ambushed him from nowhere that day and seized his will, and rendered him mentally hopeless, and positive that life was a winless, pointless game, and in the end he stared at Ben and cried before him like a little boy while hemorrhaging shame and revulsion for himself, blubbering, *You die like a dog, die like K, die horribly, so why not hang yourself, because it hurts less than living with someone you hate.*

You aren't those characters! Ben shocked him. He was so stern. He was so direct. But he was compassionate. *They were doomed victims,* Ben had said, *overcome by a destructive world that at once defined them, controlled them, owned them, and they crumbled. None possessed an inner moral compass to point their souls toward self-possession and belief in the power of their own free will to make change. So they succumbed. But not you!*

Davis remembered imploring Ben. How, how, how could he defeat surrender, keep trying, how could he find the will to possess himself?

Smile like Sisyphus, Ben had said. Smile bravely while you're down, smile bravely while you hurt. Smile, and you'll discover Davis, a responsible, compassionate, and loving Davis. Ben implored him to never forget that those fictional characters were protagonists, *but not heroes,* not Davis's heroes, not anyone's, because they all caved. *They opted out, but not you,* and then Davis confessed in a flat stammer that during the *black days* this past year, when the possibility of opting out flooded his head and tried to drown his will, were it not for Ben, he just might have succumbed. And will he ever forget noticing Ben's reddish-brown mustache broaden, reminding him of a contented caterpillar, and Ben's round cheeks and Ben's big smile and the crow's-feet deepening and the sudden feeling that he had been freed, and Ben saying after a silence, *Well, you can't opt out now,* and his own dumb blurt: *Why? Because,* Ben said, *you're smiling.*

Davis sat up and stared into nothing and slumped in melancholy. Ben's counsel over this crazy iPhone fiasco was the answer. That was simple. Resolved. And he thought about leaving for Brown, leaving home, leaving his past and how he would remain stuck in that past, forever, mired in its whirlpool of despair: too angry to love, too afraid to hate this intimate enemy that was his father. He wanted to smile.

Davis faked a smile. Maybe what happened to his father wasn't just something to freak about, he thought, but an opportunity, and he tapped hope. *If I can show him that I understand,* Davis thought, *maybe he'll open up. Maybe Ben's bridge will appear.* Maybe he could assume that responsibility and compassion would follow, and maybe, maybe he could talk to his dad, maybe even help him sort through, maybe get through this, this gay thing.

Shit, dinner. Davis stood. Soon, Ben would no longer be at his beck and call. He would handle this, on his own. Bravely. With Ben on his shoulder, he would smile.

Davis sat opposite his father, and trolled for clues: Lawrence Rayburn. Larry to friends, associates, and to his select *coterie of intellectual inmates*, is how Davis remembered his dad putting it several years back. They referred to themselves as *Lenape's dwindling cadre of anachronisms.* His father's full black and vanilla beard—precisely trimmed—had never looked remotely homo to Davis. Until now. *Chill, Davy.* He was just being paranoid. When the right moment intervened, he would, as he had promised himself, sane-lever in hand, initiate a dialogue.

Davis took a gander at their round, solid oak dining table, the three place mats, its sky-blue centerpiece—an oval-shaped platter—and his gaze froze on the Chinese porcelain-ware replica displaying two fighting dragons in the center. On the platter were two teacups—one containing sea salt, the other freshly ground peppercorns—and between them a teapot containing olive oil. All were Eastern Han Dynasty replicas that his father had told Davis he'd *purchased whimsically. Purchased whimsically?* He wondered, *Homo-speak?*

Davis assessed their small, rectangular dining room: white walls, brown carpeting, dimmed track lights. Otherwise, no photos, no artwork, no furniture—save for the oak table's six matching chairs. Was the lack of decor his father's subconscious reaction to his homosexuality? Or was this room purposefully spartan because it was *simply where you ate to live, not a museum, as* his father once said? A homosexual would decorate this place up the wazoo. The room's icy sparseness definitely matched the silence that bookended the few stilted conversations he and his father shared during mealtime. Where was he going with this? *Whatever.* Davis was out of control. Stereotyping homosexuals was all he was doing, and if there was one thing his father was not, that would be a stereotype.

His father leaned back in his chair, as he usually did, though his eyes seemed more squinty than usual, the lines on his forehead more furrowed than usual. His index finger aimlessly circled the empty oblong dinner plate in front of him. *Homo-ish.*

His father was in his usual state of oblivion. Probably engaged in his pre-meal ritual: *contemplating revisionism.* Davis felt trussed, confined, fearful, as if his father could just as easily eat his meal or him, and he recalled the very, not so long ago, hour when his father just launched into this soliloquy—measured and steely, its melody ornate and distant—on this mysterious *contemplation* ritual: *If you enjoy history as I do, you view it, not as a chronology, nor even a cacophony of clashing, competing, incommensurable ideologies, but rather, as nexus points, locations —where yesterday's immutable fact is inconveniently interrupted by the immutability of today's fact, giving birth to the new normative.* He recalled how his father's eyes actually contacted his as he continued: *Contemplating revisionism, a.k.a. immutable fact creation, trying to guess some nation's latest fact-of-life, is my way of prestidigitating dinner time into something entertaining and productive.* And then his father had uncharacteristically clucked—like a chicken being tickled silly: *That is, until contemplation is inevitably short-circuited by Nancy, who swoops in to spoon whatever salad she's concocted that day on the back of my hand, which, as always, I whisk from the plate in the nick of time!*

Davis wondered: Would he ever see his dad that loose again? "Yo, Mom!" he shouted. "What are we having?"

She boomed from the kitchen. "Fazoo!"

"What's the meat?"

"Quit hollering," she yelled. "Chicken!"

Davis spotted his father looking to the kitchen, as if his mother's voice were a fly in need of a swat.

"What else is in it?" Davis shouted back. "No fennel!"

"You could speak more quietly," said his father.

Davis shrugged. "Well, if I did, I'd have to go in there, huh!"

His father's stare slithered freakily beneath Davis's skin, and he wondered how he would feel if the man actually looked at him. His father watched his finger circling the plate in figure eights. The top loop was smaller than the bottom.

"I never told you about Gil."

No response.

"Dad?"

His father was altering the eight's configuration—the top loop was increasing in size.

"Dad?" Davis had, he hoped, drowned his feelings of urgency.

His father looked up, "He liked my course?"

"Oh yeah."

His father looked down. "Good."

"He told me the final paper was mad hard, but, like, fact creation was mind-bending."

"There were one or two provocative essays," his father said.

"Are you upset?"

His father's gaze nearly met Davis's.

"I yelled, right?" said Davis. "To Mom."

"I'm fine," said his father.

"You're not upset?"

"No."

"So," said Davis. He searched his father to glimpse a gesture, a smile, a glance, a raise of the eyebrows, some reassuring sign that he was still open to conversing. "Um, so, like Gil's smart. You gave him a B-plus."

"He's Lenape smart."

"He is—"

"Not Brown smart."

"Yeah, but Dad, he's just not a great test taker—that's the only difference between us."

"Not rigorous smart."

"He's only at Lenape to play D-3: I mean, so he can start at guard."

"Curious, but not Ivy curious."

"You know he's transferring after sophomore year, and I told him Brown is definitely not out of the question."

"He would not bore dull people."

"I know he can make an Ivy team."

His father sniggered faintly. Davis slammed his fist on the table. The teacups rattled. "Why do you put him down?"

"I assessed him, intellectually."

"Why do you dislike him?"

"I don't dislike him."

Davis stood. "If he's so dumb, why'd you give him a B-plus? That would make *you* dumb!" He trembled. "You think all my friends are stupid." He sat. "I'm not hungry."

"In my opinion, Davis—and I like Gil—"

"So why did you laugh?"

"I didn't really laugh."

"You laughed. A laugh is a laugh."

"Okay."

"So you don't like him."

Davis's father leaned back. The hollow crescendo of a descending jet plane seemed to warrant his father's undivided attention, and he caught his father's full face disappear into profile. Davis found himself staring at the window's closed green curtain, reaching for the sane-lever.

Davis thought to smash one of the teacups. "It doesn't matter what you think." He half-saw his father look near him.

"What matters," he said, "to me, is *how* I think, Davis. How. The *how* matters. More than the *what*."

He half-saw his father's index finger draw looped eights.

Davis's mom cradled a wooden salad bowl in one arm. She gripped the handle of a covered pan with her free hand. Tucked under her armpit was an Evian bottle. A dishtowel was draped over her shoulder.

Davis said, "Chicken chunks are big, right?"

"Relax," she said. "Yes. Big chunks. A-OK?"

"A-OK!"

His mother lowered the salad bowl before Davis, and he had, he thought, retrieved his sane-lever. The towel slipped from his mother's shoulder. He caught it. She patted his head, grinned, nodded. He smiled. She didn't have to say that he wasn't totally useless. She folded the towel in half and placed the pan over it. She deposited the Evian in the middle of the table, and Davis already missed her, painfully so.

Davis eased the cover off the pan at an angle. Dribbling condensation splattered the table's bare wood.

His father got up and wiped away every trace of moisture with the towel.

"Sorry," said Davis to his father's back as he took his seat.

His mother pushed his hand—still holding the cover that still dripped—down.

"Wait. Okay? Can you wait till I sit?"

"Chill, I was just checking out what's in there."

Davis tilted the lid this time, ensuring that the dribbling liquid plopped into the pan, and inventoried the mixture beneath the steam, the mélange of spinach, tomatoes, tofu, garbanzos, scallion, radish, cucumber, feta, roasted red pepper, hearts of palm, Greek olives, and chicken, ingredients he knew by heart, as this had been his father's preferred fazoo since he could remember. He dabbed the sauce with his index finger, sucked it —*white wine*—and nodded his approval.

"You're happy?" his mother said.

"Oh, yeah."

Davis's father was peering at the curtained window. *Why?*

He observed his mother's hand burrow the wooden serving spoon into the salad bowl. The initial helping began its plummet above his father's plate and, in the nick of time, his father's untouched hand vanished. And the expected: his father's expressionless wink, Mom's fake, melodramatic raised eyebrows. Their silent dinnertime ritual, reenacted nightly, unless they were pissed about something, didn't disappoint. Davis envied his mother.

As Davis ate, his parents' ritual that seemed to demonstrate their mutual affection had reassured his suspicious mind: *No way he's gay. Maybe he was ... experimenting?* Davis's memory scurried to a video loop from the *CollegeDudes* site he had found before coming to dinner. He rebuked himself—just as he recalled doing while staring, blown away, at the computer—for envisioning the two *cut* guys doing it, doing it with his dad. *So gross!* His paranoia dissolved. Images of his father's betrayal lingered.

"Mom, I don't think Dad cares if I just withdraw money as I need it."

"You can't be serious," said his mother.

"Mom, you're obsessed with this, like, rule—"

"We agreed on a monthly spending limit."

"I never agreed."

"This conversation is over," she said.

"Look. Goddammit!"

"Are you kidding? What is with the language?"

"What do you think, I'm gonna, like, what, spend all your

money? I just don't get why you won't give me a big lump? If I don't need it, I won't spend it."

"We already figured out what you get. Painstakingly! If you really need more, we'll see about it, but I want you to get used to a budget. Not a spigot!"

"This is so stupid!"

"Really!" His mother's snap bit into him.

Davis leaned in to her. He whispered, "Read my lips, Nancy. This is so stupid!"

"I will not tolerate disrespect!" Her boom was followed by an implacable iceberg staring him down.

Davis's father had stopped eating. *Bad sign.* He was corpse-still.

"So, Larry. You're gonna sit there?"

"Should I eat standing?" he murmured.

Davis shifted in his chair, as if scolded by his father.

"You're not gonna support me?" his mother said.

"I don't feel compelled to review this, again."

"Dad, you said I'm trustworthy. You told me that last week. Could you tell Mom?"

"You are that. Trustworthy."

"See," said Davis.

"Larry, we agreed responsibility was the issue!"

"I said that—"

"That is what *we* said, Larry!"

"Right," said his father.

Davis watched his father's lowered fork rest over the remainder of his salad. His hand's veins, like ink-blue tributaries, seemed like a monster's as he reached for a napkin. His father's fingers folded it like a robot would, Davis thought, and he wiped a green speck from his lips and the napkin fell to his plate, which his father's other veined hand lifted.

Silence.

Davis lowered his eyes.

"Oh, for chrissakes, Larry!"

"What?" his father said.

"Where are you going?"

"I'll finish in my library."

"Please don't leave the table."

Davis clenched his jaw.

"Discussing is one thing," said his father. "Whatever this, um, conversation has become isn't for me."

His father stood.

"Goddammit!" his mother said.

His father grasped the nearly full Evian bottle. "I'm fine, really."

"We might want some of that," his mother barked.

His nod was agreeable. The bottle touched the table without a sound, and away his father went, just like that, Davis thought.

Davis would work out the money with his mom.

I'm wildin', texted Davis. No reply. Minutes passed in agony. He checked the time: 12:10 a.m. He pressed Gil's speed dial key. *Be there.*

"Yo," answered Gil.

Davis departed his room, leaving the iPhone plugged in, hiding in plain sight, there to be discovered by his mother or father, and there for them to relieve him of a crisis that was beyond his control.

Davis slinked through the oily-smelling garage, slid beneath its door, and galloped, pushing down panic, pushing down insane contemplations if Gil wasn't there to ease him through his craziness. He opened his car door and waved off his panic.

Seated on Gil's bed, Davis faced him, and he thought he could not wish to be anywhere but here, in Gil's single-occupancy dorm room, sequestered in *the vault*, as Gil anointed it, where whatever confidences they shared—no matter how childish, how whack, how bizarro, how insane—remained *in the vault*. And his permanent access to the vault—open 24/7, open unconditionally, open at a moment's notice—reminded Davis, as he sank into the safety of his cohort's gaze, how glad he was that Gil shook off his initial guilt and bullshit his dad into paying extra for one of these coveted singles so that he could totally focus on academics.

"Gimme your computer," said Davis.

Gil's laptop morphed into a portal through which Davis introduced his best friend, whose face slackened as if he had had a seizure, to this kaleidoscopic extravaganza of naked-men sites, all starring: the dick. They even gaped alike, thought Davis, at the photos and videos of men doing it: to men, to boys, to men who looked like women, men turned into women, leather queens, jacked muscle queens, to a German Shepherd.

"Jesus," murmured Gil.

Davis stared at Gil staring at him "So?"

Their faces, Gil said, definitely all had in common what his father once told him was a dead homo giveaway: "That slightly pinched-lip look."

"Get out," said Davis.

"Seriously, man."

Davis typed: *CollegeDudes*. He clicked through dozens of video clips, all their contemporaries, whose signature endowment —"*If* they were straight," Gil concluded—would both humiliate and infuriate them.

"You believe the size of those?" said Davis.

"If you could, like, unscrew them," said Gil, "they could be used by the school's pole vault team."

Davis swayed inertly in the swivel chair by Gil's desk,

confused and terrified. He needed serious clarity from Gil, curled on his blanket like a cat, Davis thought, who had gone through the last of its lives.

"What do you think?" asked Davis.

"About the whole gay thing? Truthfully?"

"Yeah."

Gil sat up. "I'm like, whatever. Born that way. A choice. It's all good. *What ever,* bro!"

"Fuck politically correct, man!"

"It's whack, Davy!"

"Like—"

"Ludicrous, stupid. Like a goof on procreation. How could any normal dude trade a pussy for a pecker?"

"So being gay isn't normal?"

"I mean, you're gonna pass up a mad juicy backstop, monster boobs, nipples that, like, when you rub 'em, meow, fuck my brains out please? Are you cracked?"

"Lesbians?"

"Personally, *I* don't get two women. But they're like, more into relationships, so maybe carpet munching is normal to them— whatever, Davy."

"You think being gay is sick?"

"C'mon, you're sticking it in some guy's ass. Is that really what nature has in mind for your dick?"

"So my dad's a freak?"

"No," said Gil.

"You're telling me he is, man. C'mon, this is me you're talking to."

"When it's someone you know, Davy, like your dad, like the way we all know him, it changes things."

"So my dad's not a freak?"

"No. He's your dad, c'mon."

"Is he immoral?"

"I don't know."

"Yes, you do. Tell me."

"Fuck no," said Gil. "I'm not saying it's like it should be a crime."

"The fact that we're even saying it shouldn't be a crime means there's something wrong with it. Right?"

"Yeah," said Gil. "I guess."

"It's okay to be gay? Openly?"

"Yeah, whatever," said Gil. "Look, homos can get legally married—"

"So? What? What are you saying?" said Davis.

"Your dad is not immoral, Davy!"

Davis sat by Gil and watched him breathe.

"Have you looked at the photos?" Gil whispered.

"No! I can't. Maybe sometime."

Gil closed his laptop.

"What do I do?" said Davis.

"I don't know."

"What if he gets found out? What about my mom? What about me?"

"Talk to him," said Gil.

"If this was your dad, could you talk to him? Would you?"

"I would."

"Got any weed?" said Davis.

Davis tiptoed into his house through the garage door. He'd learned that, despite his stealth, his mother more often than not heard him, so he removed his sandals, then squatted to his knees. Slinking on all fours made him smaller, maximized his chances of avoiding some revelatory blip that only his mother could detect. God, he couldn't wait till he was at Brown, he thought, when he could come and go without worrying whether *Officer Nan* was going to catapult from her bedroom, as if from a slingshot, to interrogate him, sniff his breath and clothes, launch into one of her standard lectures on his infuriating arrogance, sense of entitlement, disrespect for her, excessive cursing, lack of personal hygiene, misogynistic attitude he and his teammates exhibited toward girls—each rant finally terminating, hallelujah, with the same annoying reminder of his Job One: earning her trust by consistently doing the right thing.

Assisted by the pasty moonlight slithering through the curtained windows, Davis crawled deliberately, like a crab, up the two-step alcove, through the kitchen, under the arch leading to the living room, and down the pitch-black hallway that led to his room. Mindful to keep his feet hoisted, he looked back to ensure that they wouldn't bonk anything. *Consistency, consistency, consistency!* Why now? Where was this mantra Nancy jackhammered into his skull since he could remember coming from? Why now are Nancy's corrective zaps—*When I was your age ... if I was you ... you better stop doing blah, blah, blah and start doing blah, blah, blah*—pummeling him?

Davis stood before his bedroom door. What would he do at Brown without Officer Nan's hot breath constantly down his neck? For all her annoyances—that was all they were—she was just waiting for him, as she always reiterated in the midst of every harangue, to *step up as a grown-up*. He could not fathom daily life without her. In that moment Davis wished for himself to be happy, as if he were his mom. Had his father not also been in their bedroom, he would have gone in there to console her.

Davis sat at his desk and traversed the internet, staring at those queers who inhabited his father's world, trolling his mind for insight, a clue, anything that could illuminate a pathway that led to comprehension, to what his dad could possibly have in common with gay men, even if it was just sex. His computer read 12:46, and he had been nonstop at this since 10, totally manic, and caged by paranoia: Was this obsession to figure out his dad sincere? Or was he nothing more than a voyeur? He was still a little ripped from Gil's weed, the cause of his mania, his paranoia, *the weed*, that's all. He wondered, what about famous fags? Davis googled *famous gay people*. He perused them randomly. He recognized Socrates, Greek philosopher; Andy Warhol, U.S. artist; Ralph Waldo Emerson, U.S. author. He had heard about Martina Navratilova, U.S. tennis star; Greg Louganis, Olympic swimmer. *Wow*, he thought: Candace Gingrich, gay rights activist.

Davis raised his eyes and stared at the bigger picture: There are fewer homosexuals than heterosexuals; otherwise, there's no profession they don't pop up in. He zipped through other luminaries: Elton John, J. Edgar Hoover, Hans Christian Andersen, Walt Whitman, Michelangelo, Pope John XII, Ellen DeGeneres. *Holy shit!* Jim McGreevey, former governor of his state. Married, kids, then kaboom, admits he was a homo all along. *Now he's like a priest.*

Davis sat up and imagined his preacher-daddy in a billowy frock and prancing in front of his all-black congregation, sermonizing fag fire and brimstone to a lisping throng of gyrating queens hooting back at him: *Oh yeah! That's right! Uh-huh! You go girl!* He giggled aloud. He pictured a pinched-lipped Jesus-on-the-cross—with rouged cheeks, nappy-haired Mohawk, nose ring, one hand nailed, the other limply extended, its wrist bent—attached to a gold chain around his dad's neck and swinging madly. *Honor thy father,* his dad bellowed, *oh yeah! But yo' mama? Ditch that bitch fo' makin' us sissies!*

It was 1:53, and Davis had seen an array of informative, educational, scientific, sociological websites devoted to male homosexuality. He had learned, anecdotally and from expert testimony, enough about the nature of homosexuality to curb his obsessive curiosity. He had found men *like* his dad, he thought. He had not found *his* dad.

Davis reclined in his chair, and stared into his blown mind. *CollegeDudes!* What if one of these guys was the one? He reached for the iPhone by his bed and then hesitated. He was overdosed: all the photos, the videos, and the spurting cum shots from doing it with men. *Who poses for this stuff? Why?*

Davis was wrecked, fried. Four hours' sleep would get him through tomorrow, he thought. The night's quiet mediated Davis's angst. He regarded his room. His for now. But not for long. The impermanence of his room—his *home field advantage*, where he crashed, pulled all-nighters, snuck in girls, smoked weed with Gil when his parents were away, this crib, this sympathetic nurturer of his dreams and assuager of his fears, no matter how crazy—registered, big-time. His room was his: temporarily.

Davis searched his room's four corners willy-nilly, as if solace might seep unexpectedly through some nook. He waited for the posters, photos, prints, the portraits of athletes that embodied who he was and who he aspired to become, to center him. No longer. His room didn't belong to him. Maybe everything on his wall was on loan, too.

No tests Monday; nothing pressing, grade-wise; less than six weeks of school. He could stay up another hour, center himself.

Davis straightened his back. He was not going to Brown alone. "So, who is coming with me?" Who was going to keep him centered? Which of these icons? He gazed at Muhammad Ali—sinewy chest, arms flexed, gloved fists primed and standing victoriously over a dominated Sonny Liston; Eminem—hooded, fittest of the hip-hop survivors—poet for the anglo-weary. He turned to the framed 8" x 10" photos above his bed's headboard: *The Davis Rayburn Fab Five*; The Lions' Ndamukong Suh —*Beast*; the Redskins' Donovan Jamal McNabb—*Intrepid*; the

Jets' Mark Gastineau—*Enthusiasm*; the Giants' Lawrence Taylor, L.T.—*Relentless*; Johnny Unitas, Baltimore Colts—*The Best*. They were all going to Brown.

Not Unitas! The rookie quarterback's Adonis-like blond crew propelled Davis's suspicion. *No way!* He gawked at him, kneeling on one leg, and posing: trying maybe too hard to look hetero. *What the fuck!*

Davis slept in fits that night. He awoke in the dark, apprehensive, suspended in doubt and then determined that tomorrow he would cut school—talk to his dad!

Davis walked briskly across the quad. Alliance Hall was in sight. His imagination had already arrived in his father's office. His heart galloped. His father—who had never abused him, threatened him, spanked him, pushed him, never so much as tugged at his arm or physically intimidated him, ever—had his hands around his neck, squeezing, dragging him through the open window, threatening to drop him, to let his dangling legs break if he didn't hand over the evidence, *right fucking now*!

Davis stood in front of the rust-colored brick pre-war English and Language Arts building. He smirked. Dalliance Hall, or Diddle Hall, the kids called it. You had to be careful not to slip in the basement's infamous storage cranny, there was so much jism. Davis looked up at the third-floor window. His dad was there.

It was unusually humid for May. The sun was scorching. Davis felt for the iPhone in his jeans pocket. He was sweating. His armpits squished. He stepped up the stairs leading to the front door and into shade provided by the overhead arch. He stopped. He turned around and saw some students. Also some faculty, he guessed. There was no breeze, no discernible life-affirming cadences, human or animal, just damp atmosphere, stultifying. He sat. He extended his leg. He tugged at his iPhone. He looked at the time. His dad would be out soon, soon enough.

"Dad!"

Davis's father paused on the last downward step and turned around. Shade darkened the left side of his face. He looked at his watch, expressionless.

"No school today?"

"I cut."

"Not a good idea, I think."

"Just today."

One hardcover and one paperback were clutched in his father's hand. Davis noticed the bulging left pocket of his father's gray sport coat. A dildo? *Gross*, he thought.

"Is something wrong?" his father said. "Are you okay?"

"I'm fine," said Davis.

"I'm on my way to the science pavilion. You know the mini-park behind the building—"

Davis nodded yes.

"You know how shady it is. And quiet."

"I know it, Dad."

"You know I enjoy reading there."

"I didn't know."

"I live there every summer afternoon—unless it rains, of course."

"You read for class?"

"Pleasure only." His smile seemed like a frown. "I have two books. You can read one with me. If you like."

"What books?"

"Saul Bellow biography," said his father. "You know him?"

Davis shook his head.

"Brilliant. Brilliant writer," said his father. "You should acquaint yourself with him."

"What's the other?"

"*The Women.*"

"Oh," said Davis. *He likes to read about women.*

"T. C. Boyle," said Davis's father. "Next life, I'm going to be T. C. Boyle."

"Who is he?"

"Come with me if you like. You read Tom, ah, T. C. You'll love him." He handed him *The Women.*

Davis strode a step behind his father down Crescent, a tree-lined street. He examined the author's photo on the back cover. His tweed gray coat collar was turned up. He sported a black beret. Davis noted the tiny speck of fabric on top, sticking up. His black-and-red flannel shirt was buttoned at the neck. The jury is out, he thought. He looked into the author's face. He stared uncharitably into his expression. Mealy-mouthed. Said it all. His eyelids looked gimpy, he didn't have the strength to open wide. His pinkish lips shone wussy-like between his dirt brown mustache and goatee. *Pinched.* Slightly, maybe not but definitely, maybe. *God, his expression is weak,* gay weak, thought Davis. "You're obsessing!" he murmured.

Davis thought he heard his dad say, "What?" His dad had gained several more steps on him, and Davis rushed to catch up. He tucked the hardcover under his arm. How much more evidence did he need? Earlier, when his father said, *you'll love him,* love Boyle, this homosexual author, did his father mean he loved him, as in, love him? *Never could I love a man,* Davis thought. *No way.*

Davis and his father walked beside each other in lockstep. When Davis reached the corner, he realized that his father had disappeared. Davis looked back. His father, taking small, uneven steps several paces behind him, was intently flipping through his book's pages. "Hey, Dad," said Davis. His father mumbled, "Sorry," he was just checking something, and closed the cover, and caught up to him. Davis noticed a Barnes and Noble bookmark between the pages. What was his father checking, he wondered? Several cars passed by. The traffic cleared. They crossed the street.

They meandered around the pavilion. Davis looked down and noticed the weeds poking through the cracks separating the walkway's cemented squares. He tried to see inside the mostly glass structure, but the sun's glare displayed only his reflection, and his dad's.

"I recommend you get to know T. C. Boyle's work. Ah! The syntax. A maestro."

"What do you mean?" said Davis.

"Well, let's see, compared to, oh, say, David Baldacci—do you know him?"

Davis nodded. *Who?*

"From the sublime to the banal," his father said.

"Banal?"

"Banal. As in *bah-naaaahl!*" To Davis, his father laughed gloriously, as if from a secret reservoir, a place that, were it open to him, might reveal what made his dad truly happy.

"Well, blend Baldacci and Boyle together, I imagine you'd have a rather oxymoronic genre: Banal Sublimity." He laughed again, an unbridled, happy laugh.

Davis grinned, perplexed.

They approached several slatted green benches, surrounded by American Beech shade trees, his father said. Davis's father appeared ponderous, distracted, as if it meant time now for them to read, uninterrupted by chat, without commentary, then head their separate ways.

They sat on opposite ends of the bench. Davis's book rested, unopened, on his lap. He watched his father remove his bookmark and slide it into his coat pocket, the one that bulged. His hand shuffled about a moment. He removed his reading glasses case.

"Don't stay here on my account," said his father.

"No, I want to."

"I'm happy if you do. You'll enjoy T. C. I promise."

"Is he gay, Dad?"

His father laughed. "The author? No. He's married and has children."

"He could still be gay."

"What makes you say this?"

"His photo. On the back cover."

"Really." His father smirked.

"Dad. He could be gay!" His stomach clenched.

Davis's father nestled his thumb inside his paperback. He closed the book over it. He turned to Davis. "What makes you say this?"

Davis thought, frantically: A convincing answer—a coherent one, a response that didn't magnify this blatant intrusion on his father's privacy—escaped him.

"Do you have an issue about homosexuality?" said his father.

Davis shook his head.

"This isn't about you?" his father said.

"Me? No way. I'm fine—"

"Then?" said his father.

"I'm not gay, Dad!"

"I never thought you were."

"Dad, this isn't about me."

"It's about me," said his father.

"No. What?"

"That I prefer men."

"What?"

"You've discovered I'm gay. Somehow. Have you not, Davis?"

Davis counted the exchanges that he and his father had had from when he was invited to read alongside him. One, two, three, four, five, six. He couldn't recall the last time they had spoken to each other this much, this freely. *You can tell me, Dad.* He searched the small park. He saw a woman sitting on a bench; she was too far away to notice them. Davis heard a whooshing hum. He turned to the square aluminum structure beside the pavilion. The building's AC unit, he thought. He squinted from the sun's reflection. He blinked and quickly looked down.

"Davis," said his father. "Davis. Look at me, please."

Davis did not move.

"Davis."

His father stood. Davis saw his father's feet. The front of his shoes turned and pointed to him. His left foot tapped the grass. "Davis." His father's feet disappeared. Davis looked up. His father was walking away from him.

"Dad!" he said. "Dad!" he shouted.

His father turned around and walked back to the bench. He sat at the opposite end, on the edge. *How far away from me can he sit without teetering?* Davis thought.

"What do you think you know about me?" said his father.

Davis shook his head, wary, panicked.

"What do you think you know about me!"

His father's repeated words were less a question to Davis, more like an inquisition. He took the iPhone from his pocket and tossed it on the grass in front of his father. "A kid from the school took pictures, Dad. I haven't looked—"

His father bent over and reached for the phone. He stood, then walked to the sidewalk. Davis watched as his father stomped on the iPhone, crushing it. Smashed shards sputtered from beneath the heel of his shoe.

His father returned to the bench and sat closer to Davis.

"They could be all over the internet by now," Davis said.

"I'm no longer interested in being discreet," said his father.

"Does Mom know?"

"Ask her."

"Does she?" said Davis. "Does she?"

"Does she? Could she not?"

"So you both hid this?" Davis said.

"I said, ask her!"

"I'm not going to Brown," said Davis. His volume escalated. "I don't care about me. I don't care about you. I don't care what you do. I don't care who you are. I don't know who you are. I don't care why you do anything. I care about Mom. I am so tough, so tough that I will never, never cry, not even when I hate who I am. I can't help you. If I didn't have Ben, I would still believe in you, but I have Ben, so I never, never, never have to worry about you. I never have to help you, and you never, never have to help me. Stupid faggot! Faggot!"

"You should reconsider going to Brown."

"Why should I?"

"You may discover there that gay people are people."

"I know they are."

"Doesn't sound it."

"You think I care if you're gay?" Davis stood.

"Davis."

Davis lifted a foot.

"Sit down!" his father said.

It was as though an alien had spoken. Davis had never heard words from his father that sounded this direct. He sat down.

"I will not bore you with the tyranny of a soulless life, a marriage between a man and the wrong sex, a demon that is both me and the other who lives within me. To everything, turn, turn, Davis. A time to be born, a time to die, a time to every purpose, under heaven ..."

His father droned on—a chronology beginning with the first homosexual inkling through his botched effort to somehow withdraw from his family without destroying them or himself.

Davis sat. He imagined numbing his heart, and it numbed, enough to tamp his rage, to keep him still and endure his father.

Silence.

Hope drifted from Davis. He wanted to speak. He reached for a compliment, a sentiment showing he understood, a kindness. He reached for his voice. Nothing.

"Davis."

While his father spoke, he thought of Ben. *Smile like Sisyphus, Ben will tell me, because you must.*

II

A FATHER AND SON TRIPTYCH

MAKAVELEYE'S CANON

ED STANDS in the doorway of his son's room, cataloguing every breach of his authority: the unmade bed; a mound of hardcover and softcover books on the floor; two disheveled V-neck shirts beneath a spiral notebook on the dresser; a half-visible New Balance shoe behind the door; an earth-brown leather belt dangling over the edge of the bed; several plaid boxers and four, no, five socks on top of the hamper; the rumpled pair of Lacoste jeans he'd just purchased for his son at Nordstrom's—a syrupy, violet blotch mucking the back pocket, *Moth-er-fucker*—slung over the desk chair, as if it were worthless, a remainder. The effect of the price tag, still sewn to that desecrated pocket, like that of his son's tongue splattering raspberries in his face.

Ed's animus smolders. Every out-of-place article is a rejection, not merely of his unyielding demand to keep the place from looking like *a Neanderthal lives here*, but of him. Clutter is betrayal.

He twitches his nose. *What the fuck!* He tracks down the offender. Despite the pain that sears his kneecaps, Ed squats and scours the floor beneath the bed. He removes a cup filled with curdled milk. *Jesus H. Christ!* The stink nauseates him. He waves it off. He gingerly drags the saucer forward, careful not to disturb the half-eaten doughnut teetering on its edge. His outrage coils. *Nice!* A coagulated glob of liver-red jelly beneath the saucer streaks the Provencal hardwood floor he had varnished last month. He should clean it now. *Whatever.*

Ed nudges the socks and deposits the saucer and cup on the hamper. A mound of books by the door catches his attention, and he ambles in their direction. *There must be 20 goddamn books here*, he thinks. Hands on hips, thumb tips disappearing inside the elastic of his tennis whites, Ed bends over for a closer inspection. His knees will burn. So what. Pain, he reminds himself, is a wall you either slam into or scale, and he wants a closer look.

He squats and winces while scaling the wall, the pain still debilitating, despite what he thought osteoarthritis surgery on both knees would correct. *Whatever.* He scrutinizes a collection of 18th- to 20th-century American and European history books. Nothing of interest to him. All are about revolutions—American, French, Spanish, Russian.

A paperback—Machiavelli's *The Prince*—teeters atop the pile of precariously stacked hardcovers. The title piques his curiosity. It's smaller than the other books, which makes the idea of opening it mildly intriguing.

Ed pinches the book, careful not to disturb the pile. His son need not be privy to his meddling. He stands, winces, and flips through the pages, and straightens out the dog-eared ones as he goes along. He reads several of his son's handwritten notes. The billowy script gets under his skin. *So friggin' prissy.*

He peruses a notation and fixates on the word "diary." He can't let go of his son's trademark oval that distinguishes the bottom part of every letter y. He is impressed by the loop's precision, every y identical, but what possesses his son to bother with this he cannot fathom. His catches the word "beyond," and follows the line that emerges from the bottom oval. It squiggles and then straightens to connect to the o. Squiggles everywhere! The top of capital T's. The E's: three-horizontal-lines squiggle. *Friggin'* bottom of every L squiggles. *Definitely artistry there*, he thinks. *But Jesus.* He shakes his head. *Friggin' squiggles.*

He flips to the back of the last page, which is blank, save for what appears to be a quote from the book in his son's script. He murmurs, "A prince's sole priority is to keep the people content and happy, which, in turn, will make them loyal and supportive subjects and more ready to support the ruler in times of war."

Below the quote must be the assignment: *Defend one of Mr. Edelman's debate points. 1. The ends justify the means. Or, 2. If the ends don't justify the means, what does? Due May 13.*

Ed closes the book and regards the cover. He contemplates the title: *The Prince.* He ponders the "prince's sole priority" quote. He extrapolates from it themes that typified most of the upper-management people he'd interfaced with in business: *Consolidation of power, calculation, no-nonsense, tough, winner-take-all. Oh yeah, and the ends justify the means.*

Ed sits on the edge of his son's unkempt bed and recalls his first *moral situation* in 'Nam, standing up to his redneck sergeant in front of the platoon. *No, if the gook is pissing, I wait!* It was exactly *because* he was principled, Ed thinks, that he stone-faced endured his sergeant's hyena laugh and didn't frag the fucker's ass at some point: "FNG men!" He is humiliated by their unison-chant as if it was occurring now: "Fuckin' new guy."

Ed's 'Nam stint, he would inform his son if asked, taught him that "the ends justify the means" wording isn't right. *Not the point. It's fairness.* Fairness justifies the means. *Yeah.* The day his son asks him anything, hell will freeze over, he thinks. *Whatever.* He recalls the first time he met his son's debate teacher at an after-school team mixer—cinnamon crumb cake and coffee. No booze. Edelman! *Total Yid.* Big shnoz, bald head, arrogant little wuss. He remembers clasping Edelman's sweaty palm, noting his grimace. Barely squeezed it. One notch tighter, and pee would have dribbled down and out his corduroy pants. He fancies himself straightening out Edelman on his son's assignment: *Here's the deal. Ends? Means? No. It's fairness. Fairness justifies the means. But, if you mean to fuck me by not being fair, then I will mean to fuck you any way I can. End of story.*

Ed regards the book's cover and savors his analysis. He lights on the author's name and figures that if he reads it aloud, maybe that will help him pronounce it. "Mak-ah-vell-eye."

Ed places *The Prince* where he found it, to a tee. Another title that strikes him: *The Origins of the French Revolution* by William Doyle. He checks out one more: *Chronicle of the Russian Tsars.* The author's name is obscured by a big book. *Like it matters.* These books are tokens of his son's latest craze: history. And like every craze his son gloms on to, some of which stick, why, who knows, others flights of fancy, easy come easy go, for sure this history obsession one will devour his kid with a vengeance. He will become obsessed by it. *This obsession thing,* Ed muses. *So not like me.*

A sharp spasm in his lower back startles him. This is new. *What the fuck!* He stands and despairs. He is falling apart. The pain withers. He surveys this hellhole and recalls June never failing to somehow mention during every parent-teacher conference they have attended since his son was a first-grader that John B is the *brainiac* just as she was in school, whereas his younger sister, Barbara Ann, is Eddie: *natural, gut-smarts, personality-plus.* June will use any opportunity to haul out these comparisons in mixed company, and why, he does not know. He does know, it pisses him off! Easier to let her have a laugh at his expense than say anything. *Choose your battles, my boy.*

Ed shuffles in the direction of his son's door and his left foot slides, as if it hit black ice. His ire rekindles. He looks down. How did he miss the large sketching pad? An arsenal of related materials defile the floor. Yes, this paraphernalia is indicative of another of his son's obsessions, so, what? It's okay to be a slob. He ticks off the dozen or so charcoal pencils and a couple of off-white, 11" x 14" pieces of scattered paper whose subjects reflect a hasty, albeit facile, artist's virtuosity. He shouldn't—*Fuck it!*—and bends down and flips over the cover of the pad he just stepped on. Unfinished charcoal portraits of his son's latest fixation: U.S. presidents. He flips the pages: Lincoln, FDR, Washington, JFK. *Wow!* Bill Clinton. Totally captures Bubba! His knees throb, and he lifts up the pad with two hands and stands. *Bull's-eyed that smirk and those signature pinched lips.* Like a photo. *Dumb ass.* Ed snorts. *Risks it all for that little porker.* He is gripped by a wish that he could express to John B the pride that he tells others he has in him.

He stands by his son's door and wonders if his adolescent has ever kissed a girl, much less screwed one. Knees feel okay. He looks over his tennis whites to ensure no smudges. The glory of his first time enchants him. His smile broadens. Reading *Knock on Any Door* as a youth comes to mind, and he recalls that feeling, feeling like a man, his adolescent rite of passage as he now understands it, Nick Romano, his antihero, as he now understands it, and he relishes discovering then, as he now understands it, how Nick set himself straight about the world and the world about him, and he murmurs, "Live fast, die young, and leave a good-looking corpse." Naive, as he now understands it, but not then, and it's 1956, back seat of the Buick belonging to Hani Goldfarb's parents, the car hidden under a gigantic weeping willow near the entrance to Pelham Bay Park, a little tight, a little blood, but he gets it in, all the way, and out, and in, and Hani, no slouch, showed this wise-ass Bronx kid what a virgin Hasid could do, and he wonders, who is his kid's Nick.

Ed steps outside his son's door, and the gulf separating his world and his son's, he thinks, is why, deep down, June has it right: Like mother, like son. He glances at his Aquaracer sports watch. He freaks and blows away a sliver of something from the diamond-studded strap. It's nothing. Jesus, for a second he thought it was a scratch. If he splits now, he'll just make his Saturday tennis date with Al.

Ed backs his '98 Lexus Wagon down the driveway. He will manage his temper, he thinks, and refrain from ripping his kid a new one when he gets home tonight. He steps on the brake and reaches beneath his seat and grabs a bottle of Extra Strength Tylenol. He pops three with one hand while guiding the steering wheel with the other. He drives off and is mindful of avoiding another speed trap courtesy of the fuzz. He sees it: Sequestered in a nearby cul de sac, the crescent-shaped street with its nearly contiguous split-levels all but obscures the black and white. *Ha!*

Windows are closed! AC is on low. He slides the Beach Boys CD into his car's player. He grooves. He sings along to, *Be True To Your School.* He bops in his seat.

The soul of Ed escapes, escapes into the beat. He digs it! The beat is his pathway into their souls. The beat is where meaning and rapture reside. He digs that. He digs conflating the Boys' story with his: hard-livin', fucked-up lives that are dead opposite their squeaky clean personas. How badly the world wants to be seduced by their frivolous lyrics and his *squeaky clean* suburban lifestyle. And how friggin' ironic that he and the Boys conceal their hard-livin' reality behind a veil of *squeaky clean.*

Ed tools down Old Country Road. He will be in Hicksville shortly. He stops at a light. To his right is an SUV occupied by a lone, black driver. Every window is rolled down. The rap music emanating from the SUV assaults Ed's sensibilities. The volume is so cranked up, he is forced to abandon the Boys and wait out this unintelligible, deafening shit. *C'mon, is the fuckin' light stuck?* He eyes the clown next to him—*a dark reminder*, he thinks, *ha ha!* that while Plainview is still predominantly white, it's coming. Just like in Baldwin, where his friend Marty recently split from, after telling Ed that the town was getting *spookier* by the day.

The light turns green, and Ed steps on it. He is content to be alone with an outrage he would never verbalize to his family because it would contradict what he routinely tells them is his understanding and acceptance—and therefore must be theirs—of how the world works in business and life. Having been humbled more than once by women, Asians, blacks, and Hispanics—like Jose Herrera, his self-made former colleague and tennis buddy from Spanish Harlem who, at 64, can still clean his clock—he realizes that all people are the same, they're entitled to equal opportunity and treatment, which he doesn't buy for a minute right now. "Fuckin' nigger music!"

"John B!" Ed shouts. He is in the living room and leaning against the railing by the stairs to the bedrooms. "No leaving tonight till you clean up. Got it, son?"

What follows is consistent with Ed's expectation: no response from John B. This lack of simple courtesy infuriates him more than his kid's clutter. He bounds up the stairs.

Ed opens his son's door and talks through a sliver. "I'm doing a drive-by of your room in five minutes. John B! The maid twisted her ankle in there last week, and it's a good thing she's illegal, or I'd be facing a goddamn lawsuit."

Silence.

Maybe John B didn't hear. Or he is oblivious. Ed doubts it and wonders what is it his kid doesn't get about obeying this simple rule. A towel-head fundamentalist could learn from John B's fanatical devotion to intransigence. Maybe it's just a case of:

A thing plopped there remains there. "Five minutes and counting!" Too steely, he thinks, and softens his approach. "I know you hear me because you're not answering."

Silence.

Ed opens the door a crack. His intrusion isn't noticed. *What the friggin' hell is this kid doing?* Ed looks at his watch and will give him five minutes, no more. He eases the door closed.

John crosses his legs yoga-style and gazes at the ancient black-and-white photo. He recalls the colors he saw online, colors he will forever associate with the garb the two men he is peering at wore, the weapons they bore, the things they carried. He stares into the photo. To the left, his father—*Strong. Proud. Fierce.*—posing in his uniform whose olive-green tint, he remembers, is similar to but darker than the M-48 tank he's standing in front of. Next to him, the ARVN. His uniform's black tiger stripes indicate that *Dad's buddy was a warrior, too. Best buds,* he can hear his mother telling.

His father's over-the-top Cheshire cat grin is a clone of the ARVN's, he thinks. Makes sense. *Same life, same feelings.* He considers the jaunty buddies giving the "V" for victory sign to the camera and thinks his mom was right: *Dad and Nguyen were like brothers, only closer, John.*

He stares at his father for a moment, at a figure as strange and distant to him as the *best bud* South Vietnamese soldier to the right. Would his father have ever revealed this adventure to him? He believes his mother's insistence that he'd planned to, *in his own time.* Whatever that means. Still, *wow.* Twenty-four hours ago, he'd had no idea that his father was even in the army, let alone served in Vietnam. How cool is this *beyond amazing chapter in Dad's life.* This photo definitely shows a man so different than now, he thinks: *carefree, despite the danger around him.*

John reaches for his diary. He finds his latest entry and gazes upward and recalls that it reveals his first hint ever about *Dad's inner psychological workings.* He looks again at the photo of his father and Nguyen. He appraises his father's handwriting on the bottom of the photo's white frame: *Quang Trí's Dynamic duo —'67.* Artless but legible, childlike, the way the letters are stilted.

John is drawn to his father's infectious smile. He imitates his father's smile to see how it feels. He is bemused. *Not like mine,* he thinks. Images of his dad's war adventures deluge him: the jungle's stifling heat, rotting corpses, humongous, gross bugs, shooting at a live human who's shooting at you. He imagines himself sitting by his father's side, hanging on every word, totally rapt.

John rereads his entry.

Saturday, June 19, 1999

> *Mom told me that Dad finally gave her permission to tell me someday about the "Vietnam trauma" that still haunts him. No detail, Dad told her, but he agreed on enough to help me understand him better. Before they got married Dad confessed to her that a soldier in his platoon set a villager's hut on fire because he was frustrated that his buddies were being killed by an enemy they never saw. When a family ran out, they all, Dad included, shot at the husband, and killed him. But he and Nguyen didn't shoot at the rest of the family. The others did.*

> *I was stunned when Mom told me that Dad visited Vietnam in 1985 and found the man's widow. She'd graciously accepted his apology, but she refused his offer of money and asked that he never visit her again. Dad still cannot forgive himself, Mom said.*

*I'm sketching Dad and his ARVN best friend for Father's
Day, to honor them. I'm glad Mom's someday was now.*

John begins sketching. He looks at his alarm clock. It is late.
His stomach twists. He pauses. He barks: *Tough it out.* He knows
why he is freaking. The usual: Getting *nutsoid* from competing
demands on his time. This deadline to finish the sketch by
tomorrow night is pushing against his looming French exam. *Pri-
or-i-tize!* He resolves to finish the sketch, keep moving, do it all,
because that's what he does—does it all. He will pull an all-
nighter if he has to, if that's what it takes to perfect the sketch's
detail. That's it. *Chill.*

He lowers his pencil and thinks, not another one of his wacko
sex fantasies, though he is totally good with these increasingly
frequent diversions. He is *pushing 17* and has yet to see what his
best friend, Aaron, calls *the hairy clam*, let alone do it for real. He
thinks, what will it be like, who will it be with, and *fucking when?*
He unbuckles his belt, lowers his jeans, and grabs a nearby purple
sock.

* * *

John shades youth into his father's forehead. He frets. Since he
joined the History Club at the beginning of senior year, his
sketching time has fallen off. So what. He has doubled his
volunteer workload at the Old Country Road Hospital to 12
hours a week, and he is maintaining a 96 average in his AP
courses. And he is definitely *not* going to scale back tutoring
freshmen who exhibit potential to become one of Plainview High
School's elite Mathlete Hawks!

He stops sketching and recalls freshman year with Aaron,
when Plainview stunned New York City's heavily favored
Stuyvesant Peglegs in a major state competition and wrested top

honors from the Big Dog. Doesn't get any better than clenching his fist, locking eyes with Aaron's, mouthing *Fuckin'-A* in slo-mo as it was announced that Plainview delivered the coup de grâce to Stuy in the differential calc competition's decisive round. *Booyah!*

John gets down to business: *Good is the enemy, not perfection!*

Ed prowls the upstairs hall and knows that he is obsessing about his overachieving son, cursed at birth by June's Achilles heel: *workaholism.* It's been *half a fuckin' hour already.* He *should* leave his kid alone. Screw it. He'll casually ask John B if he's, what? Seen his tennis racket. He'll kill two birds with one stone: See what the kid's up to and if he has touched his room.

Ed pushes the door open. Fine, he will talk to his son's back. Are his legs crossed in that namby-pamby yoga style? *Jesus!* Why is he leaning over his sketch? A nude? Female, he hopes.

The floor lamp his son is sitting under? All four bulbs are on high. *Why the fuck is he hunched over like he's just been stricken with botulism?* Enough germs in this shithole to kill an army.

"Room's a mess!"

His son nods.

"You paying for the electricity? Maybe turn off the lights you don't need."

His son's hand extends up. His body is otherwise immobile. His fingers find a plastic switch attached to the pole's lowest lamp. He clicks one. Medium illumination.

"Thank you," says Ed. His monotone should inform John B that he is satisfied by his son's acquiescence, *not* grateful for it.

His son grabs the pole and leans it forward. He reaches the two next highest lamps and clicks each once.

"Look," says Ed. He works the compassionate Ed. He wills compassion to transform 6-foot, hard-ass Ed into tolerant flesh and blood. "You're on the five-yard line, son. Your mother says your grades have slipped some. You need to cut back. After-school volunteering? I know you're already accepted, but you do not allow the university to think, now that he's made it, he's a slacker."

"Hmm-hm," his son mumbles.

Fuck it! Ed is incensed. "Your mother's back from Pittsburgh tonight. We have reservations at Bella Noche tomorrow at 6. Remember, it'll be packed for Father's Day, so not 6:05."

His son nods.

"And, look, John B, no jeans debate like last time. Your Old Navy khakis. You can wear those. And maybe the shirt I got you at Neiman Marcus."

The silence distances Ed from compassion. "Son?"

Finally, the head turns, he thinks.

Okeydokey, mad matador, Ed figures his son is saying to himself, like he always does, June says, *when you start bearing down on him, Eddie!*

"Or the Brooks Brothers. Okay?

His son nods.

"Any words come with the head bob?"

"Okay."

The floor vent's hum interrupts the jarring quiet. Ed notices that he and his son look in the direction of the whoosh. Ed recognizes that turning away—each from the other—to check out the escaping cool air is a mutually acceptable alternative to engagement's discomfort.

"Really humid for this time of year," says Ed. Their eyes are riveted on the vent, he thinks. "Son!" Does John B sense that he is a minute from exploding?

His son's gaze returns to the direction of his.

"I know you'd rather wear the jeans. I understand. But, remember when I pointed out Clinton wearing jeans? He was on vacation. *On vay-cation!* So you see, son, the circumstance—and I don't care if it's business, politics, or education—the *circumstance* is the driver. Not the jeans. Net-net, when you understand that the circumstances drive, you accommodate the circumstances: You win. You drive them, you try to leverage the circumstance, short-term maybe, maybe you get your way. Long-term, you lose. End of story."

The fucking nod. Ed searches his son's expression for a blip of recognition. He has learned to expect not a scintilla of genuine acknowledgment from his adolescent. Still, he has just infused this moment with the sum and substance of what has made him a success. *A teachable moment,* like June says. His son's for the taking. It could have been special. Instead, that look. His son, the Sphinx. The black hole. Whose thought bubble Ed can decipher: *Thanks, Dad, for the bullshit Sermon on the Mount. Whatever.*

His son turns to his drawing. The hunching over his crossed legs aggravates Ed, and he thinks that every time he has ever tried —like *right friggin' now*—he just can't cobble together the correct words to *relate to John B.* If only there was some common thread to link who he is—the *accident* whose working-class white father did take responsibility by marrying his Puerto Rican mother—to his son, who reeks of privilege. If only he possessed a magic bullet that could turn his life-lessons into *teachable moments* his son could benefit from. He fantasizes laying out his childhood allegiance to the America his father took it in the leg for at the Battle of the Bulge. That turns his kid's head around. *Look, John B,* and he explains that the *sociological laws* he grew up under— staying true to his flat-top, no filthy movies and atheist TV, keeping on full homo alert, *don't get chummy with niggers, direct quote*—were just his father's way of fending off the anything-goes '60s that threatened the lifeblood of his Bronx neighborhood. And how would his son like a taste of his fate when he violated the old man's regs: a shellacking! Like what he got when his dad saw he'd removed the Jesus cross from his necklace. *Yeah, John B, a lot of ignorant shit.* John B nods like he gets it, and he lays on his son this *silver lining, huh*: that his opposite-side-of-the-tracks, take-no-shit-from-anyone brashness had and still has real-life benes. Toughness, grit, standing up for what you know is right, *even when these attributes come from an ignorant asshole like me.* His dad could have abandoned him, could have quit getting up at 2 a.m. to haul cement, could have left him to be raised by a single mother. His dad didn't have to provide for his family. Yeah, his dad was ignorant, a racist, but—and his bonding index finger presses into his son's chest—he was a role model who gave me enough character-tools to rise above working-class subsistence to big-league corporate success. *Man,* Ed thinks, does he want to tell his son who he is! *Fuck it.* There is not one inkling in his son's attitude that indicates a desire to know him. Much less relate.

Ed is losing to the silence. If his son would only speak. Tell him to get out. Anything. There is some consolation, he thinks, in his conviction that his son's knowing him, and conversely, his *knowing John B,* is far less important than his son's respecting him. Maybe someday he will at least be accorded an ounce of respect. The hunching over, the crossed legs! He could shout with such ferocity that it would rupture his kid's eardrums.

Ed descends the flight of stairs and congratulates himself for reining in his temper while with John B, a temper he is right to be considering lately, his inherent temper, one that, because it went unmanaged and unchallenged, basically destroyed his two previous marriages, even though its unleashing was often justified. *You made your point; kept your fuckin' mouth shut.*

At 57, Ed is a believer in the application of business adages to his home life. Case in point, a raging temper is a loser's game. Blowing away your employees, even when it's deserved, doesn't produce the productivity and loyalty you want from them. He stops by the door leading to the basement. *Good job, my boy!*

Ed clip-clops down the stairs to his below-grade—home away from *their* home—man cave. He is jaunty. *When I'm controlled, I stay on point, I'm communicating.* He mulls over this epiphany. *When I blow, I'm off point. So with John B, stay ... on ... point. On point.* He will tell June about *on point.* This codification of his Job One mission as a parent cleanses Ed and invigorates him.

Ed approaches Oz, where everything that he has meticulously put in its place meticulously stays there, where he will sequester himself, enveloped by a coziness that is pacifying and safe and equivalent, he delights in imagining, to curling up inside a big mama's poon.

To get to his 12' x 25' oasis at the far end of the basement, Ed must navigate a shit-show of haphazardly placed crap. He wends his way past a defunct washing machine, an unplugged freezer, his daughter's ancient tricycle—wrecked beyond repair—the dank boiler room. He is careful not to stumble over the purchased but never used, the broken, the half-full cans and jars, the aluminum shelves cluttered with the crusted, rusted, busted, and useless. *Fucking gross.*

He approaches boxes and boxes of June's stashed crap: childhood memorabilia—from her Brownie uniforms and doily projects to college and grad school assignments, including every MBA paper and correspondence she can't bear to part with—to crap from her 15 years as a 3M marketing manager, to crap from her current job as senior VP of marketing for Papier Mâché Is Us.

Ed trips over an open carton of Papier Mâché specialty eggs. *Jesus fucking Christ!* Why he supported her desire to work at home for a *micro-cap public fucking company based in fucking Chicago* he does not know. It is all hilarious when, half-looped, he jokes to friends about June's crapola fetish. But were she here right now, he would unleash a tirade, in her face, and let her know in no uncertain terms that he is always, and he'd mean always, one step from burning the goddamn house down, because that's what it would take to send the message that she has no respect for herself, him, or anyone!

Ed stands over the eggs' carton, which he has a mind to crush. He must deflect his invective. He thinks, his mantra: *fairness.* Fairness maintains perspective. Fairness maintains equilibrium, especially when he considers that his screeching—*overkill*—obliterates June. In fairness, he thinks, June exhibits so many outstanding qualities—as a mother, a self-made business success. He can forgive this failing, albeit a serious one. In fairness, June has to deal with him, too. He is not for the faint of heart. He recalls his past wives, who shivered when he stormed. June will tolerate his outbursts, up to a point. But unlike his *airhead trophy exes,* as she calls them, when he goes ballistic, she'll step up, shout like a banshee.

Ed steps away from the carton and indulges his reverie over recollections of bragging about June's phenomenal patience to his buddies and associates, about her uncanny ability to back off and compromise. *What got her to the top in business.* Push comes to shove, she will bite off his balls! He gets June. Respects her smarts and spunk. Would never leverage his physical superiority. Only fair that he indulge June her crap.

Ed reaches Oz. He unlocks the door. He enters and removes his shoes. He closes the door. He wallows in no crap. He is enamored of his cherrywood bar across the room, his possession. He savors what belongs to him. He walks to the bar and with each cushiony step luxuriates over his plush gray carpet.

He sits on the middle high-back bar stool and is seized by doubt. He will *never get John B.* The bottle of Jameson atop the bar will rehabilitate him. For now.

On the cherrywood shelves behind the bar, he locates his favorite among the two dozen tumblers that are embossed with the names of U.S. Open tennis men's singles champions.

He sits and watches the Jameson fill the tumbler. It rises to

U.S. Open, 1972, rises past *Mr. Nasty,* and stops just above *Ilie Nastase.* His main man, he thinks. The mythic rogue he becomes each time he strides to the court.

He sips the whiskey. Nothing surpasses its singular, peppery taste. Jameson to the rescue. He gulps what remains. He pours another. He alternates sipping and gulping. One of these days he'll quit slugging it down, especially when he's troubled. Today he needs some rehabilitation.

Ed snickers. The buzz is freeing. He recalls regularly reminding his tennis buddy, Izzy, that life would be bitchin' if only he drank like Izzy, though if Izzy drank like him, Izzy would be dead. He is giddy and recalls Izzy once telling him how he had traced his lineage—family letters dating back 200 years to Minsk. "Any alkies?" he had whispered. Izzy busted out laughing, like, yeah, right! "So that's one way your people saved a bundle over the centuries," he had retorted. "If only I drank like a Hebe." Instead of laughing, Izzy should have smacked his face.

He refills the tumbler. He looks across the bar at his *achievement pillars*—symbols that make him *fucking credible,* corroborate his truisms and edicts and prove beyond a doubt that he was a force to be reckoned with in business. Ed's rapture cuddles his anxiety as he steps closer and encounters who he is.

One of these days he'll ask what *the fuckin' Latin means,* but for now, he thinks, the framed diploma on the wall to the left of the shelves just might mean more to him than anything or anyone. He reads: *Long Island University, Edward Miguel Howard, Bachelor of Science, 1st DAY OF JUNE, A.D., 1979.* He is *no Rhodes fuckin' scholar* like his kid could be, but after *eight fuckin' years* of night classes, this sheepskin proves not only that he is smart, but determined and goddamned proud to be the first of any relative to receive a college degree, even if no one in his family gives a shit.

To the left of his diploma, the varnished cherrywood shelf

that displays two small statues of crouched tennis players—each faux bronze champion's face ruggedly lined, hair straight back, calf, thigh, and bicep muscles cut—prove that he is a warrior, in spirit and deed. He reads from the rectangular gold plate below each player:

L.I. Senior Men's Amateur Open – 1993, *Eddie Howard,* 1st *Place*

L.I. Senior Men's Amateur Open – 1996, *Eddie Howard,* 1st *Place*

Ed turns to the framed retirement photo-portrait above the diploma, and he relives swallowing so as not to choke up the moment it was presented to him by his one and only secretary *on behalf of your staff.* Thirty years at Nippon Home and Garden made sense to him in that instant. Still does. Were it not for his team's absolute loyalty and admiration for *Boss Eddie,* who would have given a shit?

He steps back, and the imagery of his faraway, cheap-ass bosses tickles him still, he thinks. How long into retirement will it take before he no longer delights in reminiscing over the new ways to end-run his superiors' smugness while on his LIRR commute to Manhattan? *Haughty Japs,* he thinks, hung over from the previous night's binge, sitting on their asses at HQ in Nara, just dying to deep-six their up-yours-attitude V.P. of U.S. sales. Every raise came with a grudge. And only after the numbers reminded them that it was Eddie-san—*fuck you very much*—who put them on the map by getting their Nip shit into Walmart.

Ed regards the portrait and recalls the office ceremony, how it lit in him an eternal flame of pride, how the outpouring of affection from his 16 employees overwhelmed him, how they marveled over his humility, how they agreed, to the person, that what fueled their loyalty and devotion, what caused those attributes to never waver, what made them the luckiest employees alive was the single-word inscription emblazoned in script on the bottom of the frame: *FAIR*. He did not show his emotion then. He wishes he could have. He wishes he could summon his family and say to them, as he did to each new employee, *If I am fair with you, I know you will be fair with me.*

Ed stands beneath a small window, just above ground level. He notices the yellow and red flowers leaning against the pane and wishes that somehow he could be delighted by their presence. He worries that he doesn't have it in him to get what makes his son tick. He sees the mound of books, the artistic passion, the devotion to volunteer work, all the extracurricular activities that *consume John B.* He should express more interest in his son's life. He could. If he had to. He wonders if maybe the reason he doesn't demonstrate this desire isn't because he doesn't want to, but because he doesn't know how.

How much time has passed, and he is still standing beneath the window. He is lost and disoriented. He concentrates. The quiet is a salve. Why isn't he groovin' on it?

He sits by the bar, and the drink cannot rout his anxiety. He sips Jameson. *Why?* It's like he can't dispatch some intruder. He feels suckered by the sadness this uninvited guest is laying on him. *What the fuck?* He'll figure out what's bamboozling him. When he does, he'll block it. *Only pussies can't block feeling sorry for themselves.*

Ed should be groovin', he thinks, lost in alcohol-induced euphoria, reliving some old one-night stand, picturing his index finger burrowing inside her wet poon before doing the in-and-out. Why can't he block the intruder, this wondering about *who me and John B are to each other?* It's like this wondering is the enemy. *We don't have a single, solitary thing in common.*

Ed pleads with the Jameson to vanquish the enemy. *Okay. Reinforcements.* The Jameson is near depleted. He has had enough. *So fucking what!* He takes a gulp. Like a cue ball with too much English on it, his fretting bounces in directions he cannot anticipate. So the kid doesn't play sports, or watch it. So he could give two shits about tennis. So he'll never thank him for all his business insights. His egghead son has no use for anything he has to offer. *Zip! Nada!* He says to the bottle, "That's a killer." *What if he's a poofter?* he thinks. He sips his drink. He stares into the liquid. A tad out of focus, he thinks. He pops it, *a pop* more than a sip but not a gulp, he thinks. Would he love his son even if he brought home some little screamer? Would he? *Fuckin' yeah,* and he would bash any screwball who didn't. He is sure. He thinks. So, no, that his kid could be a fruit isn't what's bothering him. June? *Yeah, maybe.* Well, end of the day, she short-circuits any lasting influence he might have on his son. He has overheard her confide in him about his drinking. About his inability to quit smoking. Which reminds him, he hasn't had one yet. Maybe today will be the day. He wonders if June has gone so far as to tell him about the debauchery during his early days as a traveling salesman. June always tells Ed she'd never divulge their confidences. He hopes to God she's loyal and reckons he is capable of strangling June upon learning of her betrayal, right before *John B's wailing, red face.*

He *pops* from the bottle and thinks, June has begged him to participate in family outings, to be *a team player, Eddie.* Okay, maybe he'll repeat it in slow-mo next time she hassles him about this. He *would accompany her, Barbara Ann, and John B* on their annual trek to a different European capital were there any way that his, what she calls them to the kids, *Dad's quirky intolerances* wouldn't turn their thing into his thing. For harmony's sake, he accepts that the ritual they've engaged in the past five years cannot accommodate his *quirky intolerances. Fuck them.* Like he could give a shit about museums, anyway.

Jesus, he could use a smoke. Someday he'll honor his no-smoking-in-the-man-cave reg.

A couple of pops left. He cradles the liquor bottle and lolls on his black leather recliner. He inspects one small coffee table to the chair's left and then the other on the right. *Motherfuh! Oh.* The remote control rests atop his Marlboros.

He takes aim and fires! The five-CD holder whirs. He raises the volume and lights up. *Bitchin'.* He leans back, pops, and grooves: *Round round get around, I get around, yeah, Get around round round I get around, I get around...*

Ed is conscious of his eyes opening, of his head throbbing, how long was he zonked, he is still half in the bag, and *thud. Thud-thud-thud!* "June?" *Don't slur.*

"Dad. Mom's home!"

Barbara Ann from outside his door. "Okay, I hear you."

"I can smell the cig."

"Thanks for the warning." He juts his chin, exhales and sniffs: *Brutal!*

Each thud sounds like a howitzer. He can make out June's muffled directive: "Honey, please go feed Butch. I need to talk to Daddy. We'll review your spelling in ten."

He opens the cabinet door behind the bar and grabs the strawberry Tic Tac mints and chews two. He checks his watch. Out for an hour. He is still buzzed but can fake it.

"Eddie," June says. She sounds *perturbed, not pissed.* "I'm opening the door, don't freak!"

"Open it."

What is she waiting for? The door opens. "Okay, you opened it," he says. "You can close it. I don't *freak* when you knock first." The door latch clicks. "Okay, thanks for not slamming it."

Still dressed in her navy blue pants suit, Ed notices. Her only accoutrements are the no-frill gold bracelet and stud earrings he strongly suggested that she wear.

"You took my advice about the jewelry."

"You were right. Too much last trip. Too distracting."

"Yeah, you want the focus on your presentation, not the *ahkootermints!* Is that how you say it? Those hoop earrings you wore last time, that necklace, Jesus, you coulda passed for a—"

"You made your point."

June approaches the twin leather recliners and turns one a bit. Does she not get his scowl? "I'll put it back when I leave."

June musters the oomph to push her chair around, and why she is moving his chair he does not know, and he masters his petulance by attending to his 45-year-old wife's *svelteness* as she bends, by eyeballing her *bitchinest ahkootermints*: auburn hair like silk, and the dynamic duo rock and rolling beneath her white blouse. His erection gratifies him. "My Caucasian Pam Grier, *que pasa?*"

June raises her eyebrows. *Playfully?* "You've been calling me that ad nauseam lately."

She is flattered, he knows. She sits and leans in. She scrunches her nose.

Here we go.

"How much, Eddie?"

"One cigarette."

"You know what I mean?"

"You're in my sanctum, June, okay?"

"Eddie."

What?

"I know we have reservations for Father's Day. At 6."

She leans in further. *What is with this?*

"Look, it's your day. John goes directly to work at the hospital after the dinner. He has this beast of a French final on Monday at 8 a.m. Hospital that night. I thought, maybe if we do an early brunch? I ran it by the Brannigans. They're on board."

Ed stares away. His earlier thought of a Viagra is history. "You overmanage him, June."

"Please don't start."

Looking at his lap does not douse his rage. "What are you, in charge of his itinerary? Should I check with you from now on to make sure that what we *already* agreed to do ..." He contacts June's gaze. "As ... a ... family."

June will, she thinks, pick her battles. "Can you adjust?"

Ed allows for the passing of a tactical moment to pretend consideration of her request and ensures that his intonation is flat. "He'll call the hospital. He won't make it tomorrow night."

"I assessed that option."

"What about 'he won't make it tomorrow night' don't you get?"

"You're right, Ed." She walks to the door.

" 'You're right, Ed,' " he sneers.

"You're pathetic, Ed!" she howls. "You couldn't hide it from Rosemary or Jane. You can't pretend it away from your other kids! Why do you think they don't call you? Because you're the pathetic drunk who rips heads off, Ed. You think our kids don't know you're pathetic? Despite everything I've said? I don't give a shit about defending you anymore. Fuck you!" She wipes her eyes with her palms.

Ed jumps to his feet. She is unraveled. She is defeated. That was easy. He laps it up. He wonders, what is she thinking? How will she handle this?

June eyes Ed. She embraces her conflict-avoidance ground rule and chants its coda in silence: *Drop back, reboot, reengage.*

"You overmanage him," Ed says.

June has diffused her urge to retaliate. She stares above Ed's head and chants and reminds herself of this ritual's purpose: avoidance. Avoidance of confrontations she cannot win, and she recalls the male bosses and colleagues whose power and offending innuendos and gropes she has had to humor her entire professional life, just to survive, let alone advance.

Ed is reveling in his composure, June thinks. Composure exemplifies dominance. Ed is telling himself, she lost it, I didn't. She is done. *Let him win.* "I shouldn't have yelled," she says.

"Please have Barbara Ann and little Johnny B ready to go tomorrow at 5:30. Unless he has a boo-boo. Pleeeease."

"I apologize for what I said." She leaves.

Ed sinks in his chair. He respects June's moxie and regrets that a win *wasn't enough for you, Eddie.* Would that *piling on* wasn't in his repertoire. Would that he was the type to gloat in silence. He could have refrained from countering her apology with a nuke had his gut not bellowed as if being crushed, had he been able to suppress June's pattern of betrayal, of contradiction, of end-running his agenda with hers, of conniving with the kids to prioritize their needs over his, had he not wanted to knock her teeth out. He feels arrested by shame. *Goddammit!* He did not have to resort to the baby talk, to mocking her. He did not have to! *What is wrong with me?*

John stands outside his father's den. The guttural snoring he detects sounds predatory. He leans his ear into the door and envisions his father's shock of reddish-gray hair and imagines some wild-eyed troll in there. At least there is no chance he will be heard.

He checks out the finished sketch. Yes, it is finished. He reviews the bottom two lines and wonders if any relatives of the Vietnamese male nurse at the hospital who helped him were killed during the war. He approves the accuracy of his Vietnamese lettering: *Cha và người bạn của mình.* And next to it, the English translation's unadorned script: *Dad and His Friend.* He assesses the imperfect looping-J in the left corner, *John B, 6/19/99.* Why was he so nervous?

Maybe he will open the door and drop it—*really bad idea.* He will *slip this to Dad* at dinner tomorrow night, as planned. He feels rhapsodic and can't wait. Maybe tomorrow, when *Dad goes to the men's room as per usual,* he will trail behind him, and before the door opens, *Hey, Dad, when you come outside, I have something for you. Thank you, son. So, Dad, maybe you could tell me, when you feel like it, what happened? I blame the war. Not you, Dad, not you.*

John senses reality reclaiming him and thinks, maybe just give it to his mother to give to him when he is in college next year. For sure, now is not the time. *Bad idea, John B.*

John turns to leave and hears the telephone ring and notices that his dad's snoring has ceased. His heart thrums. Maybe he'll mention Vietnam. His obsession is official, daring to get caught in the hope of catching something 'Nam-related. *Is he nuts?* He is, and yet, he thinks, he will not deny himself this rush of anticipation, this liberation from the usual excruciating and scary boredom that overtakes him each time he is forced by his dad to endure one of his idiotic lectures. He presses his ear to the door.

* * *

"Yeah, yeah, hang on."

Ed refreshes his tumbler with Jameson and lights a Marlboro, returns from the bar to his recliner, and is extra careful to place his glass on the coffee table away from the phone.

"Yeah, so, what was that ... No way, Little Serena! I aced your ass today, I'll ace it next Saturday, and ... What?" He laughs, gales that are deep and hearty, until his lungs—suffused with four decades of pack-a-day toxins—rebel. He holds out the phone and mashes his fist against his mouth to prevent the spittle from staining his carpet. He reels from the hacking. His eyes tear. His chest feels ablaze. He catches an escaping drop of saliva. "I'm back. Serena doesn't volley *like* a man, she *is* a goddamned machine: Roboplayer! So take it as a compliment when I call you Little Serena ... Yeah, yeah, well, we're gonna get that elusive doubles trophy. There's no one next month can touch us ... Tomorrow? Yeah, us six. Your kid's coming, right? Great ... Huh, come off the bench? I thought Coach K. was gonna redshirt him freshman year ... No shit, he's gonna be the most kick-ass point guard since Hurley. Hey, congratulations again. Jesus Christ. A Blue Devil. That is the real deal ... Oh, hell yeah you're takin' me down to Tobacco Road for a game." Ed yaps his Dick Vitale impression: "Dukies versus the Tar Heels. You and me, baby!"

Ten minutes have passed. His father's clowning has been incessant, and the vulgarity frays John's image of this war hero. He is deflated and departs harm's way and the boring sports jargon that is Greek to him. Maybe he'll go on Google to check out *this stupid basketball analyst Dad always imitates: Dickie V*.

John approaches his room and imagines goofing with his dad like his dad's buddies: *I mean, what's so great about this Dickie V that you do his voice after every game? Are you, like, in love with him or something?*

Ed reaches for another Marlboro. "Yeah, we've known since May where John B's goin'. No, I'll tell you guys tomorrow at Bella Noche ... Because I wanna see his face when I announce it. He's gonna see how proud of him I am. I mean, Jesus, Al, I don't know if he's ever been kissed, let alone, you know. And even if the old lady turns him into a poofter, he's gonna see in my face the respect I have for him and what he does ... Oh yeah, but you and your kid are Frick and Frack. You know my kid and me don't have shit in common ... Hey, like I always say, walls are meant to be scaled, right, so being a man and showing respect, that overrides everything, including a kid to who you are or what you do doesn't mean shit. You dig ... Yeah, maybe, maybe he respects me deep down, but fuck if I can see it. Anyway, my friend, respect for the head of the family is why we *all* go out every Father's Day ... What? I know. June the contradictor had other ideas ... No, we're all groovy! Tomorrow, Al."

From the head of the table, Ed appraises his son, the statue, crouched, oblivious, trying to shut out everyone, ignore Bella Noche's din. His son's eyes—*friggin' sentries*—blink like he's got a tick as they search the restaurant, alert him in case someone approaches, recognizes him, like incoming, give him a chance to avert his gaze, stave off contact, stay inanimate, maintain his preferred state: *Don't look at me don't look at me don't look at me.* He sips his Jameson. *Jesus.*

John scooches his arm behind his chair, enough to make sure his backpack, loaded with his hospital uniform and shoes and the framed sketch, is securely hanging there. As if answering a phantom interrogator, he insists that he is not antisocial. He has friends. His nature is shyness, especially in public, especially in his father's presence, especially when he drinks.

June analyzes Ed's hand waving, his chirping something to the four people at the adjacent table. They laugh. Ed chortles and gesticulates and chirps on. *He's in a good mood, thank God.* Stares from Bella Noche patrons closest to Ed amuse her. They are, she knows, enchanted by his aura, never mind that he is loud and obnoxious. *Eddie's aura is catching.* She stands by this description she came up with after years of observing Mr. Personality. *Look at him. Piece of work,* she muses, super-in-control, self-assured, ingratiates himself to strangers, friends, and colleagues in an instant. That confidence—not arrogance—*never wavers, does it,* always gave him the upper hand in business, put antagonists on their heels, made them aware that Eddie knew something they didn't, but should. *He's layering charm like frosting.* She recalls him telling her that even as a stock boy at Penney's, *even then, June bug,* it was that confidence—not arrogance—that propelled his superiors to treat this brash kid with a high school GED as special. *Never let up on my manager. Just give me a shot. But the key, June bug, never plead. Be up-front, be eager to please, be single-minded. That's the mindset. Never plead.* Ed waves like the pope, she thinks, to the faithful he doesn't know from Adam, but the aura makes them think he does. Ed sips a fresh whiskey. *That's my Eddie. Was.* That is the Eddie who electrified her. *Once.* She recalls their first encounter at the Seattle conference as they strolled out of Room 231, and his hand guided her from the small of her back, and he regaled her with insights and solutions to her work-related concerns, life lessons that awarded him the unique ability to squeeze every ounce of productivity from his loyal team, his capacity to remain laser-focused on consensus-building during meetings, all the while relying on his Bronx smarts to ferret out, then discreetly marginalize disruptors, before the fact. June lowers her head. *A lifetime ago, huh Eddie,* and she regrets encouraging him to *walk away while you're king* three years ago, and she laments his retirement, his *downfall,* the alcohol stealing him from her as early as noon when he's really in a funk, tennis with Brannigan, cigarettes and TV usurping her prominence, his near total retreat from the kids' lives. He has lost his aura with her. Given their combined total of four exes, his estrangement from five other kids, compliments of Jane and Rosemary poisoning the well, she will not be the one to renege on their no-more-bailing-out-of-marriage pact. Their fidelity is an achievement, a testament to her moral strength, to his, and maybe that is enough to see them through this tough patch. She still loves him, and she wonders, were it not for their kids, would she have ditched him by now?

June notices John, who is seated next to Al's son Tory and hating it. His glance at her is furtive. He raises his hand just above the dining table and mimes cupping a glass and then it vanishes. Her nod, she knows, confirms that Dad is getting blotto.

"If I was Clinton?" asks Al.

"Yeah, what would you do if you were Slick Willie?" says Ed.

"Saved by the pasta," says Al.

The waitress approaches.

"Are you folks ready to order?"

Ed inspects everyone's tight lips. They know the drill: Just order. Twenty questions about the menu tee him off.

"I believe so," says Al. "Tory?"

The waitress—petite, a Kewpie doll, his type, can't be 20—is bashful before Al's 6-foot-7, blond Adonis, and Ed doesn't have to wonder why. She blushes and tugs the back of her ponytail, and he looks at Al looking at the waitress, and then Tory, and then at him, and says to the waitress, "He doesn't bite. But he sure can dunk."

Al rolls his eyes. Tory fumbles for his spoon, picks it up, and gawks at the thing like it will deliver him from total humiliation. This is too much fun, Ed thinks. Out of deference to Al he determines that his yuk has pushed its limit. He peeks at Tory, who mumbles stone-faced, "Um, the Chicken with Mezzaluna Ravioli."

Ed winks at Al and surveys the table and is put off by his son and daughter, both looking down, neither of whom could have missed the innocent diversion and are, *what,* embarrassed by him? *Jesus.*

The waitress stiffens and jots down Tory's order, and then turns to Barbara Ann.

"Is the arrabbiata sauce totally spicy hot, or could it be less hot?" she asks.

Ed disapproves, and Barbara Ann knows it, he thinks, so why?

"Well, um," says the waitress.

"Could I get it less hot?"

Ed leans closer than he should, he thinks, in front of Honey, who is seated to his left, and he knows that the lean has captured his daughter's attention. Honey's cleavage lures the corner of his eye, and he thinks Al's wife digs the attention or she would sit back. "She's a waitress, not your secretary. Just read the menu. Carefully. Okay, honey. And then order what looks good."

Barbara Ann points to the menu and murmurs. Ed's boil simmers, and he turns to Tory. Barbara Ann thrusts her tongue out and in. For harmony's sake, he didn't see it.

"So, UNC gonna give Duke fits this year?"

"I dunno, Mr. Howard. But when I met Coach, he did tell me his upset-minded nightmare."

His son is staring into space, and Ed is stung by the *outright scorn.* "I give up," says Ed.

"Hands down, Mr. Howard, the Terps."

"That's Maryland, John B."

* * *

The waitress leaves the dessert menus on the table. "No hurry," she says, and turns away. *Tory digs.* Ed traps Tory's gaze and mouths, *Nice ass!*

The best of all worlds, Ed thinks. He tunes out the chatter of

June, Al, and Honey. He is in the *sweet spot*. Inebriated, he knows, but in control; for all practical purposes, he is sober. He doesn't slur, doesn't declaim like a drunk, as if those around him were deaf, doesn't threaten on a dime, turn violent, or silly, like a drunk. *Why?* Because alcohol doesn't get him drunk that way. Lucky him. Never has. The only indication *Eddie might be a tad vaporized* is his inability not to scowl at June. On her third white wine. Over her limit, and she *can't hold her shit*. Look at her. *Slovenly. Harlot.* Babbling on to Al. *Grasping his arm.* Arching her back, smiling. What does she think the horny bastard is staring at, her necklace? *Fuckin' brazen.*

Tory gobbles down the remainder of his ravioli. His son's plate is half-full. Barbara Ann: bored shitless. *Jesus!* Ed turns to Al. "So, picking up where we left off before dinner, jousting over numero uno topic: Slick Willie. Bottom line, and I mean it, which is why I'd vote for Willie if he could run again: The era of big government is over, my boy."

"C'mon, Eddie, he's butt-buddies with the tax man, I still don't know what the hell we're doin' in Yugoslavia, and here's the main thing, if Republicans like me and you didn't put the brakes on this liberal, *liberal*, Eddie, he'd have socialist Hillary running government health care, he'd have, I dunno."

"Have what? What, Al?"

"Look, I give 'em his civil rights stuff, even Monica, who cares! But, and I mean *but*, if a corporate tax increase walks like a duck, guess what?" Al cups his hands, pushes them over his mouth, inhales, and blows a flatulent-like sputter. Tory's laugh is a burst, and bits of masticated food spew over his plate.

Ed claps, and everyone's mood appears buoyant to him.

John reaches into his backpack for the manila envelope. He places it on his lap. This lighthearted interlude is his cue, he thinks, to follow through on what is so opposite his wish: taking the limelight. But he is committed and takes pride, he reminds himself, in honoring his commitments. It is the right moment. He hopes.

"Look, Al, I'm no friend of tax and spend. That's the quickest way to choke off growth, induce recession, unemployment to follow. But, *but*, he's a consensus builder—"

"Triangulator, Eddie."

"Whatever you wanna call it—"

"That's why he's slick—"

"He's a realist—"

"Eddie—"

"Did I interrupt your quack?"

"Okay."

"Al, he is reducing the deficit, and I gotta say it, hail to the triangulator. I'm telling you, he isn't anti-business, he isn't anti-conservative, he's pro-liberal. Big difference, Al, big, and I gotta tell ya, you wanna know why I'd vote for him again?"

"No."

"Affirmative action."

"Say what?"

"We know what it's like, Al, to work with some black guy you know is inferior."

"Oh yeah."

"It's a done deal."

"Shouldn't be."

"But that's my point, Al, it is. Get over it."

Silence.

John grasps the envelope. *Now.*

Ed feels the spotlight. He spies on Al, June, and Tory with repetitive peeks. They appear zeroed in. His son? Is actually looking at him! Ed's aplomb takes flight. *He's paying attention.* "Al, these minorities, yeah Clinton loves 'em, but still, he deals with 'em *as a realist.* Like, the welfare cheats who game the system. Hello! Welfare reform. Makin' 'em work. Pay taxes. He deals with *their* problems ..." Ed glances at his son and frets that it was too deliberate for him to interpret it as casual. "He fixes *ours*. You dig? I want a fixer, Al, maybe not how I like it all the time, but better than these conservative Republicans who take *Give me your poor and huddled masses yearning to be free* with a grain of salt and wanna reinvent, with their heads stuck up their last-century asses, this hands-off capitalism for white guys like us."

The table's collective hush powers Ed's confidence. "Now, I'm no history major like ... Sit up, June!"

Silence.

John sits, like everyone, impaled by his father's correction, but not daring to show it. *Forget the envelope.*

"Don't slouch, June." Ed cannot stanch the rage that leaks like seepage from a fouled wellspring. He gasps inside, is the victim, defiled, impugned by June's disrespect, has had enough of her contempt for him, for all to see, and he is threatened, backed against a wall, caged. His breathing is heavy.

"Stifle it, Archie," she murmurs.

Her reply is tepid. No backbone in her threat, he thinks.

"Talk about Monica's dress," says June. She sits up. She fears him, and he is filled with misgiving. If he could start over, he would, but he can't. Honey is shrinking herself, he thinks, hoping Tyrannosaurus Rex won't make eye contact with her. His outburst has cast a pall over everyone. *Back off, Eddie.*

Al stretches his arm. "This was great."

He is grateful for Al's resurrection of the dead and observes him signal their waitress with his extended arm straight up and waving it like a metronome. He notices a patron gawking at its feverish sway, and he whispers, meaning to be jolly, "Easy, buddy, no one's choking."

"Right, right," says Al, who drops his arm, Ed thinks, as if ordered to.

June acknowledges Honey's squeezed grin at her with a nod

and she commends herself for mollifying Ed, for prioritizing Father's Day and its celebrants, whose cheeriness will dispel a darkness between them she fears will soon force her to leave Ed. For now, she thinks, let everyone's renewed camaraderie induce amnesia.

"Well," says Honey.

The waitress scurries over.

Ed doesn't do dessert and orders an Amaretto. "Imbibe in the homemade cakes, all, and the house specialty, gelato."

The waitress stands by Honey and levels her pad.

"No, thanks. My weight has cursed me since I was a teenager. Just decaf." She titters and turns to him. "Now why'd I tell her that?"

Ed has not run across a ditzier broad than Honey, but he is not about to compromise this ten-year relationship with his best friends by acting on his impulse to do what T. Rex does and disembowel her with a quip, a look. He will never disrespect this boundary. He raises his rectangular Amaretto glass.

The adults follow his lead.

"If I waited for John B to tell you, well, let's just say hell would be frozen over."

"Finally!" says Honey. She turns to John. "Your dad absolutely wouldn't tell us. I mean, his closest friends."

Tory lifts his soda glass.

John raises his glass. He smiles. He tries to evaporate.

Ed motions with his other hand like a traffic cop, John thinks.

"Hey. Guys. This is Tory's night, too. We've been keepin' it a secret long enough. Tory, congratulations on Duke. And John B. Congratulations on ... Princeton!"

John smiles enough to avoid his father's chastising. Honey gasps. Tory shakes John's hand. June and Barbara Ann clap. *Let's wrap this up.*

"When did you hear?" asks Honey.

"Well," interrupts June, "it was one snafu after the other, so first he's rejected, then waitlisted because he was confused with another John Howard who didn't get in. It took till May for Admissions to get it straight, so all's well."

"And you're still interested in history?" asks Honey.

"Oh yeah!" says Ed. "Of course, John B won't tell you— maybe Princeton will cure his shyness—but the History Department chairman told June he's already got the knowledge of a graduate student. He was blown away by the essay on Makaveleye."

"Who?" asks Al.

"Al, you know-nothing rube. *The Prince*, my man. By Makaveleye—"

"Machiavelli," says John. "Machiavelli, Dad."

Silence.

John's heart races.

Ed turns to him. He murmurs. "Mak-ee-ah-vell-ee. Is that how you say it, son?"

The alcohol on his father's breath panics John. He is still.

"*Mak-eee-ah-vellll-ee.* Am I saying it the right way? The mama's boy way?"

"Ed!" says June.

"Shut up! Son, you think I don't know I'm a hayseed from the Bronx? You think I don't know I'm an ignorant, hard-ass drunk? You think I don't know who I am! You think I don't know that's why you corrected me. Well, now you know that I know. And now you know I don't need to be corrected by mama's boy ever again."

"That's enough!" says June. She grips her water glass and holds it in front of her.

From the look of the sloshing inside, Ed thinks to say they must be in the midst of an earthquake. He is silent.

"I mean it, Ed."

He thrusts his arm at June and sees the flinch. He extends his index finger in her direction. He peers at his son, who seems focused maybe on his neck, maybe his chest, somewhere he can look without being accused by the old man of not facing him.

John lowers the manila envelope between his legs.

"Now there's a man! Look at her standing up for you, son. That's what a man does. Stands up to the enemy. Like she is to me. You understand what a man is now? You understand why she is so goddamn successful?"

"Shut your fucking mouth, Ed, or I will throw this glass in your face."

Ed looks away.

The headlights from June's SUV illuminate the garage. She slows to a stop. She steps out of her car and sees the light coming from Ed's man cave window. *He's home.*

She nears the front door and looks up. Barbara Ann's bedroom window is illuminated. John's is not. He is volunteering at the hospital, she reminds herself. She marshals her will. It has been twenty-four hours. She can no longer block her fury. She will not avoid confrontation.

Ed is crumpled in his recliner. He stares at C-Span. Madeleine Albright is speaking to a gathering of NATO foreign ministers. At least retirement has turned him on to what is now his preferred source of information. *Definitely,* he thinks. Why he is especially drawn to the complete airing of speeches by members of the president's administration, he does not know. Maybe he subconsciously wants to become a policy wonk, like the Clintons. He admires the bulldog-face Secretary of State, not only for her smarts but her tenacity.

Ed doesn't react to the knocking. He heard June's car door slam and knows she has just arrived from a late-night meeting and that she is standing outside his door, still dressed in full battle array. Sooner or later she will tear him apart. Maybe now. He takes a swig from his tumbler. He mutes the TV. He is ready. He is going to let June speak. He is going to take it. Everything he deserves. *Jesus God*, he wishes he didn't deserve it.

June enters his room holding the envelope containing his son's sketch. "John called me from the hospital. He was in such a hurry he forgot to give you your Father's Day gift."

Ed watches June place a manila envelope on the bar. She turns to leave.

The door closes, quietly.

THE PROBLEM OF ED

HANNAH'S SHOUT DISCONCERTS HIM. It isn't the urgency.

"Johnny!"

It's the *melodrama*.

"Johnny."

What! He looks up from his book and runs a hand through his hair. Fewer and fewer strands between his fingers. He frets. This yielding to vanity is becoming habitual, he thinks. *What is, is.*

"Johneeee!"

He bookmarks the page with his thumb and closes the hardcover over it and rests the book on his chest. His knees shouldn't throb. They are raised above his pillow. That can't be the problem. What is this? The cartilage? The meniscus? He straightens them. His core is taut, and he observes his legs free-fall: like cut logs. He leans against his chocolate brown backrest. The pain subsides. *You're okay.* He is okay. *Okay.*

"It's Ed!" Hannah shouts.

"Who?" He did not need to match her intensity.

"Your dad, Johnny!"

What?

"Can you please come get it!"

Hadn't the problem of Ed been resolved? So much for his father's promise to abstain from ever contacting him again. He kicks at the pillow.

The distant corner of the hallway is close enough. He observes Hannah by their kitchen counter without detection. One arm secures the waist of their 13-month-old. The baby's legs dangle. They kick helter-skelter. Both sandals fly off. He is enamored of his son's lust, his will. His love for him is fierce and beyond measure, he thinks. The seeds of his commitment to be the architect of a spirit that is unbridled by his reproach, that lives life untrammeled by limits, by caveat, by recrimination are taking root, he thinks. With her other hand, Hannah grips the pink curlicue cord, and lowers the wall phone receiver to the parquet floor. She presses the baby to her waist and bends until her mouth is inches from the phone. "Be right here, Ed," she says. She murmurs, "Hopefully." He should relieve her. The baby's forearms flail about while his hands open and close into fists. One hand clutches Hannah's pigtail and yanks it like a parachute's ripcord: "Ow, well that hurts!" Hannah's head tilts. She loosens the baby's grip in haste. Her fingers are deft and gentle. "Thank you, baby Bumblebee." Her grimace evinces a kind of long-haul resignation. She raises her head, and the baby's other hand cuffs her across the face. "For fuck's sake, Bumblebee!" Hannah's grimace sours, and she barks: "Johnny! Johnny! Can you get the hell in here?"

He appears before Hannah, though she does not see him, and he hopes his patience will tenderize hers. "I'm in front of you."

Her smile is crooked. She rubs her nose, and points to the dangling receiver and then digs her fingers beneath the baby's cloth diaper. Urine trickles down the baby's thigh.

"Bumblebee's leaking."

"No, really Johnny!" Hannah trudges off. She deserved more sympathy.

His distress is abject. Like nothing has changed, he thinks. He hauls up the cord.

He flattens his beard with his hand several times. Wasn't he over Ed? What is he afraid of?

"Hello."

His father's voice intimidates him. He endures him.

He leans inside the open door to the baby's room. Hannah is watching Nathan, who is swaddled in his black and red *doggie* blanket, like a papoose, he thinks, and asleep on his side beneath the overhead puppies-mobile. The plastic yellow, green, and orange puppies smile like humans. When, what day, he thinks, will his son's innocence be revoked? He notices talcum powder, like specks of dry snow scattered about the changing table. He hopes that what he dreams for his son is possible.

Hannah turns like a rotating sculpture. She nods. *Success.* And relief. Her lips purse. She taps them with her finger. She crouches. Her shoulders hunch. Her neck vanishes. She waddles in his direction like a duck, and he is reminded of his father's account of a *'Nam buddy who wasted two Gooks in a Cu Chi tunnel.*

Hannah stands, and turns down the dimmer. He imagines a black rain cloud darkening the room. Ribbons of light peep through cracks between the lemon-yellow curtain halves that cover the room's window. Hannah tugs the rear belt loop of his jeans. He is riven with anger. He follows her like a caboose and shuts the door.

He means his murmur to express fatigue: "Ed's got stage III emphysema."

"Will he die soon?"

"He told me he's, quote, 'a stubborn motherfucker.' His, quote, 'game plan' is to outlive his doctor's prognosis."

"Which is?"

"A year. More or less. They don't know."

They walk down the hallway and hold hands.

"You really believed banishing him from your life was possible."

"I really did."

"What does he want from you?"

He stops and looks at her nose. "Wow. Bumblebee really got you."

She looks up at him. "Do I see white in your mustache?"

"How is taking the baby to your parents' next weekend?"

"All right, I guess."

"He wants my help. A favor. 'One big favor, John B,' he said."

"Which is?"

"I'll find out when he visits."

"Are you okay with seeing him?"

"No."

"He must really need you."

"He must."

"You will help him, Johnny?"

She does not mean to entrap him. "I'll see."

He arrives at Princeton Junction train station early. Why? Trains are never early, he thinks.

What if his father departs at the far edge of the platform? He bites his thumb's cuticle and walks more to the center.

The train arrives. The passengers disembark. In the distance, the man being assisted down the car's steps by another man is his father. *Jesus.* From the top step, a uniformed trainman hands a suitcase and other objects he cannot identify to the other man. His father is crippled.

The two approach his way. His father's gait shocks him. He looks decrepit, like a decrepit ghost. *Humpty Dumpty had a great fall.*

They make their way to his car.

"No, you help your dad in his side while I load the back," the other man says.

His father is insistent. He can buckle his seatbelt without any help! The sight of his father disgusts him. They do not speak.

The other man's face appears before his open window. He thanks this good Samaritan for folding the walker, for placing it and the portable oxygen machine and its accompanying paraphernalia into the trunk of his Hyundai. He does not appreciate the other man.

His father leans into his shoulder belt. "Thanks, buddy. I'd have been a fuckin' goner if you hadn't come along."

"No problem, sir."

He snakes his car through two parked vehicles and follows the arrow to the parking lot's exit. *The voice*, he thinks. *The voice* he hasn't heard in five years that sounds to him now like sludge flushing through a corroded pipe. *The voice* menaces him. As ever.

The late morning air is crisp. The mid-rise apartment buildings that enclose his complex's courtyard secure him. He senses invincibility. The world can't get him. His familiarity with the toddler in a white undershirt and naked below the waist is a welcome solace. The boy is pushing a red plastic lawnmower—its green blades clacking like ruptured tires on pavement—in the direction of the hexagonal wooden gazebo under which he and his father sit on a small bench, half-facing each other. He waves at the boy's black nanny, who is clutching a disposable diaper and trotting after the boy. She stretches her arm.

"Turn away a second, and he's gone," she says. Her fingers extend like a hawk's talons and snatch his shirt. She hoists the boy up and carries him off.

"You were a runner, John B. Always runnin' as a baby, like somethin' invisible was pushin' you away from June and I."

June and me. Why did he smile like a jester?

"Man, John B, that woman must weigh 400 pounds."

At least this time he didn't smile. The leaves on the yard's lone sycamore chatter with the sudden gust. Some drift downward, and he thinks what vibrant color they had this fall. He wonders if the chill is deleterious to his father's enfeebled lungs. Goose bumps cover the exposed thigh just below Ed's tan cargo shorts. His father's gape lunges at him. Why? Ed appears to be eyeing *PRINCETON* emblazoned in black capital letters across the front of his gray long-sleeved T, mulling it over. Whatever, he knows this look, in preparation of a slight, something denigrating. He implores himself to contact his father's gaze. He stares at his father's chest, a crumbling barrel, at the soccer ball gut daring his plum-colored short-sleeve shirt to remain buttoned.

"So, look at you, kid. Gonna gimme the lowdown on those traps, the delts, triceps, those forearms? What, they popped up by accident? Jesus, with that beard, you look like ..." His father's coughs gurgle, and he is breathless. "Like Paul Bunyan."

Ed looks diseased, like a disease. Like death. His inhalation is labored. His cough is frantic. The hacking seems to cause him to spasm from head to toe. Ed retrieves a Kleenex from his pocket and spits. Yellowy, taffy-like phlegm dribbles into it. "What are you ... 6 foot ...?" he says through abating spasms.

"Five-ten."

"You still look like a lineman. So, what? You train?"

"I work out. Five days a week."

"Man, you probably gotta fend off the babes every day, too. And ..." He coughs. Spittle lines his shirt. "And the boys. Ha!"

Malice surges and reunites him with remembrances of his childhood. He is shamed by his father's uncertainty of him.

"So, when did you go from this scarecrow I last saw?"

"Grad school."

"Princeton, huh."

"Graduate school. Duke."

"Oh yeah. Where Tory played. Brannigan's kid. You remember him. Got drafted by the Raptors. He tore up the ACC. Me and Brannigan must have gone to ten games. They redshirted him, so, so you, were you at Duke his senior year? I never called." His father clutches his breastbone. His breathing is fettered and heavy. " 'Cause, ya know, I was—"

"I know."

"I was persona non gratis. Which, in the Bronx Dictionary, means an unwelcome douchebag."

The aluminum leg of his walker slips through Ed's grip. His fingers redden. He tugs it. The front wheels retreat. He pulls hard and the walker topples over. "Cocksucking motherfucker!"

He retrieves the walker. He sets it in front of his father, who pushes it into him.

"Fucking monstrosity!" says Ed. "Who the fuck invented these things!"

He leaves the walker before his father and sits on the farthest end of the bench from him. He can inure himself to Ed's temper. *Do it.* His father cannot seem to catch a palliating breath: His lungs gurgle; he draws a Kleenex from his pants pocket; he retches sputum that drips from his mouth onto the hanky and his wrist; it is frothy; he wipes fluid from his mouth with the hanky that appears saturated; he folds it and blows his nose; he coughs four or five times; his mouth is agape; pus or something bubbles over his lower lip; he licks at it; he snorts it all in. Ed's breathing appears less tortured. He twists around. His torso looks like a distended grape. Ed reaches for the gazebo's railing and stands and spits over it and stuffs the used Kleenex in his pocket and then sits, and it appears that Ed's hands on his knees are keeping him from collapsing. Ed's breaths are truncated and sluggish, as if there's sand in the air. The couple of tears that drip from Ed's cheeks are cough-related. On second thought, maybe not, and he wonders about the degree to which his father suffers.

"Hey, I didn't mean for that walker to hit you when I swatted it back."

"I know."

"I was pissed at it, not you."

"I understand."

"You were tryin' to help me."

"I was." He turns away.

His father mumbles.

"Sorry, what?" he says. He turns to Ed, whose face is pallid and puffy. *The Pillsbury Doughboy.* Ed's eyes are swollen. Snot is coagulated under one nostril. His lips are brownish-red, sickly, dry, dark where they are cracked. His father licks them. Liable to cut his tongue. He sniggers to himself.

"When we came in the house," Ed says. His gasp is faint. "It's not that I didn't." Ed gasps. "Need your help. I'm just not used to it. I don't like it." Ed gasps. "Not even from the doctors. And the fuckin' nurses, grabbin', liftin', ya! Shit, they'd carry my dick if I asked 'em to." Ed gasps and coughs. "I'm an. Avid individualist." Ed gasps. "How's that for a highfalutin turn of phrase?"

"Awkward, Dad."

"You mean, ignorant?"

"A little of both."

"Yeah, well I'm not a goddamn intellectual like you!"

"You've just demonstrated that."

Ed raises his arm and makes a fist and shakes his fist at him, and then places it inches from his face. "Yeah, well, if I was my old self, I'd smack your wiseass—"

"Raise a hand to me again, and I'll knock you down."

His father coughs and sways like someone shot. Snot bubbles from his nose. A strand of mucus extends from his upper lip. "Will you ever respect me, son?"

"Is everything okay, Johnny?" calls the nanny. She is waving at him worriedly with one hand and holding her charge with the other.

He nods and waves and smiles.

"If your pop needs a hand, let me know."

He nods. Her *Islands* lilt is ingratiating. The toddler picks up a white whiffle ball and hurls it up. The ball careens off the nanny's forehead. He notices that she doesn't react. "You need somethin', tell me, Johnny."

"It's okay, Mrs. Clarke." His eyes wander near his father's direction.

"You call her Mrs. Clarke?"

"I do."

"That's nice."

His father appears steady, and he wonders if his disdain for him is palpable.

"You want my respect, Dad?"

Ed murmurs, "Yes."

"Pretend you're talking to Brannigan's kid."

Ed studies the courtyard.

He doubts his father could understand his meaning and hopes only that he is shamed.

Ed grimaces. His father's muscles are atrophied. He feels sympathy for him. Ed is not a dog.

"Nice lawn, John B. Nice. Thick. Well-manicured. You must

have a good condo board." He points to a nearby oval of hedges that enclose mango-orange flowers, yellow daisies with chocolate centers, and coreopsis. "Nice flowers over there."

"One of the tenants cares for them."

Ed plods over to the oval. He carries the walker and follows behind. Ed walks like an arthritic ostrich.

"What are those?"

"Coreopsis."

"Say what?"

"Coreopsis."

"I think your mother would like 'em."

"They're June bloomers."

"Ha." Ed leans over the hedge and pets a red petal. "Your mother's name." He stands with his back to him. "It's June today, huh?"

"June 1st."

"How is she?"

You don't deserve to know.

Ed turns and looks up at him.

Silence.

Ed strains, willing himself, it appears, to stand erect. He cannot. His spine will not straighten, his legs are bowed, hairless, hoary, leathery spindles daubed with oil-blue varicose veins and scarred at the knees. His sorrow deepens.

"Good," he says. "Mom's good." His father is in pain, he assumes. He will not ask.

"Barbara Ann?"

"Good."

"Well, we got that out of the way, huh."

"We did."

"And you haven't kicked my ass outa here yet."

"Not yet."

He is aware that they are facing each other and wonders how to disengage with grace.

"I wanna head inside," says Ed.

He is relieved and reaches for the walker.

"Without that fuckin' thing."

He collapses the walker.

"Can I rest on your couch, and then I'll explain why I called—"

"You can sleep in our bed."

"No."

"Hannah took the baby to her parents' for the weekend."

"Maybe you can get my little oxygen porta-potty—that's what I call it—from the car?" Ed clasps his hands until they present a tight fist and winces. "Arthritis is a bitch!"

He looks up. The sun peeks over a cloud. He turns to Ed, who is posed like a prize fighter.

"You know I did a little boxing in 'Nam."

"I do."

He jabs the air. "In my head, I still got it. Whattya think?"

"You look like a rooster with rickets."

"I never understood your humor."

"I'm not joking."

He carries the walker and leads Ed at the pace of a snail to his building's back entrance.

Ed calls out, "I was gonna take a cab from the train station."

"No problem getting you."

"I planned on takin' a taxi here."

"It's okay." He walks by his father's side and is careful not to assist him.

"Ya didn't have to show up. I'm still an independent guy. Lucky ..." A hitch catches his father's voice. "Lucky ..." Ed cannot quite seem to control his gasps. "Lucky I saw your car ..."

"I said I'd be there."

"Or I'd have taken the cab and been waitin' by your door like the fuckin' ..." Ed sniffles and wipes his nose quickly and shakes his head. His eyes appear liquid. Ed stops. "The fuckin' what?"

He feels assaulted.

"Dipshit of a father that I am," Ed murmurs.

He opens the screen door. What should he say? He leads Ed through a grayish stucco hallway illuminated by two rows of overhead fluorescent lights that remind him of a prison. He presses the elevator button. Ed appears breathless.

"Not a weed in your garden back there," his father says. "Beautiful lawn. No brown grass, all thick, no dead spots." His father's chortle sounds like a child's. "Who takes care of it? Illegals?"

There is no room in his life for Ed.

He enters his complex's gym. He should have woken his father, should have said he would be right back. He lowers his duffel to the floor. He mimes tipping a cap to the other occupant, indicative of his admiration for the middle-aged, single mother of two adolescent boys, who waves at him from her elliptical trainer. She brushes a nub of sweat from her nose with her wristband. He winks and proffers a high fist pump. She is lithe, and her black tights attract him. He is tempted to extol her *consistent dedication,* to remind her of consistency's *virtue,* and decides not to cross the line.

He faces down the heavy cobalt-blue punching bag that the board permitted him to purchase. A squall of ire unbalances him. He faces down EVERLAST. *Do not capitulate, John B.*

He seesaws his shoulders; he jiggles his hands. Ritual anchors him. He tugs the bottom of his sleeveless T; he tightens the wristbands of his fingerless, leather gloves; he squeezes his fists; he taps his chest; he adjusts the elastic of his white boxing trunks; his waist is comfortable; he adjusts his headphones; he reaches for the mini iPod strapped above his right arm's bicep. He scrolls down the *Something Old* playlist: Dvorak, Rossini, Mozart, *West Side Story*, Janis Joplin, Stevie Wonder, Bruce Springsteen, Shakira. No. He presses *Heavy Bag mixes*: Eminem, Common, Kweli, Kendrick Lamar; *yeah.* LL Cool J. *Mama Said Knock You Out.*

One foot in front, one behind in the ten seconds of music that precedes the lyrics. *Guard up*: left arm extended an inch from the bag; clutched right fist beneath his chin. *Conquer.* He faces down *EVERLAST.* He jabs up, jabs down, up down up down up down up down, smashes into the feel of canvas rock. Hook up down up down. He quickens his punching motion. He pounds hard: up down up down up down up down. Successive blows are swifter, harder. Uppercuts: hard swift hard swift hard swift hard swift hard swift hard swift. He punches into the pain that gores his left wrist. He grinds his teeth; *fists are iron*; his reddened knuckles burn. The *clacking* against the bag's surface booms louder with each punch. *The bag is not hard.* His arms accelerate like pistons; his punches burst right left right left into the bag, the impenetrable bag that taunts him.

His arms droop. He scrunches his face against the bag and sucks air open-mouthed. *The leather tastes good.* His left knee buckles. *Nice.* He straightens and commends the bag for its resilience. Dread gnaws at him. He bends over and wipes perspiration from his forehead. He squats. He cannot account for this reemergence of devastation in his father's presence. Childhood feelings he had long since vanquished, or so he thought. He cannot account for the reemergence of this craving, this crying out to make his father understand *who I am*. Is the trigger Ed's imminent death? He does not know. No matter, he will treat these old emotions as encumbrances, as ephemeral. He will do what he can for his father, all he can and no more! He will have reached the extra mile when he feels himself becoming *a sacrificial lamb*.

"You okay?"

He winks at the woman on the elliptical. The sweat marbling her forehead woos him. "Are *you* okay?"

She nods.

"I'm getting too old for this," he says.

She grins. *Flirty.* She cranes her neck forward and maintains her tempo. "Right, Hoss, what are you, again, 30?" The rhythm of her sinewy legs and thighs conjure in him a balletic frog.

"Thirty-three this year."

"Fifty-six and six months."

She is a flirt. "You're awesome!" He waves goodbye in the midst of his father's menacing image. Can he engage Ed without sacrificing himself?

The bedroom wall's mirror reveals his father sitting up *in my bed*. Ed's shirtless back is leaning against *my pillows*. Had to use all three of them, he thinks. His father fiddles with the hard plastic headset of his nasal cannula, and fiddles with the translucent tube that connects to the portable, square oxygen machine by the side of the bed, and fiddles with the supple dual plastic prongs in his nostrils. Ed's breathing appears less troubled, and animus swims beneath the surface of his skin, so he concentrates on the machine's purr and its regular interruption by a lazy, drumlike boom-boom, and he fears, what if Ed recovers?

"Bitchin' contraption, huh." Ed sounds like gravel pouring from a mixer. "State of the fuckin' art."

"Does the job."

"Like my headset? I pretend I'm a fighter pilot."

"Your breathing is better."

"I'm a COPD lifer, what's left of it."

"What?"

"Chronic Obstructive Pulmonary Disease, buddy boy."

His father grimaces, as if he's in peril. His visage relaxes some, appears less strained, though his eyebrows are furrowed. He is helpless before him.

He moves the refurbished wooden armchair by the dresser to the side of the bed and sits. He considers the pastels he'd use to shade his father's portrait: bone-white for the thinning crew cut, a paler white to replicate the tumbleweed eyebrows; dabs of eggshell-white mixed with carnation pink for the cheeks and ears. Orchid pink and varied shades of brown for the distended, livid jowls, and for the neck skin, too, and for the ubiquitous brownish lines and hollows that age his face and neck, and Plymouth pink to accentuate them; cherry blossom pink for the distended puffs of skin beneath his eyes. *If he asked me to, I'd sketch him.*

"I'm sober."

"Really."

"First time since after I quit workin'. First time in my life. Really."

"How long?"

"A month. Go ahead, laugh."

"I'm not laughing."

"Well, you should. You don't believe me."

"I believe you."

"I don't know if I believe me. But they believe me at A.A. They believe *in* me. That's somethin'! Every night I go, they say, you can do it, you're doin' it, Eddie."

"Good for you."

"Fuck good for me! You think I don't know what getting in a shit-faced stupor nearly every fuckin' day for the last fuckin' decade spells? It spells, too little, too late! Too little, too late for June. Too little, too late for Barbara Ann. Too little, too late for

John B. Too little, too late for Eddie. You think I don't know that?"

His father appears ashen. He hadn't noticed the reddish-pink blotches that stain his complexion. Ed licks a droplet of blood from a small fissure in his lower lip. The bob of his head seems in sync with his labored breathing. The cannula's prongs detach and hang just below his nostrils.

"I can't live by myself anymore," his father says. "But I guess you deduced that, huh. You surprised I know *deduced*?"

Surprised you used it correctly. His father's coughing jag is harsh. Ed plants his hand over his mouth and hacks. His eyes squeeze shut. He seems unable to manage the spasms. Stringy mucus oozes from between his fingers. Ed reaches for the Kleenex box to his side.

Cannot, cannot stay here! Fear churns in him. "Maybe you should put in your oxygen. Dad?"

His father wipes his lip with the hanky and then fits the cannula's nasal air buds, as if they weighed a ton, in his nostrils.

He recalls the print ad in one of the local papers for Allendale Senior Living. The *Montgomery News.* He'll tell his father about it, mention that there's a nursing home attached to Allendale, a hospice unit, too. Allendale will resolve this problem of Ed, his problem, yes, not Ed's problem, his, his father cannot live with him. "So, Dad, there's a—"

"What are you a doctor of, again?" His father's voice sounds like crumbling.

"I'll tell you later."

"I'm afraid to die alone, John B."

"No one wants that—"

"God help me."

He must be direct. Tell him. "No one wants that."

His father seems to rally. He must tell Ed he cannot stay with him.

"This all boils down to," says his father. Ed raises himself up and kicks his legs like a swimmer until the blanket shuffles below his white boxer shorts. "To me breaking my promise to stay out of your life forever. So it boils down to me being a complete fuckup. There's a couple of vacant one-bedrooms in your building. I could stay here maybe, some, and when you get sick of me, just, I'll wheel myself out, how's that, I won't bother you, won't visit you much, but you'll be close, that's what, that's all I, all I'm hopin' for, huh, just close, John B—"

"Dad—"

"What do you think?"

"There's an assisted-living nearby—"

"Huh?"

"I don't think you should live here."

Ed rips away his headset and throws it against the wall. "I know there's a goddamn fuckin' nursing home assisted-fucking-living nearby. You want me to get on my hands and knees, you want me to beg—"

He is up and stands over his father, and yells, "If you raise your voice at me again, if you fucking raise your voice to me ever, *ever*!"

Ed stares up at him. "Look at you. Big and tough now. Crush me with your little finger. Make you feel good? Have I ever once in my life asked you for anything? For one goddamn thing?"

"Maybe you should have, Ed. Maybe you should have asked me for anything, for one goddamn thing. Maybe you should have asked me, I'm your fucking son, asked me for one goddamn thing I thought, one goddamn thing I felt, one goddamn thing about what I believe, who I am, for one goddamn thing about who *I* am, Ed, who are my friends, who are my enemies, who I love, who I hate, one goddamn thing about what I hope, what I dream, what I fear, for one goddamn sliver of one goddamn thing about what I do. What I do—you asked me. You did just ask me that; you asked me, what am I a doctor of, a doctor of what? I am a doctor of History, Ed, from Duke, from Duke, where your friend's son played basketball while I wrote my dissertation, and before Duke, Princeton, where I won honors and prizes and contests that you didn't ask one goddamn thing about, and before that, high school, Ed, where I won honors and prizes and contests that you didn't ask one goddamn thing about, where I sketched portraits, read books, volunteered in a hospital ward, and watched patients my age die, Ed, which you didn't ask me a goddamn thing about, and my friends, no one you'd have liked, Ed—too weird, too pinhead, too Jewish, too small, too queer, but they were my friends you never asked one goddamn thing about. And I kept a diary you knew nothing about until I graduated, and once I wrote in my diary about someone who never asked me for a goddamn kernel of anything about me but for whom I would have given everything to know, to touch, to comprehend, everything, but I couldn't, too scared, too scared, so I sketched him and his best friend from the war as my Father's Day gift, you remember, Ed. I remember, like it was yesterday: the restaurant, the food, the Jameson shots, one, two, three, four, five, Ed. I counted. I remember what you looked like, stank like, sounded like, what you called me, the exact words, Ed: 'mama's boy.' In front of everyone. Remember, Ed? I do. You like to think it was just the booze talking, don't you. Don't you! That works for me, Ed, so let's just leave it that way."

He moves the chair by the dresser and sits. He observes his clasped hands, one thumb over the other and admits his shame. His outburst will be regarded by his father as weakness. That is John B.

Moments pass.

"My whole life has been a battle for my dignity, John B. A losing one. My fault. I never felt dignity, never got it passed down, ya know. So what was I supposed to do? Invent it?"

His father's head shimmers. Tremor, he thinks. Palsy? His lip is bloody. "Your lip is bleeding."

Ed's tongue smears the blood. "I hear you're a teacher."

He nods.

"College near here."

He nods.

"What's your dissertation on?"

"The role of competing historical memories of race in late 19th-century America in shaping its pre—civil rights political culture."

"Oh."

"I will help get you situated in the assisted living."

"So, now you can't say I never asked you one goddamn thing."

He is seated before the desk in the small, triangular alcove abutting the kitchen, cocooned by the shoji screen. He leans closer to his computer and examines the homepage's *Introducing Allendale* video. A grandmotherly woman plays a piano in silence. A soulful male voice sings, "This is where I'm meant to be." He mutes the video. What was his father's first day like? A montage of healthy-looking geriatrics fades in and out: smiley old folks hand-holding; a gaggle of seniors seated at large, round tables in the cafeteria—lots of flowers—laughing, drinking, chewing, smiling—always smiling; a puckish woman's wrinkled, egg-shaped face under a salon-style, oval hair dryer, smiling, smiling, smiling while dainty, brown-skinned hands paint her nails; a uniformed, black male worker's arm draped over the neck of a white female resident, grinning at each other like leprechauns.

The montage rolls on, and he wonders what his father thinks of him. He wishes it didn't matter. Maybe he should have kept in touch with Ed, let him know he was married, sent him a birth announcement, at least, hadn't colluded with Barbara Ann to convince their mother that divorcing him wasn't about abandonment but self-preservation—as if their solution should be hers, as if they really knew. He closes his eyes. He can feel the ice in his heart.

He turns and looks up at his work. He *has* captured the cherry blossom tree's bloom and recalls his Japanese teacher's compliment: *Your design of the branches, like weeping veins.* Mr. Takahashi's smile, always beneficent, he thinks, was the safety net beneath his plummeting confidence. He really does have a flair for this delicate art. He decides, despite his promise to Hannah not to be out three nights a week, to ask if she'll approve of his taking the advanced screen-making class.

It is Sunday night, and he hasn't read *The New York Times* since Thursday, hasn't checked out David Brooks and Kenneth Brennan and those columnists whose interrogations of contemporary issues admonish his academician's nose to value the *real* world. His father, he thinks, will never know him. His son will.

Hannah's voice unsettles him. He feels encroached upon. She peers at him from the side of the screen. She is disconsolate. The baby?

"You get Bumblebee asleep okay?" he says.

"Johnny. It's Allendale. He had a stroke. They couldn't revive him."

FATHER

"JOHNNY!"

I continue to read.

"Johhhnny!"

I continue to read.

"Joh-neee!"

Joh-neee! I run my hand through my hair. *All right, so it's thinning.*

"Joh-neeeeee!"

I endure the melodrama, the outrage, my temper, my spleen, I do not lash out, I endure. I close the hardcover over my *Tigers* bookmark and crave solitude, crave the Princeton library and immersion in my world, crave cocooning myself from imposition, barrage, from the simplest request! I stare at my reflection in the wall mirror opposite the bed and endure the urge to pummel. I elevate my legs above the pillow and stretch. Free fall. Like cut logs. *Kaboom!* I breathe. Spleen vented. *You over it, John B?*

The door opens, and Hannah appears. She is fed up with her squirming, naked son. And Johnny.

"Did you hear me!"

"I did. Sorry." I get up.

"Bumblebee," I say, "baby Bumblebee," imagining my words' caress, subdued and intimate as pastel. I'm the baby whisperer. My gaze co-opts his. He is wanted. He is secure. His arms reach for me. His torso leans my way, into my outstretched arms and wiggly fingers.

Hannah watches me cradle him. She is proud of me. She trusts me. Bumblebee's legs feel pudgy-fudgy, and his bottom against my forearm is satin, and I think how vulnerable he is, and I know that how I meet this vulnerability will spawn an emotional root that becomes him as much as anything. My hand supports his back. His arms dangle. I smile. There is a gentleness in his smile. I'm grateful he is gentle. I hoist him above my head. He smiles and giggles like a comedian laughing at his own joke. I lower Bumblebee until his chin rests on my shoulder. Wisps of café au lait hair tickle my neck. "Wuz up, baby Bumblebee?"

"Sorry I shouted," says Hannah.

"No worry."

"I shouldn't shout, I was just, he was driving me nuts."

I reprimand myself for mocking her earlier, which seems a habit lately though so far only in silence before her, a habit I detest, and *habits are breakable, John B, so break it!*

I grasp Bumblebee's waist and hoist him to the heavens. "Up, up and away." His grin is goofy. The Bumblebee giggle. He's good! The slightest pressure from my fingers could hurt him. How easy, I think, to hurt him. What juts straight as a peg between his legs is pointing at my nose. "This could put a damper on a beautiful thing."

Hannah retrieves the baby. "Johnny, it was the *Times* columnist."

"Kenneth Brennan?"

"Yes."

"He said his name?"

"Yes, how do you think I knew!"

"Seriously?"

"When you didn't answer, I thought I'd disturbed you—"

"That's the *Times* columnist, Hannah!"

"He heard Bumblebee fussing. I asked him to hold on. He said call him back when it's convenient."

"You're kidding!"

"His number's on the—"

I sprint down the hallway for the kitchen landline. Not chancing the cell. Cool the hysteria. Brennan figures, well, this kid had his shot, and he wasn't available, too bad, and I cannot believe I didn't give him my cell! He thinks I'm a nut. Who my age even has a landline? *Don't leave!*

Chill, John B. The first ring warbles, like it's fucked up. *Fuck.* I realize the phone's plastic is cool against my clean-shaven face. What possessed me? He'll think I'm 14.

"Hello," I say. Before him. *Nice!*

"Hello! This is Ken."

"It's John. Returning your call."

"Dr. John Howard."

"Oh, yes, yes, Mr.—"

C'mon, John B, the chute's streaking sideways, pull the lines, equilibrium, c'mon. Yes, you heard him: *It's Ken.* And yes, he is *insisting* on how "genuinely moved" he was by my email, and rather than responding by email or speaking on the phone, "if coming to the city is convenient," would I like to meet him for dinner, day after tomorrow? How is Tribeca? A neighborhood place where he's "a habitué." Walker's.

* * *

"Hannah! Ken receives hundreds of emails and letters from readers." I knock on the kitchen table. "Hannah."

"I hear you, good, that's good."

She could let Bumblebee swallow the banana before feeding him the ground chicken. Do I need to criticize her? The baby is dressed in red shorts with suspenders—that serve no purpose— over a plaid cotton shirt, red shoes, red socks, hair she's brushed, parted, and sprayed with something that smells like an orange. *Why does visiting your parents automatically require you to turn him into Fauntleroy?*

Bumblebee spits up. *Say nothing.*

"Oh, c'mon, baby," she says and swipes his chin with her hand.

"Ken said on the phone just before we hung up that my email touched a nerve in him."

"Grandma and grandpa will love—"

"Hannah!"

"Johnny! I heard you; I'm feeding—"

"Why do you yell?"

"Why do you? You raised your voice—"

"Raised but measured. You *yell.*"

"You're joking? I'm here getting the baby ready—"

"Getting the baby ready! For what? To learn how to yell?"

"That is so unfair!"

The subway wends through the station, and I see *Franklin Street* on the tiled wall. *Hannah did accept my apology. As genuine. I meant it to be. I was unfair. What am I harboring? I can do better. I can.* The doors open.

I stand on the platform and fret. *Which way?* He didn't say. There's more than one exit. *Shit.* I check my watch. Forty-five minutes early. *I'm good.*

Halfway up the stairs, I run through my email to Ken. Did he imagine the sound of my voice? Do I sound as he imagined? I'll ask. Maybe not. Will I disappoint him? Will I wreck an expectation of me that I created? Maybe he thinks I'm someone else.

I check for street signs: W Broadway. Franklin St. *Where the fuck is N. Moore?*

The lady points. "Thank you," I say, and the gnats in my stomach vanish. I meander. Still plenty of time. Deep down I believe, whatever I say about me, we have a lot in common. Maybe this will be one and done, but maybe we could become friends. *Great, N. Moore.* He's got a PhD, I've got one, so that's another common denominator. *Calm yourself, John B.*

I pass the time wandering along named streets unfamiliar to me and occasionally peer up at the nearly completed Freedom Tower to gauge my sense of north/south and because there's no numbered grid in Tribeca to guide me, I don't want to stray too far. I would like to know Ken.

Walker's is in sight, and I imagine a small hand tugging herky-jerky at my hand and I look down and that's Bumblebee at my side, whose big steps match my little ones. He is 6 or 7. *Daddy! My foot hurts!* I assess his scowl and clenched fist, wiping tears and reddened eyes. I kneel and investigate his sandal. I locate the offending pebble that somehow managed to embed itself beneath two of his toes. I remove it. *Are you okay?* I ask. He smiles, and says, *All better, Daddy.* He is dry-eyed and cheerful again. We stroll on, and my son still keeps time with me, and then he skips ahead and looks back.

I approach Walker's. I think, if someday a pebble fixes itself between my son's toes and he cannot dispatch it and cries, how I will treat this incident from the first second until the last? I will dispatch it immediately, and I will accept his discomfort and his response to it, however that discomfort manifests itself, and I wonder, as time passes, should he recall this incident, what image of me will linger within him? That as much as vanquishing his pain, I acknowledged it, and I permitted him to experience his distress his way. *I will try to never let you down, Bumblebee.*

I enter Walker's, and the chatting patrons eating at tables and crowding the bar and the noisy TV above rows of liquors and spirits remind me that the locals will think I'm one, too. I am a deer in headlights, immobilized by a solicitous wave and an ingratiating smile from the far side of the bar.

In the decidedly more sedate section, separated by a railroad car–like middle dining area, I lift my Black and Tan, and Ken sips Malbec, and I think: *Seriously!*

The fusillade of inquiry and flattery electrifies me: Where did I go to school? My dissertation sounds "groundbreaking" and "enlightening." He'd like to read it. *Wow.* Silence. "Yes, really." I'm reassured. "And you paint?" "More draw," I say; "pastels." "And you teach?" "A small college, Lenape, near Princeton." It's my second year, I tell him, and yes, I like it. "Cool faculty, especially an older colleague of mine in the History Department." And I sum up, like he must be bored shitless, "So that's it for now." What an idiot!

"And for the future?" he asks. A post-grad teaching fellowship offer from Yale, a book maybe, and then a pining escapes from a door previously unopened, and I confide to him a dilemma I have never shared with anyone, including Hannah. "So, I'm at a crossroads actually, Ken. I take the fellowship, the book, and commit to academia. Or I support myself as an adjunct and draw. For a living. I mean, try to. You know, I go for it."

"Wow."

"I'm an artist," my out-of-body voice says. *Wow.*

He nods. His lips tighten and his eyebrows rise: *professorial.* "Who knew?" he says.

We're confidants, I think, and fret and retreat from my fantasy. "Someday, maybe, I don't know."

He is so encouraging, and I feel like a breached dam and pour forth: secret plans, crazy dreams, shelved hopes. I reiterate my conflicting ambitions: academia or art. I *blah, blah, blah*, a giddy boy on a magic carpet ride, *blah, blah, blah* about my art, my academic interests, Hannah, my baby boy, *Bumblebee*. He loves it. *Wow*.

The waitress removes our entrée plates. I glance at my watch, and I finish my third Black and Tan, and Ken sips his third Malbec. The time has flown, and I apologize for having transformed myself into a "jabberwocky." The check appears, and I realize we haven't spoken about my email, his column, his obit essay, why I'm here, and he is let down, so obvious, and I reach in my jacket pocket, and he sees my wallet. "No, no," he says. I insist and he insists: "Absolutely n-o." I'll leave a hundred dollars on the table if he pays, I say, and his laugh is so rambunctious and hearty and ice-breaking, and I laugh too and feel glorious and silly and safe in his presence, more than with anyone on earth. He understands me. He does.

Ken signs the receipt like me—legible handwritingme—and mentions again how "struck" he was by my email, yet he seems reticent to speak further, so I'm just going with wondering why. I'm not pushing. He asks, as if I'm the decision maker, "Up for taking a walk along the bike path on the West Side Highway? We can talk, or not." Whatever I prefer. He says, "Just strolling up the highway is a kind of discourse-lubricant for Terry and me. But then, that's *our* communication ritual," he says. "Or perhaps you need to get back to Princeton?" *Does he want me to?*

"No!" And matter-of-factly I hasten to add, "I like to walk." The need to confide cries out and from that recess within who I am charges forth like a soldier bent on taking a hill, damn the consequences.

We are silent and amble west through the twilight shrouding the city. *Where to begin?* I wish I'd eaten more than a steak salad, had less to drink. I'm still lightheaded. If I make a fool of myself, whatever. I'm desperate for him to appreciate me. We cross a small cobblestone street that I am surprised still exists, I say, meaning cobblestone, not small. He nods and knows what I mean. He's so at ease in Tribeca, his home, his turf, and that Simon and Garfunkel song, "Feelin' Groovy," comes to mind. Ken's feelin' groovy. Not me. I'm holding back. *Why?* I'm desperate to clarify what I meant in my email, which I'm sure he understood, but I'm desperate anyway. Wow, *desperate, John B.* His silence is the segue, meant to encourage me to initiate a dialogue, I'm positive.

We meander north along the pedestrian lane. I've said nothing and still feel encouraged. There's Canal Street in the distance, where you get the Holland Tunnel to New Jersey. That much I know, I tell Ken, and he winks and says, "Hey, you're married, happily, like me, but check this out." A young woman on rollerblades whose blonde ponytail hangs over her shoulder will glide into us if someone doesn't move, and she is breathless, sweating, bent, hands on her knees and looking up. Her breasts are *like 87 percent unencumbered* by her wifebeater T, I think to say, but don't. She straightens up moments from passing us, and printed across her shirt in peach-colored script and bookended by excellent nipples I read: "I LOVE MY STUD!"

She is behind us, and I glance at Ken and make a mouth like a fish, exhale, and raise my brows like an adolescent who could only wish.

"Next life," he murmurs.

We are just north of Canal, and there the traffic cacophony and the light glimmering from buildings on the river's Jersey side comforts me, and I think to talk now. I chance a stop and lean over the railing and stare into the water. Ken is beside me. My mouth is dry.

"My brother and I often contemplate the river. Centers us.

Helps, especially in advance of something critical, a potential disagreement. Reminds us to listen first, shoot later."

A hunger to plead my side overwhelms me. *Now or never.* I talk to the river. " 'Your father was a *good* man, a good man!' my mom said. 'He was a control freak and a drunk,' said Barb. 'Get it out now, guys, okay,' Mom said, and I lost it. 'Get what out? That he was a motherfucker, and then it's, what? All better!' Mom is a Spartan, Ken. 'Johnny, it's a memorial, not a wash-the-dirty-laundry fest.' 'This isn't dirty laundry,' I yell. I'm crazed! And then my mom interrupts me, which I fucking hate! 'Good,' she says, 'get it out because now's the time, because at the memorial we will honor him, say something generous, kind—bing, bang, boom—over and out!' And now we're all ranting, interrupting. 'So many people loved him,' Mom says, 'his colleagues, his staff.' Did I see the heartfelt email from his old staff? 'I'm not the goddamn staff,' I shout, and Barb says, 'Fuck the staff!' Barb so gets it. 'I'm not gonna turn his memorial into a circus,' says Mom—a.k.a. never-give-an-inch June. 'I will not speak,' I say, and Barb says, if I don't speak she's sure as shit not gonna, and Mom mega-explodes: 'He was your *father*, Barbara, your *father*, Johnny. He did everything for you: clothed you, fed you, paid for your education, and no I couldn't live with him, and yes he was a bastard and a drunk, okay, okay, but I loved him and I still love him, and I love you both, so what more do you expect from me.' 'Well, I hate him, I hate him, I hate him, I hate his guts,' I say, and I'm pounding the kitchen table. 'And I'm sick of you defending him,' and Mom screams at me, 'I am not defending him.' So I out-scream her: 'I said, I'm sick of you defending him!' And I see the kitchen table, wet, and for the first time ever in my life I see my mother crying, and I'm incensed. 'You are defending him and asking me and Barb to be okay with that, and I am not, *am not!*' And then she says in this whisper that sounds dead and furious at the same time, 'What do you both want me to say? What do you want from me? There's gonna be 200 people, including friends of mine, people I work with, people I love. I am not going to dishonor your father's memory.' And she just slumps and the tears flow, Ken, and I can barely hear her. 'You're both adults. You can do this for me *and* for your father, and you can hate us both if you want.' And I am up, and looking directly at Mom, and I lower the volume to match hers: 'June, what is there about *I have nothing to say* that you do not get?' Then I'm gone. And if you were there, Ken, and heard me, you'd know what Ed sounded like. I am my father's son, huh."

I notice the river, as if it had disappeared and then returned. I hear the traffic again. I am aware of the night air. And the world. Ken's hand is on my shoulder. I am not forsaken. I turn to him. "I should be like you, Ken. But I am more your brother, Terry." I tell him that I don't know where to put Ed so that I can feel free of him. "I just don't."

We continue along the pathway, and pass Fourteenth Street, and I know the silence is his invitation to talk or not. "Ken," I murmur, and he looks at me, and I wave as if to say, oh, nothing. I'm not ready.

We approach Twentieth Street, and Ken points out Chelsea Piers, this indoor sports center he likes, and he tells me it has a 46-foot climbing wall that's really challenging, especially for a geezer his age, and he asks me if I'd be up for meeting him there, maybe next week. And I say yes. *I don't believe it.*

He'll accompany me to Penn Station, where I'll get the train back to Princeton, but I say, no. "It's out of your way." He tells me, okay, he'll head to the subway, and we walk close together.

"You are your own man. You're not me. Not Terry. You know that."

"I guess."

Shame grips me. I count the crosswalk's horizontal white lines as we make our way east on 23rd Street.

"If you're not your own man, John, then whose man are you?"

"Then you know what I meant in my email."

"I think so."

I slow my pace a little. With each step I know we're closer to parting, and now I wish I'd let Ken accompany me to Penn Station.

He says, "And your email meant what I think it suggested—that you would leave your wife and son if—"

"It's like when there's a history of cancer in your family. You even suspect a tumor, better to cut it out before it metastasizes. I'm already Ed, the way I overreact to Hannah sometimes, the way I treated Mom in that argument. In my mind, I kicked her when she was down. I couldn't help it. I have a cruel streak, Ken, like my dad. So there it is. I've had enough, Ken. If I stand in front of that podium, as soon as my mouth opens, I'm John B, Eddie's kid, come to praise my captor. I'm not John, I'm Eddie. I can't do it. I won't. Because I renounce him. I want from him what he wanted from me: nothing. Nothing. Nothing. Nothing. Once, I turned and mocked my son who was crying. He was too young to notice the expression in my face, but someday he will, and then what do I do? Maybe he would be better off without me."

Ken and I don't speak until we reach 23rd and Eighth, where he shakes my extended hand and hugs me before I can thank him. He grasps my back. "Thank you," I say, and I realize how much shorter than me he is. Half a foot maybe. Taller in ways that count.

"My pleasure," he says. He will email me. His steps down the station are brisk. I feel discovered. And heard.

I stare at wispy streaks of shadow and light outside the train's window on the trip back to New Jersey and wonder how it is that I'm no closer to deciding whether or not to attend my father's memorial, whether or not to speak on his behalf. How was this not resolved? And I am overcome by feelings of inadequacy and failure. And then I think, *Do what's right, Johnny, for you.* I press my nose against the window and watch everything and nothing. I wonder why I took Amtrak when the bus is so much cheaper. I wonder if Ken's rock climbing invitation was serious. And his look, his nod, when he broke the silence after my diatribe and murmured Mom's "bing, bang, boom!" and said, "To that I can relate." Relate? Oh, yeah, his dad's name, Bing.

I place my book, *The Souls of Black Folk,* on the empty seat next to me and revel in the solitude. Ken has read Du Bois, I'm sure. Maybe we'll discuss him. I look out the window and envision bounding through my front door, calling out, *It's me, Hannah. Daddy's home, Bumblebee,* and Hannah is about to put him down and I await her return, wait until she is ready for me to tell her about Ken. I love Hannah. I don't want to live alone.

My cell vibrates. I reach in my jeans pocket and click the text. *Does next Sunday look good for climbing? Kenny.*

Bumblebee and I turn into the parking lot of The Princeton Battlefield State Park just before 10 a.m. It is August 30th, and he will be a year old tomorrow. This sojourn to a historical site is the first of many, I hope. It is my birthday gift to him.

I push his stroller along the rutted dirt path, and then onto the lawn and in the direction of the Clarke House, my favorite landmark. It is blazing hot already, and the sky is cloudless. Nathan's bare feet kick in the air after a hefty bump over a tree's exposed root, but I hear nothing, assume he is not frightened, and am relieved that I made sure to observe *Hannah's Law*: You can never apply too much sunscreen, everywhere. Despite the indisputable fact that the Maclaren top shades 90 percent of Bumblebee, I liberally slathered every inch of exposed skin under mother hen's supervision, compliant and exuding bonhomie when reminded for the hundredth time, "He's fair-skinned like you, Johnny, and we don't want something preventable to appear 30 years from now, so please, and look, see, you missed under his ankle—there."

We approach the Clarke House, and I point across the lawn to an uneven line of men—some too young to shave, a few my age, but mostly ruddy-faced, elderly, retired types—clothed in blue, brown, and white revolutionary battle uniforms and tri-corner hats, some with replicas of muskets held over their shoulders, others slouching, as if from the weight of their weapon. Another actor without a long rifle appears in the midst of issuing commands that are observed with varying degrees of uniformity and enthusiasm. "See the soldiers, Nathan."

He kicks. "Almost there." I explain that the women in colorful petticoat-style jackets, gowns, and bonnets that simulate 18th-century dress are arranging food and pottery on several rectangular wooden tables whose unpainted planks and construction also replicate the revolutionary period. I think, he does not understand the words, but he hears me.

I check my watch. Enough time to get Nathan home, put him down for a nap, wait for Hannah to return from her parents', check that I'm prepped for Monday's classes, call Mom, and get to the city by 5. I dig in my pocket.

"Hey, Ken, it's John. Got your message. We're on for Chelsea Piers at 6, and Hannah's letting me stay late, so confirming we're on for dinner. *On me.* And, oh, we're really looking forward to coming to your house Sunday night. What can we bring? And fyi, we decided on a sitter. And if it's okay, I know we're gonna talk about my book proposal on Saturday, but your analysis of my dissertation was, like, amazing. I wondered if I could run a few questions regarding it by you, too, I mean, if you have time. Oh, and, um, I have a surprise from the Ohio State University Press, so now it's not a surprise. Wow, I'm jabbering on. See you tonight."

The grounds are filling with visitors. I stop and kneel down beside my son, who is grasping his plastic bottle and appears mesmerized by the flurry of movement he sees. I wipe juice from his chin with my sleeve. "This house," I say while watching his eyes dart from what I imagine is one image now more intriguing than the previous, "was once a refuge for wounded revolutionary and British soldiers." The raggedy line of volunteers straightens, and with more gusto than precision they fulfill their commander's orders and raise their long rifles and point them straight ahead. "What do we think they're taking aim at, Nathan? An enemy? The air? An idea? What do we think? Maybe it just feels good to take aim at something, huh."

"He's impressed," a man's voice says.

I'm startled and look up. An aged face engages me.

"Dead to the world," he says. I kneel and look at Nathan. His eyes are shut, hands are splayed, palms up. The man retrieves his bottle from the lawn and hands it to me.

"Yup."

The man kneels, and I can almost hear him creak. Slush-white stubble, woolly brows, a willowy face splotched red and speckled with liver spots, and his wrinkles seem to smile when he does.

"How old is he?"

"A year tomorrow."

"Congratulations. Ninety-three more, and he and I will be even."

I stand. I offer a hand, and he permits me to help him up.

"Carl," he says. He asks me "the boy's name," and I like his old-school way. "Nathan," he says, is the "spitting image of his papa," and I am swooning, and he tells me that his son, Jerry, is a retired policeman and still living in San Diego, where "we hail from," and is 68. "My goodness, if you can believe that, 68, because I can't," he says. Jerry flies to Jersey every month with his wife and, "when she can," their grown daughter. "You see, Clara is a surgeon," he says, and they try to persuade him to move close to them and his grandchild, and he will, he promises Jerry, when the time comes, but not yet, because the truth is, it "woulda happened" if he and Jerry's wife weren't oil and water and, well, since he's set in his ways and "still damn fit for an old fiddle," he's better off here, even though living alone is nothing to write home about, and then he shakes my hand. "It was nice meeting you." He bends down, and blows at a strand of hair over Nathan's eye. He looks up at me. "It goes so fast, son. I hope you make the most of him."

"That's a good way to put it," I tell him. "I'll try."

Acknowledgments

* * *

In contemplating the Acknowledgments section, it is impossible for me not to think about *acknowledgment* as perhaps the cornerstone of any relationship that feels loving, meaningful, and emotionally connecting by all parties concerned.

I want to acknowledge: my wife, Paula, for her unconditional love and support; my son, Brandon, for his unconditional love and support, and my daughter-in-law, Lianna, for her unconditional love and support; my mother, Miriam Ruben, for her love without condition; my brother, Marty, for his love and shared vision of fatherhood. I am especially grateful to Alison Larkin, publisher, for her enthusiasm, her infectious spirit, and her belief in this collection and me; Judy Lopatin, for her superb editorial services and insights; Sheree Wichard and Eric West, for their invaluable contributions; Mary Clyde, for her close reading, analysis, and incisive critiques of several of this collection's stories, and for her encouragement and belief in me as a writer; Robin Lippincott, who worked closely with me on my first novel, for his encouragement and belief in me as a writer; Sena Jeter Naslund, for introducing me to an aesthetic bar that I now aspire to; to my best friends Les Winter and Alan Winson, and to my extended family and friends, whom I value and love.

Be True to Your School
Words and music by Brian Wilson and Mike Love
Copyright© 1963 Irving Music, Inc.
Copyright renewed, All Rights Reserved Used by Permission
Reprinted by Permission of Hal Leonard LLC

About the Author

* * *

Paul Alan Ruben has published both literary fiction and nonfiction. He has completed a novel, *Raising Philip*, and is nearly finished with its companion novel, *Family in a Grove*. Paul has produced and directed hundreds of audiobooks for every major American publisher, and won numerous industry awards, including two Grammy Awards for Best Spoken Word. He is married to Paula Parker, an actress and audiobook producer/director. His son, Brandon, is a lawyer. Paul's daughter-in-law, Lianna Gomori Ruben, is a writer.

* * *

FATHER, SON, AND THE HOLY OBIT was published by *Pif Magazine*. THE UNDERDOG was published by *Pennsylvania English*/35. A MINOR ADJUSTMENT was published by *Connotation Press*.